SAINTS SINNERS

12 tales of Crime and the Clergy

Rev. Malcolm G. Lorimer

Best wishes

Max Books

© Rev. Malcolm G. Lorimer 2011

First published in the UK in 2011 by Max Books

The right of Rev. Malcolm G. Lorimer to be identified as the Author of
this work has been asserted by him in accordance with the Copyright,
Designs and Patents Act 1988

A CIP catalogue record for this title is available from the British
Library

ISBN: 978-0-9562224-2-8

Typeset by Andrew Searle
Cover illustration by Bob Bond

Printed and bound by Anthony Rowe Ltd

MAX BOOKS
Epworth House
34 Wellington Road
Nantwich Cheshire CW5 7BX
Tel: 01270 625278
Email: maxcricket@btinternet.com

To Charlotte, Emily & Anne

The sisters of 'the wild moors' who have
always been my inspiration

Acknowledgements

I would like to thank Bob Bond for the wonderful cartoon on the front cover. He created it after I talked to him and described what I wanted. To members of my family and friends who I have inflicted these stories, and who have given advice and encouragement. To Lynn and Sally, who helped in the checking of the stories and to Andy Searle, without whom I couldn't have produced the book. Also, to all those clergy who have been my inspiration!

Rev Malcolm G. Lorimer

CONTENTS

PREFACE

WHAT'S A CLERGYMAN doing writing stories about crime? That's the question which normally people ask when they discover my interest in crime stories.

I have always had a great interest in crime writing, from Sherlock Holmes to the modern TV Detectives, Frost and Morse in particular. In many of the stories of crime writers vicars appear, but usually they are one-dimensional characters who are a bit "wet". This is not my experience of clergy. Twelve years living in Moss Side in Manchester and once finding a dead body in the church park next to the manse does toughen you up a bit!

I also began to realise during my ministry that clergy are ideally placed to see good and evil in all its forms. So the ideas for these short stories began.

They are twelve stories linked by the theme of clergy and crime. Each story is about a clergyman or woman and their involvement in crime, either as the perpetrator, victim or detective. Some of the clergy are good, others weak and some evil. The clergy are from different denominations: Anglican, Baptist, Methodist and one story is set in a monastic community. Exploring questions about good and evil in the context of life and the church, the stories are not linked together and all have separate characters. The themes involve murder, deception, lust, greed, envy, hate and witchcraft, the usual attributes found in the average church congregation!

I hope you enjoy the stories, and maybe you may see the clergy in a different light! At the back of the book are some notes about the stories which are probably better read after you have read them.

Rev Malcolm G. Lorimer
December, 2010

THE GRAVEDIGGER

———◈———

*Churchyards are where parishioners become entitled
by law to render back their remains into the earth,
the common mother of mankind, without payment
for the ground which they were to occupy.*

An old law relating to churchyards

———◈———

THE SUN WAS already high in the sky as the Rev Charles Adams took a leisurely breakfast alone on the stern deck of the cruise ship, Providence. He couldn't remember when he last enjoyed a better breakfast, not just because of the quality of the food but the whole ambience of the scene. Here he was, a humble vicar from an out of the way country parish enjoying a luxury retirement cruise around the world. It had taken time for him to unwind but now, two weeks into the voyage, he was totally relaxed. He'd always enjoyed breakfast and couldn't understand why so many of his fellow passengers stayed in their cabins and didn't surface until the best of the day had gone. He'd even managed to secure a morning paper from England and it didn't even seem to matter that it was a three day old copy of the Times. This is what heaven must be like, he mused, as he relaxed in the deckchair sipping a glass of orange juice.

The coffee and croissants were just right and Charles was pleased that the stewards were willing to serve breakfast out on deck. As he read the paper his eye was drawn to a column at the bottom of page four in the Home News section. As he read the article the colour visibly drained from his face. His sun-tanned features took on an ashen hue as he read and re-read the it, unconsciously hoping that by doing so the words would alter and make easier reading. His hands began to tremble and he felt a cold shiver running down his spine, despite the cloudless sky and deck-bleaching sun. For the best part of 20 minutes he sat in the chair hunched up over the table sobbing uncontrollably.

Finally, he composed himself and took control of his emotions. Very calmly and deliberately he folded the newspaper, laid it on the table and walked over to the rail at the side of the ship. For a good ten minutes he looked out over the sea, a beautiful vista, the sun sparkling on the water, the ship ploughing a slow furrow through the gentle waves. He seemed to be wrestling with something in his conscience, a problem which had nothing to do with the sea he looked out upon. At last his mind was made up; he knew what he must do. His jump cleared the bottom deck and the splash wasn't seen by anyone.

It would be another six hours before Rev Charles Adams was reported missing, presumed lost overboard. The cruise ship quickly turned around and re-traced its route, but it was too late! 24 hours later his lifeless body was picked up out of the water by a passing fishing boat.

The Gravedigger

****

To understand the circumstances of Rev Charles Adams's death you have to go back 15 years to a small country village in Hertfordshire, Little Perivale. Charles has just been installed rector of the parish at the picturesque church of St Stephen's. On one hot sultry summer's day Charles is to be found not in the church but six feet underground in the church's graveyard as he struggles to complete the digging of a grave for a funeral the following day. It's hard work but Charles doesn't mind the exercise, or the work, as the old gravedigger, Joe, is laid up in bed with a bad back. Charles throws another shovel full of earth up towards the sky, but suddenly the sun is blocked out and a dark shape looms over the grave.

"Is that you, Charlie?"

Charles knows the voice, but just can't place it. A hand reaches down into the grave and Charles grabs hold of it to pull himself out. Slowly, as his eyes become accustomed to the bright sunlight, his face betrays signs of recognition. He knows the voice but it has been a long time, over 20 years, since he last heard it.

"It's not you, is it? No, it can't be... Good grief! It's you Jeremy... and I thought..." Charles thought to himself that his childhood companion must have disappeared, he hadn't seen him for so long, Jeremy, a friend whom he owed so much.

"Never mind what you thought, it's good to see you, Charlie, after all these years" The two men were standing shoulder to shoulder at the side of the grave, clasping each other tightly and laughing together. They were roughly the same age, but at first glance that was all they seemed to have in common. The vicar was dressed in old corduroy trousers held up with red braces and a checked shirt, which showed the marks of the brown soil from the grave. Charles was a little overweight and was beginning to thin on top. He had a round, kindly face marked with lines of concern. He was in stark contrast to the sleek look of Jeremy, who was tall and elegantly-dressed, every bit the city businessman. The suit was obviously expensive and the black sunglasses under his steel-grey hair gave him a slight hint of glamour, even menace. You may also have noticed his left arm; slightly shorter, showing a kind of injury.

"How on earth did you find me?" asked Charles.

"I didn't," replied Jeremy. "I was driving through the village and, as I slowed down for the pedestrian crossing, caught sight of your name on the noticeboard, otherwise I would never have noticed it. I remembered that you were a vicar and thought there can't be many Charlies in the Church of England!"

"You would be surprised Jeremy, you really would be amazed at just how many! Now come on, you must have a drink with me and tell me all your news. Come up to the vicarage and have a beer."

"That sounds fine Charlie, but what about the car? I've some valuable things in it."

"Oh, just drive round and put it in front of the vicarage. We can keep an eye on it from the study".

The black Mercedes sports car swung into the drive and Jeremy parked at the front of the house, being careful to lock all the doors and switch on the alarm. Jeremy walked in and from just one glance he could tell that Charlie lived alone. The vicarage was tidy but cluttered; a women's hand was evident, but only in the dusting and cleaning and not in the choice of pictures and furniture or the general appearance of the house. These were definitely chosen by a male and someone not caring too much about image or money.

Out of the afternoon sun the beer was cold and the house cool. Charles leant back into the easy chair, one in which he fitted so comfortably that Jeremy thought it could have been moulded around him. Jeremy surveyed the study, which showed the typical work of a country parish priest. The piles of song-sheets and books, not just on the shelves but also stacked high on the floor and on the window ledges. The desk was a rather admirable antique roll-top with papers spilling out of every cavity and drawer. A large black cat was in residence on one the chairs, and it looked as if he would not take kindly to being disturbed.

"That's Jonah," said Charlie, smiling.

" I christened him Jonah because he eats like a whale and a mouse once lived after he tried to swallow it." They both laughed.

"Now do tell me, Jeremy, what you've been up to since last time we met. We seemed to lose contact after university."

Jeremy smiled, recalling in his mind how the two people sitting in the vicarage study, now so different, were once inseparable as teenagers, getting into all kinds of scrapes together but always coming through with their friendship stronger.

"By the way, the name's Jez. I found Jeremy too much of a millstone. It sounds too posh!"

"That's a pity," said Charlie. "I know your mother was fond of it."

"Jez suits me now, it's what everyone calls me. After university I went abroad to the Caribbean. I had an uncle there who offered me a job with his yacht marina."

"A bit different to Norwich Jeremy, sorry Jez. The sun, beaches and beautiful girls, no doubt." A rather wicked smile crossed the vicar's features.

"Yes, quite a few of those," smiled Jez. "And it was an incredible job for someone to walk into, straight from university. It did have its problems though. I was there six months when I discovered that my uncle liked to dance with the devil."

"What do you mean... voodoo?"

"No, he wasn't into black magic, but in some ways it would have been easier if he was, at least it's not against the law! Drug trafficking definitely is and my uncle was in as deep as you can get. Not bad cover, boats always coming in and out of the marina, different people using them, nobody asking too many questions. The only trouble was he was greedy. Not content with just the drugs, he began to cheat on the drug-runners; he was getting too powerful. If he didn't like someone he would give an anonymous tip-off to the police and they would pick them up and uncle would be rid of a difficult customer. The only thing was he did it once too often. One day someone who he'd just grassed up walked into the office. A corrupt policeman had tipped him off. He burst in and sprayed the old man with bullets. I dived for cover, luckily he wasn't interested in me. After that the business fell apart and I had to return to England with no job and no-one wanting to know me. I can tell you, it was hard. But I then came across a guy who I'd met in the Caribbean. He offered me a job with cars, selling them, which was a good break. Why am I telling you all this? You're not interested in my wanderings."

"You're very wrong, Jez, said Charlie. Everyone has a story; the only trouble is that most people don't have time to listen, that's where clergymen have an advantage. We like listening. I always tell my parish that on Sundays. I speak to them for 20 minutes and then the rest of the week I go around and it's my turn to listen to them. So I am used to people being surprised about what they tell me. You know, vicars are still men of the world, we do see something of the seamier side of life at times and it takes a lot to shock us. But go on, tell me what are you doing now?"

Jez moved a little uneasily in the chair and checked the time on his gold Rolex watch. "A bit complicated really. Let's just say I work with some big companies and I specialise in going in when things go wrong. I pick up the pieces and tidy everything up – a good clean up operation."

"A bit like a troubleshooter," remarked Charlie.

Jez smiled. "I suppose you could call it that."

A look of dismay came over Charlie's face "Is that the time?" he said, looking at the old clock. "I must finish that grave I started before it gets dark."

Jez put down his beer can. "Can I come and help? A bit of exercise would do me the world of good."

"Not in those clothes you can't, but if you're really serious I could lend you some old clothes. They'll certainly fit you, you're a lot thinner than me, probably because you don't have to undergo the temptation of Mothers' Union teas and home-made cakes like I do."

Jez laughed. "I wondered why my life wasn't complete. Now I know what I have been missing all these years."

The two men walked out into the vicarage garden, the sun setting and its rays glinting through the trees, casting a warm light on the two figures as they walked into the graveyard, each with a shovel on his shoulder. Jez was wearing some of Charlie's old clothes and looking rather incongruous. Both men would have made good characters in a film about Irish navvies.

As they reached the open grave Jez asked: "Do you even have to dig your own graves out here in the country then?"

"Oh no, not usually, but old Joe the gravedigger isn't well and I volunteered to finish this off for him. The service is at ten in the morning, so there'll be no time tomorrow. Anyway, it looks bad form for the hearse to arrive at the churchyard and for the mourners to find the vicar still digging the grave!"

They both laughed as they jumped down into the grave and began digging. It was tough, hot work and the soil hard, but after 20 minutes Charlie called a halt and declared that they had now reached something.

"What is it?" Jez asked.

Charlie smiled. "You don't really want to know, do you? Just let's say that the last time this particular soil saw the sun Hitler was striding around Europe." They levelled off the base of the grave and then climbed out, before sitting on the edge of the grave, their legs dangling over into the hole as they drank freely from the bottles of beer that Charlie had brought with him.

"So tell me," asked Jez, "is this how you always dig a grave?"

Charlie thought for a moment. "Well, it's not rocket science, just hard graft. You have to make sure the sides are shored up with wood as you dig down to prevent it collapsing, and you have to have an idea of how far you can dig."

"How do you mean?" enquired Jez.

"Well, if it's a new grave, you just keep digging, up to 12 feet. We have a small mechanical digger that is quite useful. For an old grave you first look up how many people have been buried there and calculate how much space you have left".

"Don't you just look on the gravestone?" asked Jez.

"Well, you begin there," explained Charlie, "but you must consult the graveyard register, as that tells you how many people have been buried in that particular plot, but then that's not always accurate."

Jez looked puzzled. "What do you mean? Isn't it checked by the police or council officials?"

"From time to time, but I always maintain you could bury anything here, and if you chose the right place no-one would ever know. We are in the sticks here, officialdom doesn't bother us in Little Perivale. Some of my predecessors seem to have been a little haphazard in keeping records. One vicar must have allowed pets to be buried here, the number of dog and cat skeletons we keep finding. Then, if a grave has some space left in it, you dig down until you come across evidence of the previous burial."

"I bet that can be tricky."

Charlie grimaced. "That's the worst part, when your shovel goes through the lid of a coffin that has been in the ground for 20 years. I can tell you, I don't need to watch horror movies, I've had quite enough experiences here."

"But why do you do it?" asked Jez.

"Old Joe the gravedigger is getting past it. I could get someone in from the next village but I actually enjoy it, in a strange kind of way. Makes the job complete. You think you have accomplished something when not only have you taken the service for someone who has died, but you also dig the grave and fill it in afterwards. A job well done. There's only about 20 burials a year so I can cope with that kind of number and the exercise certainly does me good; no need to spend hours on a stationary cycle or in a gym."

"So what happens now?" asked Jez. "Surely the grave has to be checked and some official come to sign the papers and see that all is in order?"

"Not here. I'm my own boss. I sign the papers and fill in the register."

"But you could do anything, even put another body in the grave," suggested Jez.

"I suppose you could," Charlie replied, quizzically, "but I would need to have one to hand and, although vicars are not always paragons of virtue, murder is not something I need to confess, at least not just yet!"

They both laughed heartily as they walked back to the vicarage. After Jez had washed and changed he went to the door, clasping Charlie to his chest. "It's been good, Charlie I'm really glad to have run across you again after all these years. I will keep in touch."

Charlie smiled. "You know, Jez, you are always special and how can I forget what you did for me when we were teenagers?"

Charlie's eyes filled up as he recalled that fateful day when the two boys, barely 16, had gone out fishing to the local dam. The fishing proved boring, and with the warm sun on the water, they decided to go water-bombing: jumping in off the side of the dam and seeing which of them could make the bigger impact. This had gone on for 20 minutes until Charlie jumped in and didn't surface. Jez peered into the water and frantically shouted out Charlie's name. Nothing happened and so Jez dived in. When he had got accustomed to the light under the water, he saw the outline of his friend at the bottom of the dam, wedged up against the sluice gate, which had obviously opened as water was rushing out. Charlie couldn't move because of the pressure. Jez reached out one hand and gripped Charlie tightly around the waist. He pulled, but the pressure was too great. All this happened in a matter of seconds, but it seemed like hours as Jez frantically pulled Charlie from the sluice gate and fought his way to the surface, clutching his friend. He pulled Charlie onto the bank, turning him on his side and beating frantically on his back to get rid of the water in his lungs. Charlie coughed and spluttered; he was alive. It was only then that Jez noticed the searing pain down his own left-hand side. His arm was hanging limply and he couldn't move it. By now other people had arrived to see what was happening. They were both taken to hospital. Surprisingly, Charlie was allowed to go home, but Jez was kept in. The strain he had put on his arm had taken its toll and he never recovered full use of it. The doctors put it down to one of those instances where people can do superhuman feats in moments of tension. So, although he could use his left hand, it was never the same again and, as the years went by, it became noticeably smaller than his other hand.

"You know you saved my life that day, Jez, I remember it every day, but you still carry the cost of what you did for me." Charlie looked intently at Jez.

A wry smile came across Jez's face. "I can still use it, as you can see with the digging, but you never know Charlie, you may be able to help me one day." The evening sun glinted behind Jez, picking out the ear stud, which shone as only diamonds do. Jez started the car and the engine roared and threw up the gravel on the path. Soon he was gone, his gloved arm raised as if in salute as he drove off.

The following morning Charlie took the service for old Alice Pinney. Only 20 people turned out and, as they lowered her into the newly-dug grave, Charlie saw something glint in the sunlight at the side of the coffin in the earth. He waited until all the mourners had gone, then changed into his old clothes to fill in the grave. First, though, he climbed down on top of the coffin, leaning over gingerly to reach along the side to find what he had seen in the sunlight. He pulled it out. It was a diamond stud earring, glinting as he held it aloft. He wondered for a few moments how it could have got there, then put it in his pocket and carried on filling in the grave.

As he was finishing it off and placing the small bunches of flowers on the earth mound, now a few feet above the ground, the churchwarden came running down the path carrying a large brown envelope and gesticulating wildly. "What on earth is the matter Derek?"

"Vicar!" He gasped. "I'm so sorry to disturb you, but I didn't know what to do. I found this letter in the church vestry; there's a scribbled note with it. But look what's inside!"

Derek held out the large brown envelope and Charlie looked inside. "Good Grief," he exclaimed as he came to terms with what he saw.

"There must be thousands of pounds here."

"£3,000 to be exact – in £50 notes. And just a scribbled note saying it's for the fund to restore the bells," Derek said excitably.

Charlie beamed. "Well, Derek, someone is certainly looking favourably on us. How much do we need to complete the restoration work?"

" Well that's the strange thing. The noticeboard outside the church says the latest figure required is £3,000, so now we've got the money!" It seemed as if Derek couldn't contain his joy.

"Come on, Derek," said Charlie as he put an arm around the shoulder of his churchwarden. "This calls for a celebration. There's a bottle of whiskey in the vicarage. Let's go and toast our anonymous donor."

****

It was three weeks later. Charlie was in his study late one Monday evening when there was knock at the door. He opened it and there before him was Jez, looking very different to the last time they had met.

"I need help. Can I come in Charlie?" gasped Jez.

"Of course you can, Jez. What on earth's the matter?" said Charlie, opening the door and welcoming his friend inside.

"Have you a whiskey? I need a drink," demanded Jez.

Jez downed it in one gulp as he sat on the edge of the chair, his hands trembling as he gratefully accepted a refill.

Charlie took a seat close by. "Now Jez, what on earth has happened?"

"I can't tell you. It's too dangerous, just a job which has gone wrong. Badly wrong. And unless I sort it quickly my life is not worth very much."

Charlie looked concerned and leaned forward towards Jez. "Anything I can do I will. I owe you that, Jez, and I'll always be indebted to you."

Jez breathed deeply and began his story.

"That time a couple of months ago when I came and met you digging the grave. What did you receive the following day?"

Charlie's face lit up.

"So it was you! I had a hunch it had to be, it was too much of a coincidence. The £3,000 matched exactly the amount which the noticeboard outside the church said we needed. Thank you, Jez, it was a very generous gift."

Jez looked earnest. "It was a payment, not a gift Charlie. For a job well done."

"What do you mean Jez?" Charlie looked bewildered. "I didn't do anything for you while you were here, Jez. All you had were a couple of beers. If it was payment for them, they must have been the most expensive beers you've ever drunk!"

Jez lent forward in the chair. "Remember the grave you were digging? Did the funeral go well the following day?"

Charlie was getting exasperated. "Yes, of course it did. Nothing remarkable at all."

Jez smiled. "You didn't notice anything different, nothing out of place, everything where it should be?"

"No, what on earth are you getting at Jez? There was nothing out of place. But wait a minute, I do remember something, the diamond earring. I have it here, just like yours. I saw it in the grave during the funeral." Charlie went to his desk and produced the earring from one of the drawers.

Jez examined it and said, "It's mine, it fell out."

Charlie looked shocked. "But when? I remember seeing the earring when you were leaving, as you got into the car, after you'd helped me dig the grave."

Jez now looked very serious and there was a cold dark look over his face.

"I returned to the grave later that evening."

Charlie looked puzzled. "But why?"

"Why else do you visit an open grave but to bury something?" Jez was speaking in a low hushed tone.

Charlie was now becoming very agitated. "But you can't have, don't you see. I had a funeral the following day? Whatever you buried can never be dug up."

Jez smiled. "That, Charlie old friend, would suit me just fine."

Charlie looked aghast. "But... what... what have you buried... in that grave?"

Jez leant back in the chair. "I hope I can trust you, Charlie, because in your graveyard you have one of the most notorious criminals in London. If only his friends knew there would be quite a procession of infamous villains coming to pay their last respects. But, of course, no-one will ever know, will they Charlie? Our little secret, Charlie." A sly smile crossed his lips.

Charlie went cold, his lips moving but no words seeming to come out, until finally he murmured, "I... I can't be involved in... this... it's a crime... I'll have to inform the police."

Jez looked at him menacingly. "And how will you explain your payment of £3,000?"

"I will say I didn't know anything about the money, or its connection," Charlie stammered.

Jez smiled. "What about the police? When they trace the connection between us, old childhood buddies, spending so much time together as teenagers. This is not a stranger appearing out of the blue, Charlie. This is your life-long friend. We both dug the grave together. You're in this as much as me. Anyway, can you pay the money back?"

Charlie sounded flustered. "No I can't, not at the moment, the work on the bells has gone ahead. We would have to take out a loan to repay the money."

Jez was silent for a moment. "What if you said nothing, Charlie? Return a favour to an old friend? I saved your life once, remember? Now you can return the favour... save mine."

Charlie hesitated, his brow glistening with perspiration, and then he said slowly, "I must know more. What are you involved in? Who is this person buried in the graveyard? Have you killed him? Will people trace you here?"

Jez helped himself to another drink. "Charlie, when I came here in the summer, believe me, it was pure chance. I was driving through the village taking the back roads, avoiding traffic, when I saw your name. I had been driving for over two hours and needed a break. I couldn't leave the car with what was in the boot, and so I decided to stop. When I saw you digging the grave I couldn't believe my luck.

I thought, here it is, right under my nose, the best possible place to bury a body, a place where you would expect bodies to be buried. In a graveyard. So simple really."

Charlie was now looking ashen and, with his voice rising, he asked, "But who is it in that grave Jez?"

Jez sighed. "Look, Charlie, you don't need to know who it is. Just know that London is a cleaner place because this scum is not breathing. When I said I cleaned up when there were problems in companies, it was quite true. What I didn't tell you is that what I clean away are usually bodies. Gangland killings, drugs murders. I am the original Mr Clean. People ring me to take care of the mess. I go in, sort it out, and dispose of the body. Ideally it is never found. But even if it is discovered it is usually in the country somewhere with no identification, no signs linking it to the hit man."

Charlie's mouth was open. "Oh no, this can't be happening to me. It sounds as if it's a nightmare which I'll wake up from. Did you... murder this man?"

Jez was beginning to lose his patience. "Look, Charlie, I have never killed anyone. I just clean up afterwards. I get paid for it. Very well. If the body isn't found it can be £10,000-£15,000."

"And that's where the £3,000 came from," said Charlie, his head still in his hands.

"Yes, Charlie. I didn't want to hurt you and would never have come back unless I was in trouble."

Charlie looked around him. "Trouble, what trouble, what's happened now?"

Jez lent forward in his chair. "I thought I was being followed out of London tonight. I managed to lose them on the side roads, but they'll be waiting for me when I return and I can't have what I have in the boot with me when I go back. I have got to get rid of it."

Charlie looked aghast. "Oh no, not another body?"

Jez smiled. "Glad you catch on so quickly, Charlie! I couldn't help but notice the fresh pile of earth in the graveyard as I drove in. Another funeral tomorrow?"

Charlie's hands were now shaking. "You can't suggest this, Jez. I can't do it. I will have to call the police."

Jez looked at his friend and his eyes narrowed. "Do that and I'm as good as dead. They may not have the death penalty any more, but when I go inside there are enough contacts in the underworld to render me a dead duck in prison. You can't let me end up like that."

Charlie put his head in his hands and felt he was must be in the middle of a nightmare. He would wake soon and everything would be back to normal. Well, that's what he hoped.

The following morning, it was a rather hesitant Rev Charlie Adams who took the funeral of a Mr Thomas Pointer. As the body was lowered into the grave Charlie expected the whine of a police siren at any moment, but nothing happened. The only sound was the tolling of the solitary church bell.

Later on that day Charlie wiped the sweat from his brow as he completed the task of filling in the grave. As he wearily, but with a huge sense of relief, made his way across the vicarage lawn he opened the door to see a large, fat brown envelope behind the door. On the envelope were written the words, 'Thanks Charlie, till the next time!'

Charlie closed the door quickly and pushed the envelope deep inside the bottom drawer of his filing cabinet. He poured himself a large whiskey and sat contemplating the enormity of what he had just done.

****

Over the next ten years there would be many such envelopes, each containing £3,000-£5,000, and Charlie got used to the extra money. He rationalised it in his mind that he had to do it for his friend, a friend to whom he owed his life. He also tried to justify it by thinking that these gangland killers and drug dealers would normally meet a bad end anyway. It was almost as if Jez and Charlie were doing a service for the police and the country at large. Society was better off without these villains.

Charlie didn't keep much of the money himself. The church had a new roof, the hall for the children was refurbished and a host of other projects undertaken. The villagers almost expected the mystery donor to fund projects, and they were even referred to when ideas were spoken about. People thought it must be someone in the village, or a former parishioner. The graveyard was kept very well, of course. The vicar continued to help with the digging of the graves, saying he liked to supervise them, a foible of his. His parishioners didn't mind or think it unusual. They just smiled.

For Jez the arrangement couldn't have been better. He'd found the perfect place to hide a body, somewhere no one would ever look. It depended, of course, on when the funerals took place, and this meant keeping the odd body in one of the old crypts in the graveyard for a week. But that wasn't too difficult! Charlie was very nervous at first, but as the years went by he seemed to enjoy the intrigue. Jez became renowned in the underworld for the cleanliness of his operations, though few people ever knew who he was. The police were mystified. Notorious criminals would just disappear off the scene, never to be seen or heard of again. There was talk of murder, but no bodies were ever found. Without one and with the way the underworld clam up tight to the police, they found it extremely difficult to mount any kind of enquiry. Off the record, they were not too bothered as long as this low life fought amongst themselves and the murders did not spill out onto the streets. Who were they to complain?

Charlie became known as 'Mr Funeral' in the area, renowned for his personal care, and families would come from far and wide to have Charlie Adams conduct the funeral for their loved one. Then one day it all stopped. As abruptly as it had started, it finished. One morning Charlie woke up feeling a strange sensation, as if a great weight had been lifted from him. He didn't know what it was, but it felt good. A few days later, while he was having breakfast and Jonah was sitting in his favourite chair by the arga in the kitchen, Charlie was reading the paper whilst munching on a piece of toast and marmalade when he stopped and put the toast back on his plate. He drew the paper closer to him and read again the headline and report.

GANGLAND "CLEANER" FOUND DEAD

Jez Ward was found today dead in his London Penthouse. A single bullet through the head killed him. Ward had been under suspicion from the police for a long time as being a

"Gangland cleaner". He was linked to a number of murders in London where no bodies have ever been found. Police knew that criminals had disappeared, never to be seen again, but no-one would speak about the murders and the police were baffled by the fact that no bodies or clues were ever found.

For the next few weeks Charlie was convinced that the police would make the connection between himself and Jez and would call on him. He had decided that honesty was the best policy and he would come clean and own up to his part in this murky business. But no policeman ever called. Jez's death was put down to just another underworld killing. Charlie also failed to recognise the professionalism and skill of his old friend, the way he had carried out his work, that he was correct he boasted proudly that "no traces have ever been left at any of his clean-up operations." As the years went by, Charlie had to believe him.

Charlie lived out the rest of his ministry in Little Perivale and retired as the popular vicar that everyone loved and respected. He decided, in his retirement, to take a cruise round the world and begin to spend some of his savings.

****

And what was in the paper that Rev Charlie Adams read on that fateful morning on board the cruise ship Providence before he jumped overboard?

EXTRA BODIES FOUND IN GRAVEYARD

Police are baffled by the strange happenings uncovered at a church graveyard in Little Perivale, Herts. A road-widening scheme in the village meant the removal and re-burial of 12 graves in the corner of the graveyard. When workman started digging they found the graves contained more bodies than they should. The records in the church clearly state how many bodies should have been in each grave, but some graves had up to two extra bodies in them! Forensic work is being undertaken to try and ascertain the identity of these bodies, and also more excavations are taking place in other parts of the graveyard. The police are anxious to trace the former vicar of Perivale, Rev Charles Adams, who is believed to be on a world cruise at the moment, to see if he can help them with their enquiries.

THE MINISTER'S BARBECUE

or What would Sherlock have done?

——⇒•◆•⇐——

*"Well, I'm afraid I can't help you Lestrade," said Holmes.
"The fact is that I knew this fellow Milverton, that I considered him
one of the most dangerous men in London, and that I think there are
certain crimes which the law cannot touch, and which therefore,
to some extent, justify private revenge."*

**The Adventure of Charles Augustus Milverton
by Arthur Conan Doyle**

——⇒•◆•⇐——

REV JAMES SHERLOCK leant back on his study chair and smiled serenely. It had been a perfect barbecue, held a few hours earlier in the Manse garden. Over 50 members of the congregation had attended and everything had gone well. Even the sun had blessed them with its presence, warming the evening and bringing a soft red glow to the garden. The food had been greatly enjoyed with his wife, Judith, serving the drinks and their daughter Fiona and her boyfriend cooking on the barbecue. James was, as usual, fussing over everything and making sure the evening went smoothly.

The study door opened and his wife came in carrying a tray with coffee cups and a cafetiere. "I thought you deserved this James, with all your hard work today. Everything went so well and it was all down to you." James smiled and pulled up another chair for his wife to sit next to him. The next half hour consisted of them both reviewing the evening, the people, the gossip and news that had been gathered. That night they retired early, content with a good day and the thought that they would sleep soundly.

At 2am the minister sat bolt upright in bed. He was soaked in sweat and feeling absolutely ghastly. Falteringly, he made his way to the bathroom where he was violently sick. When he got back into the bedroom his wife was awake and looking worried. "James, are you alright? What's the matter?"

James's complexion was the same colour as the white sheets on the bed. "I'm not sure, I feel awful, as if I'm going to be ..." He didn't finish the sentence and rushed back into the bathroom.

James didn't sleep at all again that night. When he wasn't in the bathroom being violently sick he had his head in his hands at the side of the bed sobbing. Even his wife couldn't console him. "What have I done Judith? If I'm ill, what about the rest of the village. Have I poisoned them all?"

Judith tried to console him by putting her arms around him, but whatever she said it had little effect. If it was something at the barbecue, then not for the first time in her life Judith was thankful that Fiona and her were both vegetarians.

At last, James fell asleep again but was awakened at 8am by the phone ringing. Judith reached over and picked it up. "The manse, can I help you?" James could only hear Judith's part of the conversation, but he could guess the other half quite easily.

"Yes, the minister's being ill. What? You've been up all night as well? It may well be food poisoning, we will have to see how many other people have also been affected."

James curled up, racked with stomach cramps, but that was nothing to the pain that went deeper, in the very soul of his being. What had he done? Organised a barbecue, poisoned the congregation, not to mention half the village! What a mess! What a bloody mess!

It was only later in the morning that the full scale of the catastrophe revealed itself. Over 50 people had been at the barbecue the night before and 23 of them had been taken ill with food poisoning, and of these, seven were now in hospital seriously ill. The minister was not one of them, but perhaps he should have been, as well as being physically ill the mental anguish was acute. All he could do was sit in the study in his dressing gown receiving and making telephone calls to make sure he was up to date with the news.

As the day wore on the news at least didn't get any worse; there were no new people going down with food poisoning, but then there was Mr. Sidebottom! Mr Sidebottom was the man from the Public Health Department and he arrived at the manse looking a cross between a spaceman and a time and motion keeper. He wore a protective silver shell suit from head to toe with a hood, which could be pulled up at the first sign of attack, replete with silver wellingtons. He also carried a clipboard and his visit was one not one to be enjoyed!

"Now, Mr. Sherlock, I'm sorry to have to inform you that these premises are deemed to be contaminated and until I am satisfied with the cause of the outbreak of food poisoning nothing must be disturbed, removed or anyone leave. Do I make myself clear?"

James looked at him from the other side of the desk. If he had been stronger he would have argued and said something, but the food poisoning had left him weak. He waved Mr Sidebottom away with a gesture which symbolised acquiescence.

The next development was Judith bursting into the study. "James, do you know what that man is doing? He is emptying the contents of the fridge into plastic bags and asked if we have had an infestation of mice, rats, cockroaches or fleas?" Judith was now in tears. "Can't you tell him to go and get rid of him?

James sighed. "I'm afraid not Judith, there has been outbreak of food poisoning and they have to find out where it came from."

Judith stood up indignantly. "Not from my kitchen, I keep it scrupulously clean, we've never had any problems before."

James held his head again, which was beginning to throb. "Judith, we've never had a barbecue before for half the village."

Judith stood over her recumbent husband and looked down at him. "If it was that barbecue then it's wasn't my fault. I told you to be careful. It's all your fault James and I won't be blamed. With that she stormed out of the study, slamming the door. James put his head on the desk and wished that things were not as they were.

Some time later he felt a comforting arm around his shoulder. It was Fiona, his daughter. "Dad, how are you? You are going to get better aren't you?"

James looked into her strong blue eyes and, for the first time that day, smiled. "Yes, I will get better Fiona, I have to. You know I never thought it would be an advantage until now to be a vegetarian!"

Fiona's face lit up with a broad smile and then a frown crossed her brow. "Have you seen that nasty little man Mr. Sidebottom? He's questioned me about the barbecue; he even asked if I had cooked the food for enough time before it was served? The cheek of it! I told him straight that I had a certificate for culinary skills & food hygiene from the college. That shut him up. A real nasty little man."

James smiled and patted her arm. "He's only doing his job dear, there has to be an investigation, people are very ill and something must have gone wrong."

The telephone rang and James went to answer it. It was hard to imagine that his complexion could go paler, but on hearing the news, it did. He put the phone down and looked ashen.

Fiona looked concerned. "What's the matter, dad?"

James looked very serious. "Mrs Tempest, she's taken a turn for the worse and is very ill in hospital, they think it was food poisoning."

It was Fiona's turn to look pale. She put her arms around her father and they both sobbed together.

The entire village soon knew on that fateful Friday the full extent of the 'manse food poisoning'. Of the seven people in hospital, four had been discharged and three others were on the critical list: Mrs Tempest, who was in her 80s, Anne Riley, a spinster in her early 60s, and Charles Gerling, a local businessmen in his late 40s. That night James slept, but it wasn't the sleep of tranquillity but the sleep of wanting to forget and get away from a world of rumour, guilt, accusations and innuendo.

As James awoke on the Saturday he found that he felt remarkably well, that is until he remembered the events of the previous 36 hours. The feeling of nausea had gone but was replaced with a sense of apprehension and recrimination on how stupid he had been and how careless to allow such a serious act to ruin what was a perfect barbecue.

It wasn't long before there was a knock on the door and Mr Sidebottom arrived, this time with two colleagues similarly attired. "I am sorry to disturb you minister," he said, "but this is now a serious case of food poisoning with three people on the critical list." James stood aside and let them pass into the house, detecting a faint sense of satisfaction from Mr Sidebottom. Here was a little man, he thought, and now he was important, in charge of a major investigation. Maybe he sat around his office every day waiting for such an occurrence to take place.

They left after a couple of hours, taking with them various samples in plastic bags, and after questioning everyone who had anything to do with the barbecue. Mr. Sidebottom declared that life in the manse could now resume, as he didn't think they would need to come back. James asked if they knew where the poisoning had come from. Mr. Sidebottom rose to his full height of five feet four inches, trying to look imposing and reading from his clipboard: "Staphylococcus aureus, contamination of the sausages, Mr. Sherlock." He said it with all the venom of a devout vegetarian.

James stammered: "But they were freshly bought from the butchers in Marmby. I always buy them from there..."

Mr Sidebottom peered above his clipboard. "That seems to be where the evidence is pointing. Probable contamination from the butcher's shop. It's the one common element between all the poisonings. We have closed the shop of course for further tests." James's colour again ran from his cheeks. Was there no end to this nightmare? Now a local business's livelihood was threatened.

After the 'Health Gestapo', as Fiona nicknamed them, had gone James went into the study and tried to say his prayers; it wasn't easy.

Later that morning James felt that he could sit in the manse no longer. He wanted to do something, so he decided to go and visit the hospital and the three parishioners who were still there. First, he called in to see Mrs Tempest. She was sleeping and still very ill. Next to her bed were her niece and nephew, who looked accusingly at James when he introduced himself. He didn't stay very long.

When he walked onto the next ward to see Anne Riley his heart leapt and he smiled for the first time in ages. There, sitting up in bed, was Anne reading the paper and munching on a piece of toast. "So good to see you Anne, how are you? I thought they said you were extremely ill."

Anne smiled. "Oh, I was, I felt absolutely lousy minister, vomiting and diarrhoea. I thought I was going to die. But as quickly as it came, it went. I woke up this morning feeling fine and hungry. They said they will keep me in for another night and if I'm alright in the morning, I'll be home in time for morning service James!" She winked at him and they both laughed. The tone of the conversation became more sombre when she asked about others who had been at the party. James told her of Mrs Tempest and how he was just going to see Charles Gerling. Other people in the village had made a good recovery and after 24 hours they felt fine. James told Anne about the visits from Mr Sidebottom and the suspicion about the sausages. Anne put a reassuring hand on the minister's after they had prayed and, as he was about to leave, said, "Don't take it all on yourself James, you're not to blame, everyone knows that."

James felt reassured, but it was a feeling was quickly dispelled when he walked into the single room where Charles Gerling was being cared for. He was unconscious, with various tubes and monitors attached to him. Sitting by the side of the bed was his wife Heather, holding his hand and looking very distraught. She looked up as soon as James came into the room. "Oh minister, I'm so glad to see you, but I thought you were ill?" James put his arm around her and told her that his illness had only been for 24 hours.

He asked how Charles was. Heather stopped crying and told him how they said that Charles had a very nasty bout of food poisoning which he wasn't shaking off. His heart condition didn't help and they said that the next 24 hours were crucial. "They are doing all they can to help him pull through." She then burst into tears again. James put a comforting arm around her. Heather looked into James eyes. "Is it true about Mrs Tempest and Anne Riley, are they going to be alright?" James could only confirm some good news about Anne Riley, but then relay the news that they were still worried about Mrs Tempest because of her age and frailty. Heather burst into more tears.

Mrs Tempest was a wonderful lady, generous and even though she was in her eighties, always the life and soul of any gathering at the church. Some said she was eccentric, others a bit of a character, but everyone loved her and had time for her and now she was lying gravely ill in hospital, poisoned at the Minister's barbecue! James felt the void at the pit of his stomach once more.

He stayed with Heather for over an hour and after saying prayers at the bedside left saying that he would return as soon as he could.

James drove back to the village with a heavy heart. What had he done? What havoc had he allowed to occur at his barbecue? On that Saturday afternoon, I suppose by way of reparation, he went to visit people who had been taken ill at the party. It was a long, weary afternoon interspersed with innumerable cups of tea and hearing the same story again and again. People had felt ill during the night and, the following day, it seemed as if the food poisoning was for most people a 24-hour infection which they shook off very quickly. Everyone was very understanding and only a couple of people said things like 'more care should have been taken' and 'how could such a thing happen?' They had all heard the news about the sausages and the closure of the butcher's shop. Mr Sidebottom and his aides had been busy visiting them, it seemed! A few people said that they thought the sausages tasted a little strange but put it down to the unusual flavours, pork & apple or venison & stilton.

James walked back to the manse later on that Saturday evening wondering about that quirk of human nature that is always wise after the event and that some people it seemed could have predicted problems. Why didn't they say anything then at the barbecue? As he walked up the path Judith, looking concerned, came out to meet him. "You look all in dear," she said anxiously. "You shouldn't have pushed yourself so much."

James smiled. "I had to. I wanted to show people I cared and I suppose punish myself because it is all my fault." He broke down and started crying. Judith put her arms around him and held him like she

31

would a small child, trying to comfort him. But there was no comfort. The quote, which seemed so apt came from Matthew's gospel: 'Like Rachel weeping for her children; she refused to be consoled, because they were no more.'

Sunday morning dawned with the sun shining from a clear blue sky. James was in his study early, trying to put the finishing touches to the service he was about to take in a few hours. It wouldn't be easy and he was finding it very difficult to put any coherent thoughts together.

He needn't have worried as the few people who turned up were there to support the minister in his time of need and pray for those who were still ill. There was some good news. Anne Riley had been discharged and Mrs Tempest was now sitting up in bed talking, but Charles Gerling had still not recovered consciousness and his latest condition was causing grave concern.

James didn't want lunch and just ate some fruit before dashing off once again to the hospital. He drew up outside and walked towards the ward where Charles was. He opened the door and Heather ran over to him sobbing. He put his arms around her, as she blurted out between sobs, "It's Charles, he's…dead." James could only hold her and feel once again the sinking void in his stomach. After saying prayers around the bedside and anointing Charles, they took their leave, James offering to drive Heather back to the village.

They drove back in silence; no words could comfort and nothing could make any difference now. James avoided any platitudes. What was the use? The only thing he felt was guilt and shame that he had been the cause of death of Heather's husband. The car swung into the gravel drive to Heather's house and James couldn't help parking next to Charles' Jaguar, which was still where he had left it on the night of the fateful barbecue, outside the garage.

James went into the house with Heather, a house which was silent and would remain so, thought James. He was worried for Heather. They had no family although they had been married for over 20 years. Charles was a successful businessman, travelling the world, and the house showed the marks of that success with all the material comforts, but, thought James, not much of a home or showing much character.

James made Heather a cup of tea and they sat in the lounge sipping the brew, both locked into their own thoughts. James broke the silence. "I feel so responsible for all this, if I hadn't had that stupid barbecue Charles would not be dead and 25 people wouldn't have been taken ill."

Heather smiled. "Don't blame yourself minister, you weren't to know, you've done nothing wrong. Sadly, accidents happen, that's part of life." James was quietly reassured that Heather was taking it like this. Better this than accusing or blaming him, he didn't think he could stand that. He asked if there was anyone Heather could be with, explaining that she should not be alone at a time like this. She smiled at James, her sisters were on their way, they would look after her and see that she was cared for. James left her, saying that he would call again the following day.

He drove the short journey to the manse and as soon as the car drew up, out of the house rushed Fiona in tears. What could be wrong now? Not more bad news? He wasn't sure that he could take any more.

"It's Tara, dad…she's…in the garden and not moving…" James rushed around the back of the house to see Judith bending over the prone form of their dog Tara, who lay motionless on the lawn. At first glance she seemed to be lying in the sun, but when you got closer you could see there was no movement at all.

Fiona was sobbing and Judith looked anxiously at James, "I think she's dead James."

James bent over and touched the dog that had been so much part of their lives for over ten years, like another child really. "How did it happen?" asked James. Fiona, in between sobs, said that she was in the garden reading and sunbathing with Tara. She noticed that the dog had gone into the bushes and seemed to dig up something, then she started eating it. Fiona had got up and tried to get it off her. It looked like a piece of chicken, but Tara thought it was a game and ran off and ate it at the bottom of the garden. She then came back onto the lawn and lay down and went to sleep…she never woke up.

James looked at the dog again, this time prising her mouth open and noticing small flecks of white froth around her teeth and gums. He picked her up and took her into the garage, laying her down gently in a large cardboard box and covering her with a blanket. There were tears in his eyes when he returned to the garden and all three of them were crying.

That evening, for the first time in his ministry, James felt he couldn't take the evening service and rang a lay preacher to ask if they would deputise. James stayed in his study for over two hours sitting at his desk and going over and over in his mind the events of the last three days.

Fiona brought him a drink of coffee and came and sat on his knee, something she had not done for ten years but she always did as a small child. She hugged her father and they spoke about all the good times they had enjoyed with Tara. They smiled and laughed and it seemed to help.

As Fiona got up to go her father looked at her intently and asked, "Are you sure it was a piece of chicken that Tara ate?" Fiona frowned.

"Yes, when I tried to get if off her I saw it quite closely."

James rose from behind the desk. "Could you show me where she picked it up from?"

Fiona looked puzzled. "Yes, I think so."

It was still quite light as they went into the garden. Fiona's book was still lying beside the sun-lounger with a half-finished drink. Fiona stood by the chair. "Now, let me see. I was sitting here and reading the novel. I glanced up and saw Tara go behind those bushes." She pointed to the far end of the garden. "A few moments later she came out carrying something in her mouth, and so I got up and went over to her."

They both moved across the lawn to the bushes. James bent down and looked carefully at a piece of earth where the leaves had been scratched away. "No wonder your called Sherlock, dad! What are you expecting to find?"

James examined the earth carefully, running his fingers over it. "I don't know," he said. He then picked up something that looked like a black twig but when you held it up to the light it was a bone, obviously blackened because of the barbecue. "Fetch me a plastic bag will you Fiona, I want to have this checked out."

Fiona went into the kitchen to her mother, who was watching them from the kitchen window. "What is your father doing?"

Fiona rolled her eyes and smiled. "He's not called Sherlock for nothing, you know!"

The following morning James drove to the vets in the next village. He took a large cardboard box out of the boot of his car and carried it into the surgery. He knew the vet and Roland had looked curiously at it. James put it down on the table in the small examining room.

"It's Tara, Roland, she's dead."

The vet opened the lid and looked in. "I'm so sorry James, was it sudden? How did it happen?"

"Food poisoning, I think, but I would like you to do a post-mortem."

"Oh yes, I heard about your barbecue James, are you alright?"

"For most people it was a 24-hour bug but someone has died, and now a dog."

Roland was examining Tara's' head and mouth. "Food poisoning is a strange thing. Dogs normally have a strong constitution, but she was twelve and you can never can tell."

"Roland, could you do a post mortem? I want to find out what killed her."

Roland looked uneasy. "Well yes, I can James, but I'm not sure what you'll learn. The public health inspectors will have done all the tests and you won't learn anything they don't know. The other thing is, it's not cheap. For a dog this size about £250 with the lab tests and things."

James looked intently. "Do it Roland, I'm not bothered about the cost."

James received some good news from the hospital. Mrs Tempest had recovered and was to be allowed home. James breathed a great sigh of relief and said a prayer of thanks. When he went into the front room he found Mr Sidebottom, looking even more officious. The shell suit had gone but the clipboard remained. He stood up as James entered the room, "Ah, Mr Sherlock." It seemed that he took a perverse delight in not addressing James by his title of Reverend. "I thought you would like to know the preliminary results of our investigation."

James sat down and listened intently.

"It seems," explained Mr Sidebottom, "that the problem was with the sausages, as I first thought. We checked with the butchers and thankfully it seems to be this is the only batch which was contaminated. The shop is scrupulously clean and passed all our tests. No one else who bought from that batch of sausages was ill, so we can only presume the bacteria, although it may have been in the whole batch of sausages, if they were cooked correctly then it was rendered harmless."

Fiona, who was standing by the window, burst into tears. "So it was me. I cooked the sausages, I must have been at fault."

Judith went over to console her. "No dear, it wasn't your fault, it was an accident."

James sat on the settee ringing his hands. "How could the food poisoning happen?"

Mr Sidebottom took off his spectacles, the gesture almost made him look human. "Barbecues are very dangerous things Mr Sherlock, we always have trouble in the summer. People abandon normal well-tried methods of cooking and think that because it looks burnt on the outside it is cooked, but that it is not always so, as this unfortunate incident has proved."

James continued to wring his hands, it was his fault and he had to take the blame. Just as Mr Sidebottom was about to leave James mentioned the dog and his sudden death. This resulted in a shake of the head from the man from the ministry and a tut-tutting. "Animals can also be affected Mr Sherlock, it must have been a rogue sausage left out there."

Mr Sidebottom retreated out of the house, his job done. There would be an inquest into the death, of course, but the hospital seemed to be satisfied that they had found the cause of death. Mr Gerling had a weak heart as well as the food poisoning.

Later that day James went to see about the funeral that would have to be arranged. Heather was at home and had been joined by her two sisters, Claire and Trudy. Heather was much more herself, thought James, the company was obviously doing her good. She was very composed and wanted to discuss arrangements for the funeral when the coroner had released the body. Her husband's colleagues would want to give a tribute, if that was alright. James said it was and there was to be some modern music played as Charles wasn't very religious. It was when James was in the kitchen with one of the sisters that a comment was expressed that surprised him. It was Trudy, the younger sister, who said to James, "You know minister, I won't be shedding any tears about Charles's death. Oh, of course I'm upset for Heather, but that man was a bastard. He chased anything in a skirt and he had even made passes at me and Claire."

James didn't know what to say; he had heard some of the rumours about Charles and the long business trips, how Heather was pitied not envied by other women in the village. But this was a bit strong and he found himself coming out with a cliché, unusual for him, "Best not to speak ill of the dead." They went back into the lounge and finished the details as much as they could for now.

As James walked back to manse he was in reflective mood and thinking about Heather. He even began feel sorry for her, married to Charles. If everything her sister had said was true then Heather wasn't going to miss Charles that much.

When he got back to the manse there had been a phone call from the vets. He rang Roland back and spoke to him. "We did the post mortem and yes, it was food poisoning – but there were no sausages, it was from a piece of a chicken and it was full of it, that one piece could have killed five men. I think you were fortunate, Charles, that only one person has died; this was mega food poisoning."

James put the phone down and sat in the study thinking. He was still deep in thought when Fiona came in with a cup of tea. "Thought you may like this, dad."

James smiled. "Thanks Fiona, come and sit down. I want to ask you something."

Fiona looked worried. "Not more questions dad, I had 'old smileybum' (as Fiona called Mr Sidebottom) this morning with more questions for me."

"No, Fiona, it's not like that, I just want to get into my mind what happened at the barbecue. Can we go outside and try to work out the exact sequence of events?"

Fiona looked resigned. "If we must, you play your namesake, I'll pretend to be Dr Watson."

They went out to the patio and Fiona stood by the barbecue. "Mum was serving the drinks and you were bringing food to us for cooking in between socialising. I was at the barbecue with Henry and Heather was also around helping us with the bread and salads." Fiona looked a little tired but complied with her father, even if it was only to humour him. "We cooked two lots of beefburgers first and then the sausages you brought from the kitchen. Then the chicken, which you told me we should cook carefully, you had part-cooked it in the oven."

James was writing it all down. "If I remember, I brought two packets of burgers, that's 24, then the sausages, which were on two large plates. Then two trays of chicken, which Heather brought out."

"Yes, that's right dad. You then brought out another tray of sausages and some veggie burgers."

"We did some more burgers and then finished off with the last four pieces of chicken, which Heather brought out."

James stopped writing and looked up. "But that's too many pieces of chicken." James looked puzzled. "You must have miscalculated."

Fiona looked puzzled. "No, I didn't. Heather brought out the last pieces of chicken for herself and her husband. She told me not to let anyone else take them. I cooked them and she put them on two plates. We then let the barbecue go out."

James closed the notebook "Thanks Fiona."

"Can I go now dad? Henry wants to take me out tonight, or do you want to question him?"

"No, I don't want to question him, have a good time."

James sat a long time in the garden and wondered. Was it possible? But how had the health inspectors missed it? Was he the only one who knew what had happened? The shadows crept across the garden and it grew cold. James went into the house, a plan forming in his mind.

The next day he decided to call to see Heather again. The sisters had returned home and were coming back the following day; she was alone. James made the excuse that he was just calling in to make sure she was alright. James made sure that he dropped into the conversation the fact the dog had died and they suspected food poisoning. "He probably picked up a stray piece of food on the Sunday after the barbecue." James said that they would have to mount a thorough search of the garden tomorrow to make sure there was no food left there which could poison anyone or make any other animal ill. He watched Heather's face closely when he said this but could detect no subtle change. Shortly afterwards, he left.

The Minister's Barbecue

That night Judith, by good fortune, retired to bed early saying that the events of the last few days had worn her out. James said he was going to work late in his study and would try not to disturb her when he came to bed. At 10.30 he switched all the downstairs lights of the house off and sat in his study. The windows overlooked the garden and there was a patio door, which he opened slightly so that he could hear any noise. He wrapped himself up with a blanket and waited. It was a night with a decent moon and not many clouds, so it was quite light. The first thing he saw was a fox cross the lawn and head for the bushes, then what looked like field mice scamper across the lawn, followed by a hedgehog meandering. It was now after midnight and he felt his head nodding. Then he heard it. Someone was walking very quietly up the gravel path along the side of the house and into the back garden. They had a torch and the figure dressed in black made their way along the side of the lawn straight to the bush where Tara had dug up the piece of chicken. The figure bent down and, with what looked like a small trowel, started digging. It was a few minutes before they stood up and returned the way they had come. James slipped on his coat and followed at a distance, keeping in the shadows.

The figure was just putting the key in the lock when James came up behind them. "So that's how you did it is it Heather?" Heather Gerling gave a gasp and turned around, startled.

James and Heather sat in her large kitchen. Heather had her head in her hands. "I thought it was a perfect plan, but it all went wrong. How did you guess? "

James was sitting a few feet away from her. "It was the dog's death and the four extra pieces of chicken. I could have believed it was the sausages, the health inspectors did, but when Tara died after digging up a piece of chicken, it just didn't add up. How did you do it, Heather?"

Heather looked resigned to the fact that she had been caught out. "It was quite simple. I had planned it for months. Charles was a first class bastard. He flaunted his affairs in front of me, and he made no pretence to hide them. He enjoyed seeing me squirm. The last straw was the hospital test I went for to see if we could have a baby three years ago. The hospital informed me I had a sexually transmitted disease, which made me infertile. I had been faithful in our marriage and I confronted Charles. He didn't even have the courtesy to lie. He said he found sex with me boring and had been taking every opportunity for the last two years to sleep around. There had been many occasions with all the business trips. He even admitted picking up call girls and lap dancers. He must have picked something up then. 'Picked something up' like a cold. This was about our family, or lack of it! I was so angry I was going to leave him then and there. I thought about it a lot, but then I wanted revenge and so I started planning how I could get rid of him without throwing suspicion on myself. I studied all about poisons, read all the books. I'm quite an expert now. I waited for an opportunity when food was being served and Charles would be there, away from our home. Your barbecue, minister, was the ideal opportunity. I volunteered to help Fiona and Henry and waited until all the food had been cooked."

"What about the sausages?" interjected James.

That was a mild form of food poisoning. Charles couldn't be the only person ill, could he? I had grown some bacteria on some rotten sausages. I just sprinkled some of it on your sausages before they were cooked. It was only meant to give people a queasy tummy, not kill them." Her eyes filled with tears. "Believe me minister, I didn't intend to endanger other lives, it was the last thing on my mind."

"But Heather you were playing a very dangerous game, trying to give mild poisons. Especially to elderly people."

"I know and that's where it went wrong."

"Tell me about the chicken."

"I prepared those at home. There were four pieces laced with staphylococcus aureus. Enough to kill someone with a heart condition. I waited until everything had been cooked, then brought out the poisoned chicken pieces, asking Fiona to cook them for me and Charles. I stood at the side and waited, not daring to move away from the barbecue. I had told Charles the wrong time for the barbecue so that he would arrive late and most of the food would have gone. He liked spiced chicken anyway, so when the four pieces were ready I took them and put two on a plate for Charles with some sausages. I then took mine to the bottom of the garden and, when no one was looking, slipped behind a tree and pushed them into the ground with my foot. I never thought about the dog. I am so sorry James, I never meant to kill Tara."

James looked at her intently. "What happened then?"

"We went home and I sat downstairs and drank wine while Charles went to bed saying he didn't feel very well. I unplugged the phone and hid his mobile and waited. It didn't take very long. He was shouting and pleading with me to get a doctor. I pretended to ring and then he passed out, unconscious. I did ring early in the morning and they took him to hospital, never to regain consciousness. You know the rest."

James made a deep sigh and looked at Heather. She would be facing at least ten years in jail for this, if not more, he thought.

Heather looked at James and spoke. "Don't turn me in James. I've had my punishment, all the years with Charles. You can't begin to realise what I've had to endue in my marriage. I'm sorry for making the others ill. I deserve to be punished for that, but not for Charles, he only got what he deserved."

"Heather, we can't take the law into our own hands, whatever the provocation."

"But what about the things he did to me? The beatings, the humiliation, the fact that he took everything away, even my self-respect. He was a bastard and I'm glad he's dead."

James knew he should ring the police, but hesitated.

"Heather, I'm going home to sleep on this. I will tell you what I'm going to do in the morning."

James walked home feeling a very heavy burden on his shoulders. He went into his study and picked up a book from the shelves and turned to one of his favourite stories. It wasn't from the Bible but from the collected stories of Sherlock Holmes. The story was 'Charles Augustus Milverton', a rather unusual story where Sherlock Holmes, after discovering who committed the murder, lets them off and doesn't turn them over to the police, believing that they have been punished enough and prison would do nothing for them. They have been blackmailed and the blackmailer gets his just deserts.

James Sherlock closed the book and switched off the study light. As he went up the stairs, he pondered if Heather Gerling had been punished enough! He wondered: 'What would Sherlock have done?'

DOUBLE DELIGHT

Alice emerged from the 'Wood Where Things Have No Name' and began to see double. She followed two signs which led her in the same direction. The first sign read TO TWEEDLEDUM'S HOUSE and the second TO THE HOUSE OF TWEEDLEDEE. She realized that, although the signposts were separate, the house she was calling on was one and the same.

'Alice Through The Looking Glass' by Lewis Carroll

"HI GUV, CAN I look after the car for you?" the small grubby boy enquired, gazing up at the tall sleek-looking man stepping out of the silver Porsche.

The man smiled as he took off his dark shades. "Yes, sure and here's something for your trouble, and they'll be the same again if it's OK when I come back." He handed the boy five coins and he smiled, expecting them to be ten pences – that was the usual rate in Moss Side for looking after cars. "Thanks guv, it'll be OK."

It was only when the man had begun walking away that the boy uncurled his fist and saw five yellow coins, five quid for one car! Wow! He'd be able to retire soon with a few more like this, he thought.

The man reached the door of a large detached Victorian-looking house, a bit shabby but substantial, which had obviously seen better days. He knocked on the door.

As it opened it was like looking at a mirror, for the two men facing each other were identical in every respect, their looks, even the way they parted their hair. The only thing that distinguished them was their clothes. One was expensively dressed with a hand-cut suit, the other wearing clothes that had obviously seen better days, and while not scruffy, were certainly not the height of fashion. And, of course, one was wearing a dog collar.

"Brian, how good to see you, what a surprise this is, do come in."

"Thanks Giles. I was passing through so I thought I would call to see you."

Giles grinned. "Come off it Brian! How many times do you pass through Moss Side? You must be here for something."

"Just a brotherly chat. After all, we are twins and shouldn't they always stick together?" He sat down in the comfortable armchair.

Giles smiled and gave his brother a friendly pat on the shoulder. "Nice to see you Brian, you know we should see each other more, after all for the first 16 years of our lives we were never apart, we shared everything."

Brian grinned. "Those were the things I'd rather forget, like being dressed by mum in the same identical clothes, being stared at all the time, and those ghastly conventions of identical twins we used to go to, like a circus freak show."

Giles frowned. "They were also good times, the scrapes we used to get into, people never knowing which one of us was responsible when something went wrong. I even seem to remember you had a very good way of pinching every girlfriend I ever had by impersonating me."

Brian laughed and they shared a drink together, talking for the next half hour as if they had never been apart. A casual observer would notice the uncanny knack each brother had of anticipating what the other one was going to say; it was like two intimate friends who were extremely close and knew each other well spending a lot of time together. But these two brothers had not seen each other for over a year.

After about an half an hour Giles stopped in mid-sentence and looked intently at his twin brother. "Brian, why are you here? There must be a reason."

Brian moved uneasily in the chair. "I suppose it's no use trying to hide anything from you. After all, we can almost read each other's minds like a book. There is a reason why I'm here out of the blue and I'll be up-front with you. I want you to do me a favour."

Giles looked amazed. "Me, a humble clergyman, doing you, one of the great financial magnates in the City, a favour. One who buys and sells companies worth millions. I hope it's not to do with money, because I don't have any, as you well you know."

Brian laughed. "No, I didn't come here for money, just the thing you alone can give me."

Giles looked intently at his brother, trying to delve behind the well-manicured exterior and burrow down into his thoughts. "I can't believe after all these years you've come for spiritual advice and counsel. Are you in some kind of trouble?"

"No, not at all, things are going well. In fact, life couldn't be better, but let me explain: You know I deal in takeovers in the City. They can be high risk, but I know my job and I have been successful up to now. It's a cut-throat business and you've always got to be ahead of the opposition and making plans for the future."

Giles looked puzzled. "I know all this Brian, but where do I fit in."

Brian took a deep breath. "I'm coming to that. I have just found out through a contact that in exactly one month's time a large British-American company will go into liquidation. It will happen on the Monday morning when trading opens on the stock market in New York. If I can steal a march on my rivals I can clinch the deal, not just of the year but also of the century. To do it I will have to be in two places at the same time."

Giles's jaw dropped and his bottom lip quivered, but no words came out.

"News will leak out on the Friday before and if people get wind of me being in New York that weekend then others will try to muscle in on the deal and it will collapse. If, however, I am seen to be in London then people will think it is a rumour and not act upon it. When the news breaks on the Monday morning I will have tied up the deal in New York and no-one will be able to do a thing."

Giles had now recovered his speech. "Let me get this right Brian, you're asking me to impersonate you for a weekend with all your friends. I, who don't know what a stock or bond is! You think I can deceive people like this. Oh come on brother, you must have been watching too many Hollywood films."

Brian looked intently at his brother. "If I hadn't gone over and over this in my mind I would never have come to you. It can work, I know it can and I have thought out everything."

Giles shook his head. "Brian you're mad, how can it possibly work, even if I was to agree, my cover would be blown with your first friend who greeted me and I wouldn't know from Adam?"

"I've thought about that. One other person has to be in on this, my personal assistant, Laura, who will be at your side all weekend. She will steer you through any difficult conversations."

Giles looked a littler sterner. "Brian, even if it were possible, have you thought about the real reason why I wouldn't do it? It's deception. I'm a clergyman and I don't set out to deceive people and commit crimes."

"This is not a crime, Giles. I am not defrauding anyone. I am just laying a false scent and if people choose to believe one thing then it's up to them."

Giles stood up. "This is preposterous. I can't do it."

Brian clenched his fist and banged it down on the chair. "Giles, I know you can do it. Remember all the times in our teens when we used to fool people. What about that exam?"

Giles turned and looked angrily at his brother. "That was different, we were teenagers, we were just fooling around. This is the real world. We are adults now, responsible ones, at least one of us is, and has some morals."

Brian looked crestfallen and beaten for the first time in the conversation. "So that's it, you won't even consider it, your high and mighty morals say that you can't do it. Even though it would make such a difference to the people around here where you work."

Giles looked puzzled. "What do you mean?"

Brian felt he was back on level terms. "Didn't I tell you there would be something in it for you?"

Giles paused and gathered his thoughts. "You know Brian, I thought we had something – you know as twins we understand each other, but the City certainly has corrupted you if you think you can win me over with a cheap bribe. That's one temptation I have no inclination to fall for."

Brian had one last throw of the dice. He reached into his jacket, pulled out a chequebook and wrote a cheque and then handed it to his brother. Giles's eyes narrowed and his nostrils flared. "Brian, I told you I'm not to be bribed."

Brian lowered his voice, trying desperately to take the sting out of the argument. "Not for you, Giles, but for the church and your work here. I have been doing some research. You're doing a good job here, well liked by everyone and working hard in the community with little resources. Here is the one chance you can have to make a difference, that new Youth Club, even the Nursery for the children, not to mention repairs to the church. I ask you to do one thing brother and that is just look at the cheque." But Giles's hand closed on the cheque, screwing it up in his clenched fist.

Giles looked angrily at his brother, feeling that the love and kinship that had been there through everything, in all the ups and downs of life, one thing had been certain and true, the bond between them as identical twins.

Giles uncurled his fist and slowly unfolded the cheque. He didn't know what he expected: a few thousand pounds, £10,000 maybe! He was not prepared for the figure he saw. The cheque for £250.000 was made out to the church.

Giles sank into the chair. "Good grief! I've never seen such a cheque." His glance met his brother's. "How much is this deal worth?"

Brian clicked his teeth. "Many millions. It will set me on a different course for the rest of my life. This will not be the end Giles. I will help you again, whichever church you're at."

Giles's hand again closed on the cheque and screwed it up. "You don't understand Brian...I can't do it...When I left university I could have gone into the City like you, probably done as well as you, but now things are different. I've given all that up, so don't ask me to do the one thing I can't do and that's be untrue to myself and live a lie, not even for you brother."

Brian turned and left the room, for once in his life beaten, and he knew it would be useless to argue, for who knew his brother better than himself?

For Giles that night was a sleepless one. He could have put it down to the storm outside, the trees bending in the wind and the rain lashing down on the windows of the vicarage. But he knew it was the request from his brother being tossed to and fro in his mind. How could his brother even ask him? Giles had rejected the high-flying life to become a clergyman, much to the chagrin of his parents and friends. All his teaching at seminary, all he knew about being a Christian, how could he deceive? How could his brother even ask him? He knew he was right to refuse the offer, but to reject his brother! For the first time in their lives they had parted in silence and tension. Giles didn't like that and it felt like he had cut off his right arm.

The following morning, on his way into church for the early morning service, Tom the verger, looking worried, met him. "Bad news, vicar, the storm last night did some damage to the roof and water has started to come in. Giles's heart sank. That was all that was needed. They had just had major repairs done and there was no money left. He went into the church and was met with what looked like a sea of buckets catching the drops of rainwater. All the way through the service the only sound he was conscious of was the plip-plopping of the water into the buckets, each one seemingly laughing at him and saying I told you so.

On his return to the house he phoned the diocesan architect. Giles thought he had good relations with him. The work that had been recently done on the building had gone well and although the church was now in debt, it was nothing unusual for an inner city parish. The phone call didn't go as planned. The architect wouldn't sanction emergency repairs; he wanted to come round later that week to assess the viability of the building. This emergency had meant that St Aiden's had just moved up the ladder on the diocese hit list – as it was jokingly referred to – the list where the viability of the church was put into question with all that would involve. Giles put the phone down and sighed, his eye catching the crumpled piece of paper on the floor. He unfolded the cheque and gazed at it. He wondered if his principles were worth the sacrifice.

Brian was in his office high up in Canary Wharf, looking out over the London skyline, when Laura, his PA, came in. "I have your brother on the phone and he says it's urgent."

Brian made a dive for the phone and snatched it up. "Giles!"

"Brian. I'll do it, but I have some conditions. I want to be assured that this will not backfire on me and I am not committing any crime."

Brian was exuberant. "Giles, I give you my word, you won't regret this, and you don't know what it means to me." They arranged to meet later to go over the plans.

As Brian put the phone down he leapt into the air, as a footballer does when he scores a goal, and shouted, "YES!!!"

Over the next three weeks Giles made several trips to London to meet his brother at his offices on Canary Wharf, always travelling first class on the train and with a taxi waiting for him at the station. He had to disguise his appearance a little so he wouldn't be confused with his brother – just yet! Giles had great misgivings that he could actually carry it off and, although he looked like his brother, they certainly didn't think the same or act in a similar way. He was reassured that during the weekend in question, Laura would be by his side, guiding him through conversations, reminding him of people's names. Giles knew he could do the small talk. He was a vicar after all and his social life consisted of countless parish fêtes and coffee mornings when he couldn't remember people's names but managed to disguise the fact and put on a convincing display.

At last the weekend arrived. Brian had arranged for Giles to meet him on the Thursday evening in his London penthouse for a last minute briefing before he flew to New York the following morning.

Giles was nervous as he rang the bell outside Brian's flat. Going through his mind were all the questions and worries. Why was he doing this, getting involved in this way? If it were exposed, he could lose his living as a clergyman, or at least be severely disciplined. Was he really doing this for the church roof, or was it that deep down he shared the same excitement for danger as his twin brother, a bond that they had shared all their lives and which couldn't be explained to anyone who was not an identical twin? It was one person trapped inside two bodies, not that they thought alike, but they could understand and anticipate each other. They could sense the other twin, even when they were not there, and often did not need verbal communication to understand each other. A thought grew and took shape, a reason for this venture. No, it wasn't the church roof he was doing it for, it was for his brother. It was as if his brother held a magnet, which drew Giles closer, and he knew he was powerless to resist. He rang the bell.

There was a strange feeling of separation and a frisson of danger as Giles and Laura stood at the departure gate to see Brian off to New York. They returned to the car park silently, each wrapped up in the events of the coming weekend and the part they would play. Giles felt that already he knew and liked Laura, someone who was devoted to his brother and obviously arranged most of his life. He hadn't asked Brian how close he was to his PA; he didn't have to ask. Giles had picked up the signs in the body language, the eye contact as they talked. He knew he could trust Laura.

As they drove back to Canary Wharf, Giles posed a question. "Laura, why you are getting involved in all this? It goes far beyond what is expected of you as Brian's PA."

Laura smiled. "I guess I know your brother better than anyone, apart from you of course. He has a gift for inspiring loyalty, people will do anything for him. He's also fun, he lives on the edge and although it's a dangerous place to be, it's also exhilarating. I would rather be here than some PA to a boring City banker."

Giles interjected: "Or secretary to a clergyman?"

Laura laughed. "I bet you have your wild side, and if you're Brian's twin your parish will not be run-of-the-mill. I bet you take risks and have fun. I don't see you as a fuddy-duddy, not at all the image of the conventional clergyman."

Giles laughed. No, he wasn't at all like the conventional clergyman! What other member of the clergy would be setting out to deceive and hoodwink many hundreds of people masquerading as someone they are not?

They went into the office at Canary Wharf. This time, though, Giles was not the casually-dressed visitor with shapeless clothes, but Brian, with a £1,000 suit and hand-made shoes, the head of one of the leading finance houses in the city. Giles quickly realised his new status as they walked into the lobby. People moved aside as they walked through. They almost bowed and acknowledged them with a smile, or stood aside. If this is what power and status were, Giles thought, he could understand why some people almost get drunk with it.

He was brought down to earth in the lift, so to speak. Laura had almost managed to make sure they were alone in there when, at the very last moment, a breathless man jumped in. He straightened his hair, looked Giles straight in eye and said, "Hi Brian, how's tricks?" Giles's mind was racing, who was he? How friendly could he be? Laura hadn't had chance to whisper his name. He found his mouth opening and words beginning to form.

"Fine, I'm looking forward to the weekend."

The man smiled. "How did it go with Anglo-American?"

Giles felt sweat beginning to break out on his brow. Brian hadn't said anything about Anglo-American. How vague or specific should he be? He couldn't just say fine again. Before he could speak Laura broke in. "Oh Jeremy, it wasn't completed. There was a problem with the line to Boston and it broke up after a few minutes."

Jeremy nodded and, thankfully, got out of the lift at the next floor.

Laura and Giles went into Brian's office. Giles was looking pale. "I can't do it Laura. It was stupid to think I could carry it off. I froze in that lift. I didn't know what to say because I wasn't sure how close he was to Brian. I can't go through with it. We'll have to ring Brian when he gets to New York and tell him it's off, it's not working out."

Laura gave a deep sigh. "Just sit down Giles, you did fine. That was all you needed to say and aren't you pleased that someone could stand only inches away from you and think you are your brother. Your cover wasn't blown at all. Let me pour you a drink and we'll go through the details for the weekend."

Giles felt reassured. It would be stupid to give up at the first hurdle and, yes, he had never thought about being able to carry off the physical impersonation. Giles took it for granted that the physical likeness would work; he never doubted that people would mistake him for his brother.

They went through plans for the weekend. They were to stay in the office until mid-afternoon, taking any phone calls, which would be easy as Laura could listen in and almost dictate an answer.

Then back to the flat to get changed for a City dinner that evening. This was the big one, to show that Brian was in London, not 4,000 miles away wrapping up the deal of the century. It was important that as many people as possible would see Brian at the dinner. On the Saturday it was the races at Newmarket and then, in the evening, a casino at the hotel where they were to stay overnight.

The Friday progressed well, a few phone calls with Laura sitting across the desk writing down answers and what questions to ask. Giles's confidence began to grow, so much so that when Laura suggested a trip to the staff restaurant for a light lunch. Giles agreed and was confident enough to chat idly to people. One colleague ventured his support for a particular football team and Giles knew his brother supported Arsenal, so he could tease him about the results.

That Friday evening saw Giles sitting in the back of a taxi with Laura looking ravishing in a long black dress, off the shoulder. The same uneasy feeling came over Giles as they neared the Guildhall for the dinner. What if he was found out, embarrassed at the dinner, thrown out even? Giles tried not to think about all the things that could go wrong.

The evening started with a champagne reception. Giles broke out in a cold sweat as he surveyed the room, in front of him scores of people he didn't know but most of whom knew him. Laura gave him a comforting squeeze of the arm and then, like jumping into a swimming pool, they were in the thick of the throng. "Ah, Brian, you must come and join us." A rather large man with a red face gestured for them to join him. Laura had just time to whisper, "Charles, head of a Citybank" in Giles's ear. Giles held out his hand. "Charles, good to see you again."

Charles was obviously someone who didn't want answers to questions and immediately started a long story about his fishing weekend last month in Scotland. Giles sipped from his glass and tried to look interested. He thought he had done well when a tall, thin man with deep penetrating eyes came across. "Not speaking, Brian?" "Sorry," stumbled Giles. "I didn't see you there." Then he realised that there had been eye contact between them about five minutes before. Giles bit his lip and thought again, this isn't going to work.

The tall man then said something which made Giles think his cover was blown. "You know, Brian, I didn't expect to see you here tonight. I'd heard a whisper that things were hotting up across the big pond and there could be some rather large fish being landed." Giles knew he wasn't talking about a fishing weekend and so he went on the attack. "You know, you shouldn't believe every rumour – especially in the City. You could end up landing minnows and not salmon."

The other man smiled and moved away. Giles looked at Laura, who spoke quietly as she put her glass to her lips. "That was James Sobers, Brian's rival and long term adversary. They were both in the same line of business and he would also have had a sniff at what's going on in America. If he hadn't seen Brian here tonight he would have been on the first flight to New York in the morning."

Thankfully, they were called in for dinner and Brian had arranged that they were sitting at a table with people who didn't know him very well so small talk could be exchanged, something which Giles excelled at. As the wine flowed during the five-course meal, he found himself regaling the rest of the table with stories about his wayward 'older brother' who was a clergyman and got into all kinds of scrapes. Laura kept an amused eye on the proceedings, making sure Giles didn't have too much to drink.

The dinner finished with awards and speeches. During the port Laura whispered to Giles, "Be ready to get up and receive an award." Giles felt his stomach drop and he went cold. He looked at Laura, furious that she had only just warned him, and then the speaker called out his name to receive an award. Giles didn't know what to do, but he could only do one thing as everyone around him clapped and cheered. He found himself getting up out of his seat and making his way to the front, cursing his brother under his breath all the way. On the stage he was presented with a handsome marble bust, which was obviously made for the office desk. Giles thanked the organiser, who then handed the microphone to Giles. He then remembered that he had seen the Oscars the previous week on TV and made everyone laugh by telling them that he wasn't going to cry or thank everyone from the cleaning lady to the post boy. "No, he was a selfish bastard and the award was for him and him alone." That had everyone banging on the tables and cheering and he smiled at people on the other tables as he made his way back to his seat. He breathed a great sigh of relief.

"How long did you know about this?" he asked

Laura looked sheepish. "We knew it was going to happen and Brian thought it was a good idea for everyone to see that he was here."

Giles gritted his teeth. "I'm going to have a lot to say to Brian the next time I see him."

The rest of the evening passed off peacefully, with the wine flowing and people getting a little tipsy, if not drunk. Giles kept on mineral water; he wanted to keep a clear head even if everyone around him did not. At a reasonable time, when the dinner had ended and the cabaret was just beginning, Laura and Giles excused themselves and walked towards the door for a taxi. As Giles turned to go his eyes caught the steely glance of James Sobers as he stood in the foyer. Giles smiled and went outside, into the cold night air, which had the effect of sending a chill down his spine.

In the back of the taxi, Laura was exuberant. "You were wonderful, Giles, it worked perfectly."

Giles turned to her and suddenly he felt absolutely drained and exhausted. "How did I ever agree to all this? No more surprises Laura or I walk out."

Laura looked serious. "I'm sorry but Brian and I thought you'd panic if you knew beforehand about the award and the best way was an impromptu speech, and that's what it proved to be. Brian couldn't have done it better!"

The taxi drew up at Brian's penthouse. Laura smiled at Giles and gave him a peck on the cheek as he got out of the taxi. "Go and get some rest. I'll pick you up at 11 in the morning. Newmarket tomorrow is easypeasy compared with tonight."

Giles smiled. "Now, Laura, why don't I believe you?"

The taxi went off into the night with Laura waving from the back window.

Giles went up to the flat and poured himself a very large drink, that night he slept soundly.

He was wakened with sun streaming through the window and the telephone ringing. Should he pick it up? It could be Laura. The decision was made for him as the answering machine clicked on and then Brian's voice came on. "How's it going, bruv? Heard you won an Oscar for your performance."

Giles made a grab for the phone and picked it up.

"You have just given me one of the most frightening nights of my life. I must have lost years, and that stunt of the prize and not telling me!"

"Relax, Giles, it was fine. Laura tells me everything went like clockwork. The rest of the weekend will be a cinch."

Giles suddenly realised he was standing without a stitch on in front of the window twelve stories up looking out over the Thames. Suddenly, he felt very naked and exposed.

"Look Brian, I think James Sobers suspects something; he gave me some funny looks."

Brian laughed. "Don't worry about him. He was just surprised to see me in London when he thought he had worked it out that I would be in New York, and if I hadn't been there last night he would have blown the whole deal by coming out on the next plane. Now he thinks there must be some delay and it's happening next month."

Brian rang off after giving some hints on who would be at the races.

Right on the dot of 11 o'clock, the buzzer went and Giles went down to meet Laura, who looked very different from the night before. She was wearing a two-piece lilac suit with a very pretty hat and definitely looked the part for the races. As they got into the taxi Giles couldn't help noticing the fragrance from the perfume she was wearing.

Newmarket racecourse was a splendid sight. The sun was shining and Giles was feeling much more relaxed. They were going to be entertained by an old friend of Brian's, Sir Roland Smith, who owned a number of racehorses. He had retired from the City and was not up to speed with recent news, so nothing untoward was expected. It was the first time that Giles had been to a racecourse and he didn't want to show his naivety. Laura had been before and promised to guide him through. Over a delicious lunch Giles again was the bon viveur of the party, regaling the company with the story of his acceptance speech the night before and stories about his 'older brother' the clergyman. It seemed to Laura that the stories were getting more colourful and this brother seemed to be putting Brian into the shade! Soon it was time for the races and the talk was of the racecard and which horses to bet on. Giles decided to himself that he would go just by the name and choose all the horses that way. Laura put the bets on and, not surprisingly, all seemed to have an ecclesiastical connection.

> 1st Race. The Saint.
> 2nd Race. Angel Dust.
> 3rd Race. Bishop's Folly.
> 4th Race. Pennies From Heaven.

In the fifth race he couldn't find any ecclesiastical connection, but once he saw the name of 'Double Delight' he thought he must be on to a winner. Most were outsiders, but in the first race his horse came second. Angel Dust was third in the second race, Bishop's Folly won at a canter and Pennies From Heaven came in third. In the last race Double Delight started from the back in a field of six and looked beaten, but a mile from home it came with a flourish and in a thrilling finish won by a short head. Everyone congratulated Giles and Laura went off to collect the not insubstantial winnings. The host ordered champagne and asked Brian how he managed it. "Just beginners luck," said Giles, and suddenly realised what he had said. He hadn't been to the races before but Brian certainly had and was a regular at Newmarket. Frowns began to cross the faces of those round the table and Sir Roland was about to say something when Giles interjected. "Beginners luck for my brother, I had such bad form last time I was here that I asked for divine intervention. I rang my brother up and asked him to pick the winners. The money is going to his church steeple fund."

"Well," beamed Sir Roland, "he will be pleased", and reaching into his wallet produced two £50 notes. "Here, let him have my winnings as well." Of course, the others followed suit and, rather sheepishly, Giles crept away from the races with a pocket bulging with notes.

Laura burst out laughing when they were in the taxi. "Let that be a lesson to you, Your Reverence."

Giles shook his head. "Not you as well, Laura. I think I'll drop that brother of mine. He seems to get me into all sorts of trouble – that is the clergyman one, of course!"

They both laughed as they sped back to London.

That evening they were due to go to the hotel casino, which didn't open till 9pm. It was after 10pm when they arrived. Giles smiled as they alighted once again from a taxi. Normally on a Saturday evening at this time he was having a cup of cocoa after putting the finishing touches to Sunday's sermon. Here he was going into one of London's top casinos with a very attractive woman on his arm and the night still young. He just hoped that the final part would go as well as the rest.

This again was a new experience for Giles, but Laura said she would stick with him and guide him through. Giles's heart missed a beat, for there standing by the gaming table was James Sobers with a bevy of women around him and looking straight at Giles. The penetrating eyes again bored into him. Trying to find a chink in the appearance, thought Giles, he smells a rat, he must do, and he's just waiting for me to slip up. Laura guided Giles to the blackjack table and they began to bet with small stakes. The evening progressed well and apart from one interchange with James their paths didn't cross that much. Other people greeted Giles and each time Laura either whispered their name or used their first name in greeting them. All was going smoothly. Giles was trying each game and going through his chips like he was eating them. Laura made up for him, astutely winning where he was losing and it looked as if they would finish the evening evens. It was now after 2am and, although they were booked in the hotel for the night (separate rooms of course), Giles felt he should have one last fling on the roulette wheel. He began by choosing rouge three times in a row and winning, then changing to noir and winning again. He now decided to be more confident, choosing evens and again winning. A large pile of chips was mounting up in front of him and other players were trying to follow him, thinking he was obviously onto a winning streak. Then it happened.

Giles felt a pinch on his bum and a girl giggled. He thought it was unusual for Laura – she was not so familiar – and he turned around to gaze into the deep blue eyes of one the most gorgeous women he had ever seen. His mouth fell open and, before he could speak, the woman threw her arms around him and gave him a huge kiss. "Brian, I didn't know you were going to be here, I've missed you so much. What's matter, don't you recognise me?" Giles managed to shake himself free gracefully and looked quizzically at Laura, who had turned as white as a sheet and looked as if she couldn't speak. Then things moved very quickly. Laura fainted and lay in a crumpled heap on the floor. Giles saw his chance and went to her side. He lifted her up and carried her out to the veranda, saying she needed air. He laid her on a bench outside and as he bent over her she whispered: "Brian's girlfriend Susie. you're on your own for this one."

It was Giles who then almost passed out. He turned round and Susie was standing next to him. "Susie, be a good girl and get Laura a glass of water." Seeing that she had now recovered, the other players wandered back inside, including James Sobers, who had been on the edge of the group observing all that had gone on.

Laura leant up on her elbow. "Giles, this is dangerous and not at all planned. You'll have to take Susie out of here. She's a walking time-bomb, the one person who could blow your cover in a few seconds. You'll have to deal with her, get her away from everyone."

Giles was numb. How on earth was he to do that? A women who he did not know? If she broached any subject it would be the wrong one and he was expected to keep her away from everyone else. Then he had an idea. "Laura, insist that you have to go to your room, your not feeling well. I'll get Susie to help me with you."

He caught sight of a wink from Laura as Susie returned with the glass of water. "Oh Brian, is she alright? She didn't half keel over in there. I thought she was dead."

Giles looked pensive. "No, she'll live. Help me get her to her room, will you?"

They both helped to half carry the feigning Laura up to her room. When they got there Laura seemed to recover slightly and said she would be alright and that she would sleep it off, whatever was wrong with her. She wished them goodnight and closed the door.

Giles turned with a heavy heart to his new-found companion. "And where is Brian sleeping tonight?" she replied in a very inviting voice:

"This room here."

He pointed to the next room down the corridor, but before he realised what he had said, Susie looked demurely at him "And does Bri... want me to tell him a goodnight story and tuck him up in bed?"

Giles's heart and mind were a mixture of raw animal energy for one of the most beautiful women he had ever seen, but also of fear, bewilderment and confusion about how he was going to extricate himself from this predicament. He opened the door of his room and Susie strode straight in and collapsed onto the bed, stretching herself out on it. The door was still open when footsteps came down the corridor and there was a short knock on the door, followed by James Sobers putting his head around, taking in the scene of Giles standing at the foot of the bed and Susie stretched out upon it. Though she was fully clothed, it did not seem to disguise the intimacy of the situation.

"So sorry, Brian. I just came up to see how Laura was, but I see you've got your hands full. I've also brought you these; you left them on the table in the confusion." He produced a napkin full of chips from the casino.

Giles could only mumble, "Thanks, its very kind of you, James."

James gave him a smirk. "Have fun," and with that he went out of the room and closed the door.

Giles did not surface for breakfast in the morning. Laura sat by herself, anxiously looking at every new arrival that entered the breakfast room. At last she got up and went into the foyer, catching Giles walking down the staircase. She rushed over to him. "Is everything alright Giles. How was Susie? Does she suspect anything?"

Giles just smiled at her; it looked a very tired smile. "No, everything is fine Laura. Look, do you mind if we just leave? I want to get back to being good old Giles. I find playing Brian is just too exhausting."

Three days later Brian returned from New York with the takeover contract signed, sealed and delivered. Fellow financiers in the City didn't know how he had done it. News had only broken on the Monday of the availability of the firm when it went into liquidation, and who was it who there in New York ahead of the rest of the pack ...Brian. The deal was done before any of his rivals could order plane tickets.

When he returned to his office, Laura gave him a run down of the weekend and later that day Brian picked up the phone to ring his brother. "Giles, I don't know how to thank you – the cheque is in the post, but more than that you were superb."

Giles smiled. "Perhaps, Brian, you could cover for me for a weekend and see what your preaching is like. You could also do a Baptism or a wedding for me! Oh, and by the way, I think I got even for the surprise at the dinner!"

Brian laughed, not sure of what his brother was talking about for the first time in their lives as identical twins.

Later that afternoon a parcel arrived at Brian's office in Canary Wharf. It was a pair of diamond cufflinks with a note attached. It was from Susie.

'Brian, I just want to say thank you for the most wonderful, exciting and unbelievable night we have ever had together. Nothing could match last Saturday, you were so affectionate and loving I couldn't believe how heavenly it all was. You were divine. I was so sad when I awoke and you were not there, then I went into the bathroom and found your message! How romantic, to write in lipstick on the mirror! The answer to your question is yes, yes, yes, I will marry you. Till the next time I see you, all my luv. Susie xxxxxxxx'

Brian looked out over the Thames and smiled muttering under his breath, "You've well and truly got me this time brother."

A TWINKLE
IN THE EYE

———◈———

*He died surrounded by a dozen of his closest friends, celebrating
his 70th birthday at a seven-course dinner at the Athenaeum Club.
He suffered a heart attack between the dressed crab
and the boeuf en croute.*

**Obituary Notice for Canon Brian Brindley
Daily Telegraph, 2001**

———◈———

Saints and Sinners

THE PARTY WAS in full swing and it was 2am in the morning. Loud music echoed from the rooms, lights blazed from all the windows and cars packed into the small driveway. That the party was being held in the vicarage and was not an isolated occurrence would cause a few eyebrows to be raised. Certainly the churchwarden, Walter Pinchthorpe, was still awake, peering from behind the curtains of his house less than 300 yards from the vicarage. Dressed in his red striped winceyette pyjamas his hands shook as he clutched the curtains.

"He's at it again, Mildred."

"Oh, come back to bed Walter and get some sleep, you shouldn't let it bother you," implored Mildred as she tried to pull the covers further over her head.

"Bother me, bother me!" exploded Walter. "Our vicar holds wild parties, even orgies, and you tell me not to bother!"

Mildred turned over in her single bed. "I'm sure you're exaggerating now Walter. He's only having a bit of fun, surely he deserves that."

"Fun, fun! How can you call depraved orgies in the vicarage a bit of fun?" Walter was now walking around the bedroom rubbing his hands together, his face contorted with rage. "He's a pervert, a winebibber, a disgrace to the cloth, depraved, debauched and I'll see that he's de-frocked!"

Mildred had turned over again and was now sound asleep, her mouth open and snoring gently to the rhythm of the music, which still echoed from the vicarage.

The following morning The Rev Roger Phillips gently tiptoed around the lounge picking up the odd wineglass and plate, trying not to disturb some of the guests, mainly young men who were still asleep on the sofas. As he opened the curtains there was one even curled up on the rug in front of the fire. The smell of bacon and freshly ground coffee permeated the air from the kitchen. It had been quite a party – one of the best. The vicar certainly knew how to throw a good one, and he even served a cooked breakfast the morning after!

As the last of the guests departed, Sally, his cleaner, cycled up the drive. Her long brown sun-tanned legs moving in rhythm, her summer dress blowing gently in the wind, a quite delightful creature, thought the vicar as he viewed her from the window. Sally was a young, attractive and cheerful girl of about 19 who had just left college and now took a few cleaning jobs around the village.

Roger met her at the door. "I'm afraid there's a lot to do today, Sally, we had rather a good party last night," he said, looking rather sheepish.

"I know," she said, smiling. "I heard the music when I went past the church last night."

"Oh dear! Oh dear! I hope it wasn't too loud." The vicar smiled mischievously with a twinkle in his eye. "Otherwise I will be getting another visit from the churchwardens. It really is a good job I only have parties occasionally!" joked the vicar.

Sally lent the bike against the wall and smiled again. "I expect their idea of a good party is a game of scrabble and a cup of hot cocoa before going to bed at 9 o'clock."

"Now, Sally, I expect they have a good time in their own way." The vicar tried to look stern. "I have to go out now Sally. Can I leave you with the debris? I will pay you extra this week as it is rather a mess!"

Sally smiled; she was used to the vicar by now. It would be a mess and there would be a lot of extra work, but she didn't mind. The vicar treated her well and she enjoyed working for him. When she first came, she thought she would have to mind her 'ps and qs' working for a vicar. But not a bit of it! Rev Phillips was not like any vicar she had ever known. He wasn't straight-laced, prim or proper, he liked a good laugh and he was renowned in the village for it. People found they could talk to him in a natural way; he also liked a drink, not to mention the parties he threw at the vicarage. He was even known to swear!

Rev Phillips took a hat from the stand and walked out of the vicarage, thankful that he had someone like Sally who he could rely upon. He thought he'd better walk today, he was still feeling a bit tender after last night and there were the remains of a hangover.

He strolled down the main street stopping to chat with a number of people, and it seemed as if there was not a person in the town who the vicar could not talk to. He went into a few shops and it was in the butcher's that he encountered Mildred Pinchthorpe.

"Good morning, Mildred, and how are you today?" asked the vicar, as he raised his hat.

Mildred turned to glower at him with her two small but piercing eyes set in a wizened face, which looked as if it didn't smile very much. "Well, vicar, since you ask, a little tired and worn out. We didn't get to sleep till after 2 o'clock this morning."

The vicar smiled. "Not out partying again, Mildred? Dear, oh dear! You and Walter do lead such riotous lives," the vicar said with a glint in his eye.

Mildred stiffened and her cheeks flushed. The boy behind the counter had to turn away so she couldn't see the broad smirk across his face.

"Vicar, Walter and I couldn't get to sleep because of the loud music coming from the vicarage," she said in a shrill tone.

The vicar, looking sheepish, said, "I am so sorry, Mildred, I didn't realise the sound carried so far. But I don't have too many parties." The vicar's head sunk a little lower on his shoulders.

"Your predecessor, Rev Venables, didn't have any!" Mildred said with a note of triumph, and, now rising to her full height of four feet ten inches, she scented blood.

"Mildred, the man was over 70 and rather deaf, if I'm not mistaken."

"Well, he didn't keep me awake till 2 o'clock in the morning." Mildred was now sure of a kill.

The butcher's assistant smirked again and gave a wink to the vicar.

The vicar shook his head sorrowfully. "Living up to one's predecessor is always so difficult. I always seem to have the misfortune to follow men who have been such saints."

"Canon Venables had his faults, but he was a well respected vicar of this parish." With that Mildred turned on her heels and marched out of the shop.

The assistant smiled. "Not sure you've won that one, vicar. I don't think she'll be enrolling in your fan club, or buying you a pint at the Red Dragon."

The vicar looked thoughtful. "I expect not, Darren, but you know even our Lord wasn't too worried about what people thought of him." Privately, he thought, Canon Venables! He could write a book about that man. He had been priest in the village for 20 years and, although a few people spoke well of him, most were glad when he had retired.

By most accounts he preached the most boring, dry, dull sermons, he hardly ever left his study and the church had stagnated during his incumbency.

The vicar continued his journey down the High Street, stopping and talking to people he met, and then he turned into the housing estate behind the shops. He made a couple of visits, a baptism enquiry and a follow-up from a funeral; all the usual kind of pastoral work, but things that Roger enjoyed. He liked people: meeting them where they were, going to their houses in times of crisis, and also joy, sharing those difficult moments of grief and brokenness, and also their joys in baptisms and weddings. People in the village liked the vicar because he was always there for them, he loved them as they were, and you didn't have to put on special clothes or go to church to be accepted by him. Indeed, it seemed sometimes quite the opposite; the vicar seemed to relate better to those outside the church, or on the fringe, rather than some of the church stalwarts. He went in the local pubs and was not averse to having a drink with the locals, always taking an interest in what was happening and able to talk to people in their own language. Old Canon Venables had kept himself tucked up in his study writing scholarly books and sermons that people didn't understand. He rarely visited parishioners and ordinary villagers saw him as a rather stern, austere and distant figure.

Roger was just turning into the drive to the vicarage when his way was barred by the churchwarden, Walter Pinchthorpe, looking even more tight-lipped and offensive than usual.

The vicar thought attack was better than defence. "How are you, Walter? You'll enjoy your dinner tonight, I'll be bound! Mildred was buying some very good looking pork chops in the butcher's this morning."

Walter looked flustered. "Vicar, I didn't leave my warm fireside to come out here and talk to you about pork chops. I came out to complain in no uncertain terms about the noise coming from the vicarage last night."

Roger now looked resigned to being harangued for at least ten minutes.

"I'm sorry Walter, we did get carried away a bit. You see we were celebrating Adrian's new appointment as curate in Melchester."

Walter's face became a crimson hue. "I cannot see why the appointment of a curacy to an ordained priest of the Church of England should involve riotous parties and music to the early hours. I thought it should signal a time of prayer and meditation!"

Roger's head sunk a little lower as he began to eat more of the humble pie. "Yes, it was a bit loud, but I didn't realise the sound would carry."

Walter was now in full force, his small body rocking from side to side as he seemed to want much more than a mere apology.

"You know vicar, your behaviour leaves a lot to be desired. I tire of apologising for your actions around the parish. It's a scandal, and it's not a good example for the village. Not to mention the young men who always seem to frequent your parties. You could do with taking a leaf out of your predecessor's book."

Roger held his breath and only mouthed beneath it the reply he would like to give. 'Now, Walter, which leaf would that be? Sitting in the study all day writing books no one ever reads? Writing boring sermons, or maybe never visiting parishioners?' Instead he heard himself saying, "I'll try to keep it quieter in the future."

Walter still did not look satisfied. "I may have to take this further when I have spoken to the other churchwardens." With that he turned sharply to leave.

Roger breathed a big sigh of relief. Walter had only gone a few paces when he turned around and again returned to the fray, like a dog with a good bone he is reluctant to leave.

"And by the way vicar, my wife does not like being accosted in the butcher's shop in front of shop assistants and made to account for herself. She felt totally humiliated and embarrassed. Parish business should not be on display in the village butcher's shop and be discussed by common people."

"I...only..." Roger felt that he shouldn't bother. It would be useless trying to explain that it was Walter's wife who had initiated the conversation.

Walter receded down the drive and Roger looked at the small, wiry, hunched figure, going back to his fireside. He saw the curtains twitch and wondered if he should wave to Mildred, but thought better of it.

A Twinkle in the Eye

He returned to the vicarage to find it a very different place to the one he had left. It was clean and tidy. Sally had done a splendid job in tidying everything up and you wouldn't have known there was a party there the previous night. She had done all the washing up, and even brought some fresh flowers from the garden to put on the kitchen table. He made a mental note that he really should give her something special for all the extra work he had caused her. There was a handwritten note underneath the flowers.

Hope you like the flowers. They will help to take away the smell of cigarette smoke. It must have been quite a party! Why wasn't I invited? By the way, I think the churchwarden is looking for you (Old pinchface!). He didn't look too pleased when he called. I didn't invite him in but he walked right past me, saying that as it was church property he had every right to come in and he insisted on surveying the scene. I'm afraid it was before I had started tidying up!

See you next week.
Sally.

Roger felt his heart sink. More trouble ahead he could see. He had never hit it off with the Pinchthorpes, even though he had really tried in the early days: inviting them round for drinks, trying to be friendly, but it never really worked. They had been close to Canon Venables and no one else would be able to fill his shoes. They used to go on holidays together and were inseparable, he later learnt. Roger didn't have a chance really, and it was made even worse because he was so different to his predecessor. The other churchwardens were OK, if a little weak; they were easily swayed by Walter and usually backed him up if there was any kind of disagreement or vote to be taken. Thank goodness the Parochial Church Council seemed to like Roger and responded well to the new ideas he had introduced in the parish.

The vicar put the matter of the party at the back of his mind and over the next few weeks nothing out of the ordinary occurred. The parish was getting quite excited about the blessing of the new bells, which everyone in the village had raised money for. It had taken five years to raise the money and now the bells had been installed, there was going to be a symbolic blessing at a celebration service.

The person suggested was Canon Venables, now well over 80 and, in Roger's eyes, a bit past it. But Walter had got his way with the PCC and almost insisted that he be asked back to perform this ceremony. Roger was not happy but chose not to go against Walter on this one.

The big day finally arrived with the church full. Walter and Mildred insisted on entertaining the Canon, who everyone had said they were pleased to see return. Things, though, seemed to go wrong from the start of the service. Walter had told the vicar that as it was such a special service he, Walter, should lead the procession carrying the cross. Roger felt it best not to argue and had to placate the verger, who normally did this duty. The usual format was that the procession would set off from the choir vestry and go around the side aisle and enter by the back of the church, down the main aisle. Walter had forgotten that this would change today, as there were so many people packed into the church. The procession would have to go via the foyer and it would take a little longer. Walter walked down the side aisle, solemnly carrying the cross, and then saw to his consternation the aisle at the back of the church was full of chairs. What was he to do? The vicar and the other dignitaries were at the back of the procession and unaware of Walter's dilemma. Walter's response was to panic and lead the procession through the first door he saw, the bell tower that didn't have another exit. Very quickly the bell tower was full of singing and giggling 12-year-old girls from the choir, who thought this was a real hoot. Roger at the back finally realised something was wrong and the procession had to back out of the bell tower and reform. The congregation couldn't hide their laughter and by the time the procession finally reached the choir stalls, it was rather ragged and the organist had to play the opening hymn twice. Roger just smiled and made a joke about it in his opening remarks to the congregation. Walter's face looked a strange kind of purple as he tried to sink lower in his pew.

The choir sang special items and then the Canon ascended the pulpit steps ready to preach the sermon. Roger sat at the front in the choir stalls and tried to look attentive, something that was very difficult as he couldn't remember when he had heard a more boring and uninspiring sermon. Mildred sat beaming on the front pew in her new hat, seemingly enjoying every moment, which is more than could be said for the choirgirls. They were giggling and passing notes to each other. Sally was in the midst of them. He tried to catch her eye to give a disapproving look but failed. Thankfully, at last he heard the Canon pronounce 'Amen' and the sermon ended.

Then, for the blessing of the bells, Roger, the Canon and the churchwardens processed to the belfry where the new bell ropes hung down, looking resplendent with new red brocade. Roger had wanted to climb the bell tower and really bless the bells with holy water, but because of the fragility of the Canon, it was decided that it would all happen down below. Walter came forward and opened the large service book, holding it in front of him so that the Canon could read the blessing. All was ready and the Canon, in a croaking voice, began:

"We bless this font and all those who will baptised ..."

Roger interrupted. "Wrong page," he mouthed to Walter. Walter looked angry, thinking that the vicar was telling him off for something, and he just scowled. The Canon droned on and the congregation were shuffling uneasily and murmuring to each other. Roger felt that he must do something, so he stepped forward and took the book from Walter.

"I'm sorry, but there seems to have been a mistake; it's the wrong page in the book." Walter looked livid and muttered that someone must have put the marker in the wrong page after he had checked it.

Order was restored and the blessing of the bells commenced. At the end of the blessing, one of the bells was to be tolled three times. Walter had volunteered himself for this task, even though he wasn't part of the bell-ringing team. He had been told which rope to pull, but after the confusion of the wrong page he now chose the wrong rope. Before anyone could intervene, Walter had given a firm pull and immediately shot ten feet in the air, clutching the bell rope and shouting words which were certainly not contained in any church book of blessings. The bell-ringers managed to get him down and a loud cheer rang out from the congregation. Even under his ashen-faced pallor you could tell Walter was very angry.

After the service there was an informal reception in the church hall where the celebration cake would be cut. The vicar made a short speech of thanks to those taking part in the ceremony, making everyone laugh with his comments about the mishaps, except Walter, who stood beside the Canon, his top lip twitching at what the vicar was saying. Afterwards, Walter & Mildred slunk away home, figures of fun to all.

That night the vicar again chose to have one of his parties, entertaining people well into the night, and Sally was invited this time. At the other end of the vicarage garden, Walter had no thoughts of sleep. He paced around the living room, his features becoming more twisted as the music wore on; his mutterings more venomous, his hostility to the vicar plumbing new depths.

Walter didn't appear in church for the next few weeks. Like an injured animal he chose to lick his wounds in private. Six weeks later he returned. There was something different that Roger noticed, a silence. Walter just ignored him. He never even spoke or argued anymore.

That summer the vicar was to have a sabbatical for three months. He had long wanted to pursue his interest in writing a novel and he was going to a remote Scottish island for most of the time, living in a small monastic community. While he was away the churchwardens would run the parish with help from other local clergy. While Roger was away, Walter felt that he could assume control and started to dictate to the other wardens what should happen. As regards the vicarage, Roger did not feel he could entrust the churchwardens with a key. He arranged that Sally should go to the vicarage twice a week and any church post should be handed to the churchwardens. This arrangement seemed to work well, until three weeks before Roger was due to return. One Tuesday morning Sally cycled up to the vicarage as usual. She let herself in and was sorting out the letters when the doorbell rang. It was Walter. She didn't like letting him inside the vicarage so she kept him on the step.

"I don't see why I can't sort out the post?" Walter snapped.

"The vicar told me it was my responsibility and I'll do it until he returns," Sally replied, thinking that she could see why Walter was so unpopular in the village.

Sally sorted out the letters, the official-looking ones she handed over to Walter and kept back the ones that looked personal. There was one she hesitated over, a white envelope with the address written in green ink. Across the top of the letter was the word 'IMPORTANT'. Walter saw her hesitating and snatched the letter. "If it's important it must be Church business," pontificated Walter.

He tore it open and in it was a single sheet written in green ink:

YOU'RE A PERVERT VICAR

KEEP OFF YOUNG MEN

I'VE GOT EVIDENCE

DO WHAT I SAY OR I WILL TELL THE BISHOP!

There was no signature, no address. Sally's stomach turned over and her mouth dropped open. Walter looked very different. A look of triumph crossed his pinched features and a sickly smile emanated from the side of his mouth.

"I've got him... I've got him at last, the pervert. I knew I was right. Let him wriggle out of this one if he can." Walter strode back down the vicarage path, holding the letter aloft in triumph as if it was a trophy. Sally sunk to her knees and sobbed.

Two weeks later Roger returned from Scotland. He had told Sally the expected time of his arrival and she was there at the vicarage to meet him. As he got out of the car she came down the steps, looking very nervous and her features were pale and drawn.

"How good to see you, Sally, you had no need to be here." Roger smiled at her, his face sun-tanned and weather-beaten.

"Oh vicar! Something awful has happened and it's all my fault." Sally was now crying and the vicar put his arm around her trying to comfort her.

"What on earth's the matter, Sally? Come on in and let's have a cup of tea, surely it can't be that bad?"

Over a cup of tea Sally told the vicar about the letter, of Walter Pinchthorpe snatching it from her, and his reaction and her worries ever since that it was her fault that he had seen it.

Roger smiled. "Sally, don't be a silly girl. It's not your fault, you're not to blame yourself, and more importantly there is nothing I need to worry about. I have done nothing wrong and this must be some kind of prank."

She felt a little reassured and went off home. When she had gone Roger busied himself with unpacking and then making himself a meal. It was while he was having a cup of coffee afterwards and was wading through the mountain of correspondence that had arrived in his absence that the phone rang. It was the Bishop.

"Look, Roger, I'll come straight to the point. I need to see you urgently. Can I come over now?"

"Yes, of course," answered Roger, rather puzzled. The Bishop normally summoned you, he didn't come to see you, and certainly not with only an hour's warning.

Within the hour a red Rolls Royce swung into the drive and came to a stop outside the front door. Roger went out to greet the Bishop. "A bit of surprise, Bishop, but I'm always glad to see you."

When they were both seated in the study the Bishop began: "This is very difficult Roger and there is no easy way to say it, but I'm going to have to suspend you from the living here. Hopefully it will be for not too long, but we must clear this matter up."

Roger lost some of his colour and looked worried. "What on earth's the matter, Bishop? I haven't absconded with the church funds or run off with a choirgirl, have I?"

The Bishop moved uneasily in his chair. "No, and I understand how hard this must be for you, but after receiving the report from the churchwardens I have no option."

Roger exploded. "What report? What on earth has being going on while I have been away?"

The Bishop looked troubled. "I thought you knew, about the anonymous letter, the allegations and the churchwardens' report?"

Roger was now getting very angry. "I've only just got home after being away for three months, I've seen no-one." He then remembered the letter that Sally told him about. "My cleaning girl told me about some silly letter that arrived while I was away that a churchwarden seems to have purloined. But you can't be taking that seriously, can you?"

The Bishop looked apologetic. "I am afraid, Roger, that these days we have to treat any allegation seriously, but there is also the report from the churchwarden."

Roger stood up and paced around the study. "And what does that say? Written by one Walter Pinchthorpe, I'll be bound, the person who hates me and will do anything to get me out of here."

The Bishop looked at Roger. "I am afraid I am not at liberty to divulge the nature of the report until the court case begins."

"Court case!" Roger looked aghast. "Has the world gone mad while I've been away? What am I supposed to have been charged with?"

The Bishop sighed. "I'm not saying I agree with the charges, but I have no option, Roger. You know about the letter?"

"Some crank writes a letter and the church believes them, without even asking me what I have to say? This is sheer bloody madness." Roger was now going red in the face, the anger welling up inside him.

The Bishop looked dismayed. "If it was the just the letter I would not be here now. But the churchwardens have laid charges which cannot be ignored."

"What charges? That old fool Pinchthorpe complaining about my parties. He's been wanting to get at me for a long time."

The Bishop drew a deep breath. "The charges relate to conduct unbecoming of a clergymen. Of having parties here, yes, but the word orgy was used in connection with young men frequenting these parties. Of being an open scandal in the parish and of corrupting the young and impressionable."

Roger sunk into the chair, his head between his hands. "I don't believe this is happening to me, it must be some kind of nightmare."

The Bishop looked at Roger. "I have been asked to convene a consistory court to examine the evidence and hear from the different parties. I will be writing to you with the details. In the meantime I am afraid you are suspended and you are not allowed to do any work in the parish. I suggest you find somewhere to go, and you will need to consult with a solicitor about your defence."

Roger looked bewildered. "I can't believe this is happening to me… it must be some kind of nightmare."

After the Bishop left, Roger poured himself a large whiskey and just sat in the study, his eyes glazed and registering no emotion.

The following morning there was a knock at the door. As Roger opened it he could see four people standing on the doorstep, the churchwardens. Two of them didn't make eye contact and stood there staring at their shoes. Their spokesperson was Walter Pinchthorpe.

"We've come for the church keys. You won't be requiring them due to your suspension," Walter said curtly.

Roger detected just a hint of triumph in the tone of voice. He knew he was beaten and went to get his set of keys. Coming back to the door, Roger decided to attack. "I suppose you're all pleased at this. At last a way has been found to get rid of me."

Walter glared at Roger. "We have been told not to discuss anything with you until the court hearing," he cut in quickly.

The four of them turned and began to walk away, led by Walter. John Grace was the last one and as he turned, he reached out his hand to Roger. "I 'm sorry, so sorry, vicar," he said. Walter turned and gave his fellow churchwarden a look that would have frozen hell itself.

So much for Christian fellowship, thought Roger, as he closed the door, seemingly resigned to his fate.

The next three weeks were the most difficult in Roger's life. What was he to do? To go away seemed to show guilt, slinking away in the night afraid to look people in the eye. He decided to stay; he spent time by himself, still in shock, not believing that this was happening to him. Sally called twice a week and tried to cheer him up, but for Roger there was only a dull ache in the pit of his stomach. Of course, he could not go near the church and the churchwardens had warned off fellow parishes from contacting him. Roger felt alone and bereft; it left him questioning his faith and also his calling to the priesthood, things that before this seemed so secure.

One morning there was a knock at the door. Roger had risen late and wasn't even shaved or dressed when he opened it. It was Darren from the butcher's shop on his delivery bike with a huge basket on the front.

"Hi, Vicar, just thought you should know that we think you're innocent and I've got a petition together. Over 100 people from the village have signed it"

Roger smiled as he received the form. "I don't know what to say Darren, except a big thank you."

Darren produced a carrier bag from the basket. "Here's some best rump steak to cheer you up, and remember, don't let the buggers get you down!"

With that Darren rode off down the drive and when he passed the Pinchthorpes gave a large 'V' sign to the twitching net-curtained window.

Roger smiled as he watched him go, the first time he'd smiled since his visit from the Bishop.

There were other visitors, however, who were not so pleasant: the sound of breaking glass in the middle of the night and Roger came downstairs to find a brick thrown through the lounge window with a note attached.

WE DON'T WANT YOUR SORT HERE IN OUR VILLAGE – PERVERT!

It seemed that not all the village shared Darren's faith in the vicar. There were some who were only too ready to believe the worst in a person and draw conclusions from even an anonymous letter.

The consistory court was set to meet on the Monday morning and expected to last three days. Roger had refused legal help, saying that he would represent himself.

It was a strange feeling to sit in a normal church hall of a neighbouring parish and for this to be regarded as a legal court. The judge was the Chancellor of the Diocese appointed by the Bishop. There was also a panel of examiners and assessors, consisting of three solicitors. For the prosecution the diocesan solicitor sat demurely dressed in black silks flanked by her aides. The churchwardens were there and other members from the parish. Roger wondered if he should say hello, to acknowledge their presence. He wondered why he was thinking like this. Of course he should, wasn't attack always the best policy? He went round and shook each member of the church by the hand, obviously disconcerting some and embarrassing others. When he reached out his hand to Walter, he found him turning away and refusing to shake.

On the vicar's side Sally and Darren had come to lend their support, much to the indignation of at least one of the churchwardens.

The proceedings began with the solicitor outlining the case for the prosecution and the case the vicar would have to answer to. "Conduct unbecoming a clergyman" was the charge and she started on the prosecution's case: of how the vicar had corrupted young people by holding parties where dubious things had happened, loud music seemingly being the least of the problems. The anonymous letter was referred to and how young men had been seen going to these parties. Witnesses were brought forward testifying to the frequency of the parties and also the participants. Young men had been seen going into the vicarage and the vicar, it seemed, liked their company. It was also noted that the vicar had various young men staying with him on a number of occasions. The number of net-curtain twitchers in the village quite surprised Roger as he heard the evidence laid out before him with times and dates. It seemed as if it wasn't just Mildred and Walter who kept the vicar under close scrutiny, but half the village also noted happenings at the vicarage. Roger thought he had perhaps been naive to believe in his popularity in the village when at the first sign of trouble so many people could turn against him.

Walter's testimony was vitriolic and his remarks went far further than any evidence he could bring forward. It was as if this was his day and he was going to squeeze it for every drop of enjoyment. He also mentioned how the vicar had undermined him and made him a laughing stock at the blessing of the new bells.

Roger surprised the court by not cross-examining any witness, just allowing their testimony to stand unchallenged. The feeling after two days of prosecution evidence was they had mounted a strong case and unless the vicar came out fighting he would be found guilty of the charges and could, ultimately, be de-frocked.

On the third afternoon the court reassembled and the Chancellor looked to Roger and asked him to start his defence and call his first witness.

Roger stood up and said, quite calmly and simply, "I offer no defence except silence."

There were gasps of astonishment from around the court and a sly smile emanated from Walter Pinchthorpe's features as if victory was almost at hand. Roger's action had quite non-plussed the Chancellor and his panel of examiners. They declared a recess in which they would consult about how to proceed and said they would reconvene in the morning.

Sally put her head in her hands and sobbed. Darren put his arm around her, but to no avail. When she came out of court she looked determined. "Darren, we've got to do something to help Roger. We can't let him dig his own grave like this."

"But what can we do?" asked Darren. "They won't believe anything we say in his defense."

Sally looked thoughtful. "They may not believe us, but I know who they might believe."

That night Sally let herself into the vicarage knowing that Roger was staying in town at the hotel near the court. She went to his study and looked in the top drawer of the desk, from where she pulled out a battered and well-used address book. As she thumbed through it, she picked up the telephone and dialed a number.

The following morning the court reassembled and the Bishop asked Roger again if he wanted to present any defence. Before he had time to answer, a voice from the public benches spoke up, "Yes, I will speak for him." A young clergyman came forward and presented himself before the court. "If he won't speak for himself then I will speak for him."

Roger smiled at him and asked, "Jonathan, why are you here? There was no need for you to come all this way." The Chancellor asked if Roger was agreeable for the young man to speak. Roger smiled and said he had no objections.

The Rev Jonathan Guest was sworn in and proceeded to tell his story. He had known Roger for more than seven years after he had befriended him at the youth club which he had attended. Roger had encouraged him when he was thinking about the church and had paid for him to go on courses. Yes, he had attended parties at the vicarage and stayed there, but nothing untoward had gone on.

Over the next two hours there was a procession of young clergyman, each with a similar story of how Rev Phillips had helped and encouraged them into the ministry, often out of his own pocket; of how they had attended the vicarage and gone on holidays with him, but never had anything taken place for them to be ashamed of. It wasn't just Anglican curates who testified, but Roman Catholic priests, Methodist and Baptist ministers.

As each one took the stand and held the Bible aloft to swear the oath, Walter Pinchthorpe visibly winced and sank deeper into his seat. After witness 15 the Bishop mopped his brow with a large red handkerchief and said, "I think we have heard enough. This defence is quite unparalleled and these young men who have come to testify each speak of Rev Phillips in such glowing terms it is hard to think where these scurrilous accusations come from. I think we can find the defendant innocent, and what's more he leaves this court without a stain on his character and is able to resume his responsibilities in the parish forthwith."

Rev Phillips was carried aloft from the court in triumph back to the vicarage, where that night the party to end all vicarage parties began. It seemed that Sally, fearing for the vicar, had gone through his address book and rang clergy she knew had been to stay at the vicarage.

Roger took Sally aside in the middle of the party. "I should tell you off for what you did without my permission, but instead I would like to thank you" He gave her a big kiss. "I would like you to think about becoming a church-warden as I think I will be having a vacancy in the near future."

From across the vicarage garden the curtains in the Pinchthorpe's house remained tightly closed and nothing was heard again with regard to complaints about the vicar.

A (RATHER) MACABRE CRICKET MATCH

———❖———

Cricket is an ancient pastime, it ripened sweetly, it has endured nobly. The keen white clash of warriors, who can come together and laugh as comrades when all is over. Small wonder if those that join in the bloodless conquests of a world whose name is Cricket are inspired with a love and devotion deep enough to astonish the stranger.

Thomas Moult from 'Bat and Ball'

———❖———

DETECTIVE INSPECTOR George Craven was waiting impatiently by the side of the car in the police yard. He had just been told that he had to go immediately to Sunbury Cricket Club as there'd been a suspicious death reported. He waited, his fingers drumming on the roof of the car, for the police constable who had been assigned to drive him and be his No.2 in the case, a PC Sam Lacey, who the Chief said had specialist knowledge that might be useful. He would give him a real telling off for not being there at the double when he finally arrived. George was one of Sunbury's old-fashioned detectives. He was dedicated to his job, which could be deduced from his rather large paunch – too many pints in pubs trying to find out information. Not for him sitting behind a computer screen. No, crimes were solved face to face. He also was regarded by other officers as 'a bit difficult to work with'. A woman came out of the building and, to George's amazement, saluted and went to the driver's side of the car.

"Police Constable Sam Lacey reporting for duty, sir."

George's mouth dropped open. "Is this some kind of joke? First you're late and then I find you're a women. What the hell are they trying to do to me?"

They both got in the car and, with blue lights flashing, they sped off. There was an uneasy silence between them until they reached the turning for the cricket club.

"I can't say I'm happy with being given a woman to work with, but I suppose you'll have to do," Inspector Craven said in a resigned sort of way.

PC Lacey raised her eyebrows slightly and rolled her eyes in the rear-view mirror.

"What is your specialist knowledge anyway?"

"I captained the school and college cricket teams, guv."

There was no sign of appreciation from George as the car ground to a halt at the back of the cricket pavilion and he reached for the door handle.

"Do women play that infernally tedious game as well? I can't stand it myself."

With that the doors slammed shut and they both walked over the gravel car park towards the policeman standing by the rear door of the pavilion.

"Well, constable, what's happened?"

The constable took out his notebook. "We received a call at about 7.30pm reporting a sudden death here at the club. I was in the vicinity so I came along and found the body of one of the players in the dressing room. He was dead and his team-mates had tried to revive him by mouth to mouth and heart massage. The scene was a bit of a mess I'm afraid, and what evidence there was had been trampled all over. I cordoned off the area and rang for assistance. The doctor is up there now."

George looked pleased. "Good man, you obviously did your best. No-one's left the club have they?"

"No sir, they are all in the bar. I told them that no-one could leave until you arrived."

With that they both went into the clubhouse, glancing briefly in the bar where a dozen or so white-flannelled figures sat hunched up over the tables and the other officials were congregating near the bar.

They climbed the steps to the dressing room and were met with the burly figure of the police doctor bending over a rather limp looking and obviously dead body dressed in white cricket clothing, which was widely spattered with blood.

"Ah Dr Bennett. At least they've not replaced you with a woman."

Inspector Craven had now reached the dressing room and entered, followed by PC Lacey.

The doctor turned and smiled. "Still the same George, they've not managed to straighten out your prejudices yet then?"

"No, but they're having a bloody good try. Look what they've given me for this case, a PC in a skirt!" He pointed to PC Lacey, who blushed slightly, although you couldn't tell if it was with embarrassment or anger.

The doctor smiled at her. "Don't worry about George, luv, he must have been dropped from a great height when he was young by his nanny and has never recovered. Anyway, George, it will make those undercover surveillance operations in the car at night more interesting."

George grunted and muttered something under his breath. "Cut the wisecracks, what have we got here, a murder or what?"

The doctor rose to his full height, which was over six feet. "I'm not sure; a bit puzzling really. He was either struck with something on the back of the head or hit his head on the floor or on the wooden bench. There's so much blood around here I can't really say until I do the post mortem."

George turned to the policeman at the door. "Who found the body?"

The policeman took out his small notebook. "A Rev Fanshawe, sir, who was in the bar downstairs and heard a loud crash. He came up to investigate and found the body here. He's practised at first aid, so he tried to give mouth to mouth and pump his heart thinking it was a heart attack."

George's jaw dropped slightly. "That's all we need, a bloody religious Florence Nightingale on the scene. Where is he?"

"Downstairs, sir, with the rest of the team," he replied.

PC Lacey interjected. "Who was playing in this game?"

From his notebook he read out, "The Grantchester Diocese cricket XI verses the Duxbury Diocese XI. It was a friendly match."

George scowled. "Some bloody friendly match when someone gets killed, and two teams of bloody vicars to boot! What a bloody strange case this is going to be."

PC Lacey again interjected. "Where's the other team? There's only one team in the bar."

"They went home before the body was found. This fellow here (pointing at the dead body) waved them off from the car park."

George felt he wasn't getting on top of this case. "Who the bloody hell is this anyway?"

The PC again consulted his notebook. "Rev Ashley Giles, sir. Vicar of a parish about four miles away."

"A bloody vicar dead, a team of bloody vicars downstairs, and all at a bloody cricket match. And a bloody woman to drive me around! Someone has set me up on this one. All we need is Jeremy Beadle to appear from behind a cupboard with a clipboard!" George felt he was losing it.

The police doctor stood up. "Well, that's it for now, I can't do anything else here. Get the body moved to the mortuary and let's hope forensic can turn up something. It could be a heart attack, but I'm not sure until I've examined him."

George turned to PC Lacey. "Sort that out will you. Get them to do a search of the grounds outside as well. See if anything has been thrown away. After that we'd better start taking statements from the holy club downstairs."

They descended the stairs to the bar to be greeted by a cluster of cricketers who gathered around them looking for news.

George addressed them. "We are not sure what's happened yet so we would like your co-operation. No-one can leave until I say so and I need statements from all of you." Looking over to the bar and the barmaid he continued, "Don't serve any alcohol. I think we need clear heads for this one."

Inspector Craven and PC Lacey interviewed each member of the cricket team in turn. They all told a similar story. They had been playing for the cricket team for many years, usually friendly matches, and used this club for their matches. Today's match had been a good-humoured affair with the opposition winning a close game by two wickets. Afterwards they had a drink in the bar and then the Duxbury's coach had driven off with Ashley Giles waving them off with the rest of the players in the car park. They had all adjourned back to the bar and about ten minutes later they heard this noise from upstairs. It sounded like someone had dropped something. No-one was very alarmed as cricket bats were always falling over in dressing rooms. After a few minutes Rev Fanshawe went up to see, as he didn't think anyone was in the dressing room. He then shouted down for the others to come quickly and when they arrived they found Ashley lying face down on the floor in a pool of blood. They thought he may have had a heart attack and hit his head on the wooden bench so they tried reviving him, but to no avail. He was dead. Someone had called an ambulance and the police car closely followed it. They all had known Ashley as a fellow clergyman. He was single, popular, a high-flier, even in the church, destined for high office and well respected by his fellow clergy. A very able and likeable chap.

After the interviews were finished they were told they could go home after leaving their addresses with the police. Their belongings would have to be picked up later as forensic were busy in the dressing room. Slowly they departed from the clubhouse. George then turned his attention to the barmaid. "And what's your name?"

"Maxine West," she said, looking rather pale and washed out.

PC Lacey looked at her sympathetically. "It must have been quite a shock, all this?"

Maxine admitted that it was all a bit beyond her. "The only excitement you usually get at a cricket match is when someone hits a six through one of the windows." She confirmed the stories of the others and was sad it had to happen here at this club as she had been so happy here. She could add nothing new to the enquiry. She heard the crash, like everyone else, and was in the other room collecting glasses, and then she was shocked to hear of Ashley's death. He had been a member of the club at Sudbury and was a very popular player.

Back at the police station Inspector Craven and PC Lacey reviewed what they had learnt from the day. George leaned back on his chair behind the desk, tilting it at an alarming angle.

"Well, what have we got? The death of a vicar at a cricket club while he's playing for a team of bloody vicars against another team of bloody vicars! No one sees a thing. The police doc says it's not a heart attack or a brain haemorrhage. Rev Giles was either hit with an implement unknown or fell down and hit the bench at just the right angle and place to kill him."

"But why did he fall?" asked PC Lacey.

George smiled. "Exactly, that's what we don't know. We also don't as yet have a motive. Do vicars go around bumping each other off at cricket matches?"

PC Lacey laughed. "Not as far as I know, guv. But there could be person unknown who came into the dressing room."

"The only problem with that is the dressing room is on the first floor with a balcony outside. The only way in and out is the narrow flight of steps. It is closed in at the bottom and doesn't lead straight into the bar. But would someone have the time to run down the steps after he hit the floor and before anyone from the bar went to investigate? It's a very slim chance but we'd better check it out."

PC Lacey checked her notebook. "Anyone could slip out of the bar and go up to the dressing room unnoticed and come back down, or even hide in one of the other rooms and then join the rest of the players. In the confusion no-one would suspect anything."

"Good point, but that leaves ten bloody vicars as prime suspects. I'm sure someone set this case up, just for me!"

PC Lacey smiled. "What about forensic? Have they come up with anything?"

"Not a bloody sausage. Half the team must have tried resuscitation by the bruises on his body and they think he had two broken ribs, but all that can be accounted for. The crime scene was so contaminated by the other players that there was nothing. Not even any weapon, although there were a lot of cricket bats and stumps lying around which could have done it but were all clean. If he was hit then it was removed and taken away, not even a search of the grounds revealed anything."

"What about motive? The usual ones, love or money?"

"We are talking about clergymen here, PC Lacey. Aren't they supposed to live better lives than the rest of us?"

"I suppose so, guv, but it's not unknown for a clergyman to be a killer."

George looked tired and resigned as he said, "That's it for today. Let's see what the morning brings."

The following morning saw Inspector Craven and PC Lacey sitting in the office drinking coffee. George was brooding.

"The Chief wants the investigation scaled down already. He can't see any use in tying up valuable resources on this one. He's going to allow us three days for the two of us with any additional help we want, within reason, and then it goes down as a suspicious death – case still open."

"Just another statistic and another unsolved case." PC Lacey shrugged her shoulders.

George looked thoughtful. "You said something last night which kept me awake for quite a while. You said, 'It's not unknown for a clergyman to be a killer'."

PC Lacey smiled. "Haven't you got to keep all avenues open, guv, until you're certain?"

George looked up. "Yes, and that's why we're going to interview ten clergymen today and see what the buggers have to say for themselves."

The day progressed rather tediously; the pattern was identical for each one. Building up a picture of the deceased from what the vicar knew, where he was when he heard the crash, what he did in the few moments following, who he also noticed, and if he could explain why anyone would want to kill Rev Ashely Giles, Archdeacon of Sudbury.

At the end of a long day, both Inspector Craven and PC Lacey sat in the office back at the police station. George put his feet up on the desk as he looked through the statements they had taken.

"Like ten bloody parrots! They all say exactly the same thing, all shocked, wringing there hands like bloody clergy do, saying what a good guy he was and all saying they saw each other at the crucial time. A bloody waste of a day PC Lacey!"

PC Lacey looked at her notes. "Not quite, guv. I'd say that we are looking in the wrong direction."

George looked up, surprised that anyone should challenge him, especially a mere woman PC. His mouth fell open slightly.

"And what theory does little Miss Marple have?" He couldn't hide the sarcasm in his voice.

PC Lacey swallowed. "Shouldn't we really take a look at Ashley, see what's in his background, what possible motive there could be for anyone to murder him? Take a look around his vicarage?"

George put his feet down off the table. "Alright, tomorrow we take a look at Rev Ashley Giles, his house and parish. Any other ideas police constable?"

PC Lacey thought she'd better say everything on her mind: "Well, I did think we should put some pressure on the barmaid. She was there and from her position behind the bar could see everything. It's the only place in the bar you can see the door leading to the dressing room."

"So is this what a woman's intuition is then?" George looked enquiringly.

PC Lacey smiled. "Not really, guv, just basic police work." She didn't really mean it to sound as critical as it came out, but the resulting silence told her that her remarks had stung and she would probably be off the case very quickly.

The Rev Ashley Giles's vicarage was an imposing Victorian detached house standing in its own grounds next to the parish church. An elderly woman, who was very upset, met them on the steps.

George got out of the car and went up to her. "Ah! Mrs Button, have you the keys?"

She looked up; she had obviously been crying. "He was a lovely man. What are we to do? He was a wonderful vicar to everyone, what a tragedy!"

George thought he'd better get on. "How long did you know him?"

"The four years he's been here, I've cleaned for him twice a week."

"When was the last time you were in the house?"

"The Tuesday morning he was playing cricket, I cleaned while he was out."

"Did you see him before he left?"

"Yes, he was his usual self, laughing and joking. Didn't seem to have a care in the world and then this."

"Mrs Button, would you like to come in the house with us and tell us if anything has been disturbed and it is how you left it."

"Why, yes, he had an alarm put on the house after the last incident."

"What incident?" George looked interested.

"Oh! It was a tramp, gentleman of the road they used to be called. Attacked the vicar right on the front step, left him bleeding and a right mess."

"When was this?"

"About six months ago, I think."

"Was anyone caught?"

Mrs Button looked accusingly at both of them. "No, I expect your colleagues were too busy catching speeding motorists or TV Licence dodgers."

George looked none too pleased. "Thank you, Mrs Button. Would you like to go in?"

Mrs Button did a quick survey around the house and confirmed that it was just as she left it.

"Thank you, Mrs Button. We'll return the key when we've finished."

When they walked into the study Inspector Craven gave a deep sigh when he saw the lines of books and piles of paper stacked on every surface. "This will take weeks to go through and we don't know what we're looking for."

PC Lacey smiled. "Don't worry, guv. I'll have a go. Why don't you try the rest of the house."

An hour later Inspector Craven came back into the study with two cups of coffee. He found PC Lacey deep into filing cabinets and perusing various documents.

She looked up. "Oh thanks, guv. Did you find anything?"

George looked weary. "Only a penchant for bright ties when he's not wearing a dog collar and a strange choice of after-shave, but apart from that, nothing. How about you?"

"Nothing yet. Just the normal church papers, but I think I need to carry on a bit further and stay here a little longer."

George removed some papers from a chair so he could sit down. "I'll go and see the barmaid again and then we can compare notes back at the station."

PC Lacey smiled as she drank from the coffee mug. "Sounds alright to me. I'll try and be back by 4 o'clock."

For another three hours she went through papers in the study, putting some aside to take with her and smiling only once when she read a letter at the bottom of the filing tray.

Back at the station George was sitting at his desk reading the local paper.

PC Lacey strode into the office. "Hey, guv, had a good time with the barmaid."

George looked up over his glasses. "That remark young lady could be misconstrued and get me, not to mention you, in a lot of trouble with the Politically Correct Brigade. But since you ask, yes I did find out that she knew quite a few of the vicars and I think she's hiding something."

"Did you find anything in the vicar's papers?"

"Only that he was up for promotion. It looked as if he was in for being Dean of a rather prestigious cathedral. His name amongst others had been put forward."

"Do you know the others?

"No, and unless you have access to the Prime Minister's church appointments office I don't think we will know either."

George grunted. "Bloody Church of England. What's it to do with the Prime Minister who is bloody Dean of a cathedral?"

PC Lacey smiled. "Not for us to reason why, guv."

George grunted.

"Guv, do you think the barmaid could be one of his women?"

George looked thoughtful. "She does seem rather upset about the death. I just put it down to women being more emotional about these situations."

PC Lacey frowned. "Some women, not all."

George, as if to ignore the rebuke, went on: "It may be worth you seeing her, women to women she may let something slip."

PC Lacey sat up, pleased at last she was being given some responsibility. "Yes, a good idea. I'll go round first thing in the morning, or maybe I should see her at her home. She may reveal more, and anyway, it would give me the opportunity to see how she lives."

George sat back in his chair. "The doctor was on again, results from the post mortem still don't show anything really conclusive. He thinks the vicar died with a single blow to the head administered by implement unknown. He could have died when he hit the bench, but to do so with such force he must have been knocked over. Anyway, there are two blows on the head and although they both could be from the bench and floor it seems unlikely. It all points to someone else being there and some kind of argument."

"What do men normally argue over?" PC Lacey looked enquiringly.

George looked thoughtful. "Women, money and power."

"Exactly," confirmed PC Lacey, "and those are the motives we'd be looking for if we weren't dealing with a bunch of 'bloody vicars', as you call them."

George banged his fist down on the desk "By God, woman, you may be right! I've been treating this like a vicar's tea party instead of a murder investigation!"

"We need to find out who else was on that list to be appointed Dean. One of our cricketing vicars and it gives us a motive." PC Lacey could see now her ideas were being accepted.

"Leave that one to me. It will have to come from the Chief Constable, but I think he will agree to request the information. After all, we are only talking about a list of bloody vicars and not state secrets."

PC Lacey stood up to leave. "On my way home I'll call in and see the delectable Maxine and see what I can glean."

"Good thinking, batman." George smiled.

PC Lacey left the office with a spring in her step and with a renewed sense of purpose.

The following morning PC Lacey was in the office first as George burst in clutching a piece of paper. "My God, woman, you were right!

I've just got the list of potential candidates from the PM's office and four of our vicars are on the list. If you weren't a women I'd give you a kiss!"

PC Lacey smiled. "And I've got news for you, guv. Our Maxine seems to have a thing for clergy. Ashley, she says, had been very supportive after the break-up of her marriage, although she only admitted to me that she saw him for counselling. But she had visited the vicarage."

"The randy sod! And him a vicar!" exclaimed George.

PC Lacey smiled. She felt they were now working as equals. "Tell me, who are the other three vicars on the list?"

George unfolded the paper. "Timothy Fanshawe, the one who found the body, which makes him suspect No.1, a Graham Rose and a John Campbell. All four names were going to the PM with a recommendation for Ashley Giles to be chosen."

"Well, at least it gives us the beginning of a motive. Did anyone know the composition of this list and who was to be recommended?"

"Apparently the Church of England works likes some gigantic old boys' network with nods and winks flying round quicker than at a Valentine's party for queers!" George shuffled in his seat uneasily. "Sorry about that, no offence I hope."

PC Lacey smiled. "No offence taken, guv." She was amazed at how an apology from George Craven could be said in such a way that it threatened her sexuality! He really was a male chauvinist dinosaur.

George went to get up from the desk. "So we need to interview these three again. Shall we go together young woman?"

PC Lacey was puzzled at the way he addressed her, and even more amazed when he held the door open for her. Maybe some of the dinosaur scales were falling off.

At Timothy Fanshawe's they were met with a puzzled expression from the vicar. He was surprised to see them again so soon. He had told them all that he knew. When they got into the front room the line of questioning also surprised him.

"Are you married?"

"Yes, I have been for over 12 years and we have two children."

"How well do you know Maxine James?"

"Only as the barmaid at the cricket club."

"Did you ever meet her other than at the cricket club?"

"No, certainly not." The vicar was now getting angry. "Just what are you getting at Inspector?"

"Nothing at all, just the usual line of questioning."

He now altered tack unexpectedly.

"Did you know you are in line for the Dean's job at the cathedral?"

Timothy's jaw dropped. "How could you possibly know that? It was told to me that I was on the list but no-one, not even my wife, was to be told until the decision had been made."

"Who told you?"

Rev Fanshawe looked flustered. "I am not at liberty to say."

George looked angry. "Look, vicar, I am conducting a murder investigation here and not getting very much help from all you bloody vicars, so either you start talking or I get you all down at the station until you're a bit more co-operative."

Rev Fanshawe now looked frightened. "Alright, I'll tell you. It was John Campbell."

"Did he tell you who else was on the list?"

"Yes, Ashley Giles, himself and Graham Rose."

"Did he tell you the name that was going forward as the preferred choice?"

"No, he couldn't know that."

George sat back in the chair. "All cricketers together playing your jolly match and one of you gets murdered. Isn't that a pretty picture?"

"I don't like your tone, Inspector."

"And I don't like it when an innocent man gets murdered, Rev Fanshawe. Do I make myself clear?"

"When you found the body, who was there in the room with you?"

"No-one, they all came in after me."

"Who assisted with the mouth to mouth and heart massage?"

"Graham, myself and John Campbell."

"Now, isn't that a coincidence PC Lacey? The same men on the list get their hands covered in blood trying to help revive someone they have just murdered?"

"I didn't murder him…" Rev Fanshawe broke down, sobbing, his head in his hands.

"So you say, but we have only your word for it."

. George got up to leave. "We're going to see the other two on the list now and just in case you're thinking of warning them, I'm going to ring the station and have them send someone to sit with you for the next two hours. Is that understood Rev Fanshawe?"

He lifted his head from his hands and nodded. "I wouldn't do that and I can give you my word."

George turned as he was leaving to face him. "You know vicar, promises and words from vicars don't mean much to me at the moment."

As they were sitting in their car waiting for the other police car to arrive, PC Lacey turned to George with a look of admiration on her face. "That was quite impressive, guv. I don't know what it did to him, but it certainly scared me."

George smiled. "They may call me an old dinosaur, but I haven't lost my teeth or my bite just yet!"

PC Lacey laughed. "What, you a dinosaur, guv? What could they be thinking of?"

They arrived at Rev John Campbell's just as he was about to leave the house.

"Oh, Inspector, I'm sorry but I have a meeting to attend. Will it do another time?"

PC Lacey could see the anger rising through her guv's features.

"No, it bloody won't! A man's been murdered and you vicars think that life can just go on. I want some answers – and bloody quickly!"

Rev John Campbell paled visibly. "You'd better come in. Let me ring the church and tell them I won't be coming."

He ushered them into a room with modest furnishings. Around the walls were the usual pictures, team photos of cricketers and on the mantelpiece various trophies, which looked like they had been won for sporting achievements.

John Campbell came back into the room. "Now, Inspector, I don't know how I can help you as I told you all I knew the last time you came."

George looked at him intently. "Did you indeed? Like telling me who was in line for the Dean's job at the cathedral?"

Rev Campbell shifted nervously and sat down. "You never asked me, and anyway, it's not known until the Prime Minister's office chooses from a secret list."

"Is your name on the list, Rev Campbell?"

"I'm... I'm... not sure... I obviously hope it is..." He looked nervous.

George turned on him. "Now why then did you tell your friend Timothy the full list with four names on it? There didn't seem to be much doubt about it then. And when the Prime Minister's office faxed me with their list, they were identical. Perhaps an explanation is in order Rev Campbell. Shall we have it here, or at the station?"

Rev Campbell put his head in his hands and exclaimed. "I've been a fool! Yes, I did know the list. I got it from a former girlfriend who typed it up for the Bishop and sent it in to Downing Street. She will lose her job if this gets out."

"I'm not particularly interested in that, just the web of lies and deception which seem to have been woven around it. Isn't it a coincidence that you were all playing in the same cricket match? And all three of you there when Rev Ashley Giles's dead body is discovered."

"We all knew each other very well. We wished each other the best in getting the job."

"Did you know which was the preferred name?"

"No, and you can check with the person who gave me the information if you like."

"Oh, don't doubt it, Rev Campbell, we will check. We take nothing on trust, especially from a vicar."

"Did you tell the other three about the list?"

Rev Campbell hung his head in shame. "Yes, I did. I thought it would prepare them."

"Are you married?"

"Yes, my wife Heather is a teacher. We've been married six years."

"Do you know Maxine James, the barmaid at the cricket club?"

"I've met her at the cricket club."

"You've never met her anywhere else?"

"Now what are driving at, Inspector? First it's suspected murder, now what is it, being unfit for office? What will you accuse me of next, stealing the collection?"

George was now angry. "You don't come out of this smelling of roses and I'm sure the Bishop will have something to say to you about your lies and deception. I'm leaving a police constable here for the next hour while we contact the third clergyman, just so you're not tempted to ring and warn him!"

With that the two of them walked out of the vicarage. As they left, a police car swung into the drive and another police constable stepped out.

Back in the car PC Lacey realised just how angry her boss was.

"I've never been given the runaround like this. I'll get the bastard who's done this and when I do, just let him hide behind his dog collar and see what good it does him."

At that precise moment PC Lacey was mightily pleased that she had chosen a profession in the police and not in the church.

The last call of the day found Rev Graham Rose in his study. A tall, thin, almost gaunt, figure, his dog collar looked at least two sizes too big for him. He ushered them into his study and, after a cursory glance around, PC Lacey hoped she wouldn't have to search this room. It was full to the door with piles of books and papers on the floor and the desk. In order to be seated piles of papers had to be removed.

Rev Graham Rose smiled at them both. "Now, how can I help you Inspector?"

George thought he would try a different tack.

"Do you know Maxine James?"

Graham smiled. "Why, yes, the barmaid at the cricket club. She's been coming to the church and sings in our choir."

For a few moments George was taken aback. The thought of Maxine James in a surplice singing angelic songs was one that didn't spring readily to mind.

"How well do you know her?"

"Like any other parishioner, I suppose. She's a good laugh."

The Inspector leant forward in his seat. "Even in bed?"

PC Lacey sucked in her breath; this line of questioning was going in very hard, she thought.

Graham Rose laughed out loud. "Really, Inspector, that's the most preposterous thing that anyone has said to me for years!"

George looked perplexed. "Why? It's a normal question to ask in these situations."

Graham was still laughing. "Even to the secretary of the Gay Clergy Caucus? I'm sure that some of my parishioners would prefer me to sleep with the choirgirls, but I'm afraid Inspector the answer is a resounding 'no'."

George was realising that he'd better get back on safer ground. "Were you aware that you were in line for the position of Dean at the cathedral?"

"Yes, I was told I was on the list, but along with three others."

"Who told you?"

"I expect you know already, Inspector. Rev John Campbell. John's a bit of a gossip once he's had one or two whiskeys."

"Did you expect to get the job?"

"Not really. Gay clergy still suffer some discrimination, a bit like women in the police service," as he pointedly looked at PC Lacey, who blushed slightly, more out of anger than embarrassment as his comment was correct.

George leaned forward. "Who was favourite for the job of Dean?"

John Campbell smiled. " Why, Ashley. He was head and shoulders above the rest of us. He'd have been a bishop, our Ashley, had he lived."

George got up to leave. "Thank you for your help."

And with that they departed.

Back at the station they both sat looking over their notes. George looked reflective as he poured himself a large whiskey. "Tell me PC Lacey, sum up the case so far and let's see if we both agree."

"Right, guv. This is how I see it. Ashley is in the dressing room at the cricket club. He's not alone, someone is there with him and there is some kind of argument. He is killed and falls to the floor. The murderer gets out of the room fast and probably goes into the opposite dressing room to hide, joining the others in the main dressing room when everyone else arrives, and they are so concerned looking at the body they don't notice someone else slip in. All three of Ashley's 'friends' administer first aid, but to no avail. Each one has the opportunity to make things worse and also cover themselves with blood. Each one has a motive to get rid of Ashley, as he's favourite for the job of Dean. But I don't think that's the only motive, I think there is something else. Even vicars wouldn't kill each other to get promotion. Remove Ashley and no one knows who would be second on the list. We need to look again at the suspects."

"John Campbell. He's lied once. He knew the list. If he was going to murder Ashley though, would he tell the other two that they were on the list as well? A married man, but with an eye for the ladies."

"How do you know that?"

"I caught him looking at my legs, guv."

"Women's intuition again! Go on."

"If he did it there must be something else, another reason as well as the job of Dean."

George mumbled in agreement.

"As for Timothy Fanshawe. A bit squeaky clean for me. He lied and he was the first on the scene. Good cover if he was the murderer. Was he in the bar or halfway down the steps? None of the other players can quite remember where he was when the crash happened. He had the same motive as the others."

"As for Graham Rose. Bent as a 'nine-bob note.' But being gay does not mean he is not a murderer. Could be being blackmailed, that's always a possibility. He's ambitious for the Dean's job. And another link, he's got the delectable Maxine singing in his choir."

George gave a long sigh and sat back in his chair.

"Just a bit of feminine intuition, guv, but I think Maxine holds the key to this. I do think there is something we've not seen and it's right in front of us. I think she may know more than just the one vicar, and if she does, it may give us a new motive."

George smiled. "You've been reading too many detective novels, my girl. Real life crimes are solved through hard work and keeping on top of the suspects, and that's why we need to sleep on this one and see what we come up with in the morning. And remember, we've got to get some leads soon or we'll be taken off the case."

The following morning George was at his desk early, going through the statements seeing if he had missed anything, when PC Lacey came in.

"Morning, guv. I've been awake half the night and I've got a hunch. Can we go and interview one of clerics again?"

George looked up. "Sure, what's the hunch?"

"I'd rather not say because it's so outlandish you'd only laugh at me. But I would like us see Rev John Campbell again, and this time, can I ask the questions?"

George sighed. "If I wasn't desperate for some light to be shed on this case I would say no, but just to humour you I'll go along with it."

They found John Campbell finishing off his breakfast and he showed them into the front room.

"It's a bit early, isn't it, for questions after yesterday?"

PC Lacey stood by the mantelpiece and picked up one of the trophies that were sitting on top. "Quite a collection. You must have been a very good cricketer?"

John Campbell smiled. "I played for the university and was offered trials by two counties but decided to go into the church."

"Quite a sacrifice?"

"Not really. I find it very rewarding and enjoy my work."

PC Lacey sighed. "I loved cricket at school and it would have been a dream come true to play it full-time."

"There aren't the same opportunities for women."

"Wouldn't you be disappointed if you didn't get the job as Dean of the cathedral?"

"God has many jobs for us. We have to be content with what he calls us to do."

Suddenly, and without warning, PC Lacy took the cricket ball and hurled it towards Rev Campbell. He caught it one-handed in front of his face.

PC Lacey smiled. "Very good. Still got the reactions then?"

"You never lose them," John Campbell said as he threw the cricket ball from hand to hand.

Inspector Craven thought he had seen enough. "I think we should be going now."

PC Lacey wasn't finished though.

"Do you know Maxine James?"

"Only at the cricket club."

"Thank you, that will be all."

When they were back in the car George turned to PC Lacey. "If you ever pull such a stupid stunt as that again my girl, I'll have you out of the force. If his reactions hadn't been good that ball could have killed him."

"Exactly, guv. He's our murderer and the cricket ball is the murder weapon."

George's mouth fell open and for once in his life he was speechless. "What do you mean?"

"Those trophies in the room, some of them were for throwing the cricket ball. I made enquires from my friends in the cricket world. Rev John Campbell was the best fielder seen at the university for years. He could hit a single stump from 50 yards with a running throw. He was magnificent. If you can hit a single stump, a human head is easy."

"What do you mean? He hit him on the head with a cricket ball? But where was he?"

"Out on the cricket field. Below the balcony. I'd say about 20-30 yards away, but someone had to entice Ashley out of the dressing room onto the balcony, and his head would have to be turned away to hit it. There was someone else in the dressing room talking to him while this was going on. I think it was Maxine. Let's suppose he falls forward when the cricket ball hits him and crashes onto the floor. She rolls him over so that it looks as if he's banged his head and then disappears into the other dressing room. Everyone runs up the stairs and she slips in at the back along with John Campbell, who by that time has had time to pocket the cricket ball as it bounces back to him. He runs inside and then up the stairs."

George was amazed.

"But what about the link with Maxine?"

"That's what I'm not sure about. It could be that both clergymen were in love with her. More probably, though, that one of them had discovered the other and was going to tell the authorities."

"My God, what a clever girl you are. But we still don't have any evidence. We would have to break them down with confessions."

"Not necessarily, guv. You've let me run with one idea, will you give me permission for another?"

George shrugged his shoulders. "Why not?"

"This one involves you and you may not be so keen."

"Try me."

"First, we've got to get a tap put on the cricket club phone."

"No problem! As it's not a private phone there should be no trouble."

"Then, we go into the club at lunchtime and we both look as if we're getting drunk. You start chatting me up, guv, and I start responding. We let slip that we think we know what happened. That a tramp had been hanging around Ashley's vicarage and been aggressive. We think he's done it and cleared off and we're putting a nationwide alert for this guy and scaling down the operation locally. We make sure Maxine hears all this and then you suggest that we go back to your place for the afternoon as the case is almost wrapped up, for a bit of overtime!"

For the first time she thought she saw George Craven blush slightly.

"Then we adjourn to the car, stopping round the corner, and await the arrival of our murderer. With us safely out of the way the chances are that our Maxine will be dying to tell lover boy about what has been said. If she says it over the phone we've got them."

"Sounds good, if a little unorthodox, PC Lacey. I'll go along with it. I'll arrange for the phone-tap straightaway."

A few hours later they drove back to the cricket club. Maxine was the only person in the bar.

George looked at her and smiled. "You couldn't get us two large whiskeys, could you my girl? Oh, and put a bottle of champagne on ice, a celebration is called for."

PC Lacey looked sheepish. "Do you think this is OK, guv?"

George beamed. "Of course it's called for. All the hard work we've done on this case and now it's almost finished."

They went to sit down, choosing a table that was within earshot of the bar. Maxine continued busying herself behind the bar, obviously listening to the conversation.

PC Lacey took a sip of the whiskey. "A real find that tramp, and him attacking other clergy as well?"

George drank his whiskey in one large gulp. "I had an inkling from the start it was someone outside the club."

"Where's that champagne girl?"

Maxine looked flustered. "Coming Inspector, it's almost ready."

A few moments later she brought a bottle of champagne with two glasses. "Will that be all?"

George started pouring the champagne. "Yes, that's all. Here's payment and get a drink for yourself from the change." He gave Maxine a £20 note.

PC Lacey looked coy. "You know sir, I shouldn't have champagne during the day. It makes me go all giggly."

George leant over and touched her hand. "Call me George, we're off duty now. Can I call you Sam?"

She started giggling. "We'd better not get too familiar, what will people say?"

George leant closer. "I don't give a damn. You're a fine looking women and I bet you have to fight the boyfriends off!"

Sam started giggling again. "Oh go on, you're a real tease guv, or George. Tell me about the case. Is it really solved?"

George sipped from the champagne glass, noting in the corner of his eye Maxine's close proximity behind the bar.

"We were first onto this fellow when some of Rev Ashley's congregation said he'd been bothered by a tramp, not the usual kind, someone who had demanded money with threats. We'd even got on file a complaint by another priest about this fellow with a very good description. It seems as if Ashley tried to help him but wasn't thanked and the guy turned nasty. Threatened him with all sorts of things. We also got a witness from one of the houses opposite of a strange bedraggled man running away from the cricket club just before the police and ambulance arrived."

"That's amazing, guv. To think I've been and helped solve my first murder case."

George was now holding onto Sam's hand and kissing it. "You know I could help you in your career if you wanted? You don't have to be a PC very long."

"Really, guv! I think I might like that. What would it involve?"

George smiled. "I think we need to continue this conversation back at my place."

With that he downed the rest of the champagne and stood up. When PC Lacey stood up she fell over and had to be helped to her feet. She just managed to stagger to the door with George supporting her, and in his other hand he held the half-empty bottle of champagne.

George turned to Maxine and gave her a lustful wink. "Goodbye, Maxine, may see you again sometime!"

When they got into the car they started laughing. "I think we should do a turn on the stage after that. What do you think PC Lacey?"

"Do you think she fell for it?"

They drove round the next corner and waited in a cul-de-sac within sight of the entrance to the cricket club. In the back of the car there was what looked like a large radio. They turned it on. They didn't have to wait long. After a couple of minutes they could hear a phone ringing.

It was picked up. "St Stephen's vicarage."

"John. It's me, Maxine."

"I thought we agreed not to contact each other until it was a bit quieter?"

"I know, but I had to ring you. I've got some tremendous news. Come down and pick me up at the cricket club."

"I can't do that, not with Cagney and Lacey around. They came to question me again this morning. I'm sure they suspect something."

"No John, you're wrong. They know who's done it. They were in here just now, both of them celebrating!"

"No, it's too dangerous."

"Listen, they were chatting each other up in here and they took the rest of the champagne back to his place to finish it off. By now I expect they will be hard at it in bed. Oh, John, I do want to see you again."

"OK. If you're sure. I'll be there in ten minutes."

The red Volvo swung into the cricket club car park and Maxine got in. As they turned to leave another car blocked their exit and two police officers, looking very sober, got out and walked towards the car.

George leant in through the window. "I think you two have some questions to answer down at the station. Would you mind stepping out of the car and coming with us?"

Four months later Inspector Craven and PC Lacey were sharing a bottle of champagne.

"A good conviction and not a bad sentence. Maxine, of course, got off with the lighter sentence, being an accessory. It came out at the trial that Ashley had discovered Maxine's affair with John Campbell and threatened to expose it to the Bishop. Of course, it would mean that there was no chance of the Dean's job for John Campbell and he could be expelled from the church. He had to do something and Maxine had to be in on it. I think she lured Ashley back to the dressing room on the pretext of a confession. Once there, they talked with Ashley's back to the field. Our cricketing vicar took aim and wham! A cricket ball driven into the skull at over 90mph. You wouldn't stand much chance. Ashley staggered forward and Maxine laid him flat on the floor. John Campbell pockets the ball and walks into the pavilion to follow the others up the steps. He even administers first-aid, or makes sure he's dead. Good police work, Lacey. In my report I'm recommending that you join the plain clothes branch with promotion, of course."

"Thanks guv. I've enjoyed working with you." She got up to leave and then turned back and came and gave Inspector Craven a kiss on the cheek.

"I bet you've never had that from a fellow officer before, have you?

"No, but I think I may request to work with women in future."

"Now that would be a real turn up for the book, guv!"

THE BODY IN THE LIBRARY

or Butch Cassidy and the Old Patagonian Express

Books are a delightful society. If you go into a room filled with books, even without taking them down from their shelves, they seem to speak to you, to welcome you.

William E. Gladstone

THE REV TOBIAS Maybury sat slumped forward at the desk in the library. The librarian had gone in to lock up for the night and found him. At first she thought he was asleep, but when she gently touched his shoulder she realised at once that this was not gentle dozing but the deep sleep of death. The doctor was called and arrived within 20 minutes. He knew Rev Maybury well as he had been one of his patients for over 12 years and, in a way, the doctor had been expecting this to happen. Tobias had a weak heart but wouldn't slow down, even continuing to work long after retirement. At 75, Tobias could have no complaints, the doctor thought. The old boy had enjoyed a good innings and what a good way to go, falling asleep in the library, a place he loved and which was such a special part of his life.

The Rev Lisa Farthing received the telephone call shortly before 10pm from the library informing her of the death of her vicar and asking about the next of kin. She was shocked, but in a way she had been expecting this for many years. He had been a creaking gate for most of her curacy here in Greenford. Now the gate had finally closed and she was sad. He had been a good parish priest, accepting and teaching her with those kindly blue eyes and soft voice. He had almost become a second father to her. After she put the phone down she thought she must go and see him for one last time. The relations, a couple of elderly cousins in Dorset, could wait till the morning.

Lisa had been Tobias's curate for the last four years. She was a bright, attractive girl in her mid-20s who enjoyed life in the church. She had a great zest for life and her vivacious personality had fitted in very well in the life of St Gemma's. She was the perfect foil for her more studious, if a little more serious, vicar.

The Library at St Deny's was around ten miles from Greenford. A residential theological library originally endowed by WE Gladstone, it was a regular haunt of Tobias. He would go there for days off and often just book himself in for a couple of nights. With over 250,000 volumes even Tobias, with his great enthusiasm for books, was sated.

The library was in darkness, she thought, but then she noticed a light in one of the downstairs rooms. She rang the bell and Sarah, one of the assistants, came to the door.

"Oh hello, Rev. Farthing. I'm so sorry about Father Tobias, it was such a shock to find him in the library like that."

Rev Farthing entered the dark corridor of the Victorian mansion.

"I know, it must have been very hard for you to find him like that. I thought I would come to pay my respects and say prayers with him, I owe him so much."

Sarah looked crestfallen. "I should have told you when I rang, but the doctor arranged with the funeral director to take Rev Tobias to the chapel of rest. You see we have no facilities here so we couldn't keep the body overnight."

Rev Farthing thanked Sarah and took her leave, saying that she knew the undertaker and would go straight there.

The light was still on in the undertaker's premises in Greenford as her car drew up outside. It had a rather austere shop front with a window, where, she thought, there was always a problem of what to display? After all, what do you put in the undertaker's shop window to attract customers?

The door opened and a smile of recognition came across the sanguine features of John Pedley. "Oh, it's you Rev Farthing, do come in. It's a sad night and one which we have feared would happen for a long time." His voice took on the funereal tones of his profession.

She agreed and asked if it would be alright if she anointed Rev Tobias and said prayers with him.

"Of course, of course it's alright," John Pedley said and then ushered her into the back room where on a long metal table the body of Rev Tobias was lying.

She had seen and anointed many dead bodies before, but as she approached the table it was with moist eyes and faltering steps. John excused himself and left her to anoint her friend and mentor and say the final prayers for the dead with him. She was there for a long time, thinking about Tobias and his ministry. His face was at peace. The only thing that was missing was the smile, which usually lit up his features. She finally kissed him on the forehead and held his hand, smiling at the ink stains on his thumbs. Even in death she thought he would bear the marks of his beloved books.

It was after one o'clock when she finally managed to get to bed and sank beneath the covers exhausted, not from physical effort but emotional fatigue. But she didn't sleep long.

She awoke in a cold sweat, sitting upright in bed and wondering what it was that was troubling her. Could it be the shock, perhaps? The death of her friend and mentor? The problems the vicar's death would bring for the parish and the increased workload she would have to shoulder? The changes when a new vicar was appointed? The way everyone in the parish would mourn the vicar's death? It was all of these and yet none of them. For the remainder of the night she only slept in small bursts, her mind troubled by the events of the previous evening.

Lisa woke with the sun streaming through the window and only one thought on her mind. Ink! Why had Tobias got ink stains on his thumbs? From the pen he was using in the library, of course. But pens were not allowed in the library at St Deny's, only pencils, to copy notes from books!

Lisa dressed quickly and set off back to the undertaker's. John Pedley was only just eating his breakfast and not prepared for a second visit from the vicar's curate. He was a little puzzled as to why she wanted to see the body again but agreed. There was no logic in requests from the bereaved, something he had come to realise very quickly in this business.

Lisa went in and went straight to the vicar's hands, examining closely the black smudges on the ends of his thumbs. "What do you think these marks are John?"

John looked bemused. "I'm not sure. Ink, I suppose. That's what the doctor said. I will wipe them off when I prepare the vicar for the chapel of rest."

Lisa was looking thoughtful. "No, don't wipe them off. Could you get me a sample of whatever it is?"

John scratched his head. The requests were getting stranger, but he always liked to accommodate the bereaved. "I'm not sure. I suppose I could if you really wanted me to."

Lisa smiled. "Thanks, John. Have you some cotton wool, neat alcohol and a small bottle with a sealed lid?"

John scurried away wondering whatever next he would be asked to do in the cause of helping the bereaved!

Lisa looked at the face of Rev Tobias, still at peace and looking serene. What she was about to do seemed like sacrilege, but it would have to be done. She gripped Tobias's jaws and squeezed. Rigor mortis had set in and the body felt quite stiff, but the lips parted under the pressure and Tobias's tongue was revealed. Lisa gave a gasp. It was stained a deep and sombre black. She released her grip and the tongue went back inside his mouth and his face resumed its peaceful countenance.

Rev Farthing came away from the undertaker's carrying a small sealed bottle with cotton wool inside, stained black with the substance found on Rev Tobias's thumb. She returned to her vicarage and, after ringing the vicar's cousin to inform him of his death, she started to make arrangements for the funeral. Glancing up at the clock she dashed into church to take the 9.30 communion service and announce to the parish the sad death of their vicar. It was agreed that the bell would be tolled after the service 75 times in memory of the vicar, one for each year of his life, to alert the village of his death.

Lisa went back home and remembered she hadn't had any breakfast. She made herself some coffee and toast, taking them into the study as she intended to make further phone calls. She would have to ring the Bishop and other clergy, but there was one other phone call she wanted to make first.

"Kate, is that you? It's Lisa."

Kate sounded pleased. "I've not heard from you for weeks Lisa. We'll have to go out for another drink, but I expect you'll be too holy for the likes of me now!"

"Kate, I want you to do me a favour. Are you still working in the lab?"

"Every day, up to my eyes in test tubes and funny smells. I didn't expect this after university!"

"Could you test something for me if I dropped it off at the lab?"

"Sounds interesting Lisa. You've not been experimenting with wacky baccy, have you?"

"No, nothing like that. I think it's ink but there's something I'm not happy about."

"Drop it in and we'll find out what it is, mark my words!"

Lisa then rang the Bishop informing him of the vicar's death. She then made another half a dozen calls and then put the answering machine on as she left the house, knowing that parishioners would be ringing up all morning, so in a way she was thankful that she was going out.

Lisa drove the 20 miles to Dorrington to drop off the package at the lab where Kate worked. She didn't see her but just left the package at the gatehouse and said it was urgent. She then turned the car around and drove back to St Deny's Library.

Peter the warden opened the door. He was a tall, angular man with friendly open features. He expressed his sympathies and Lisa asked to be shown the desk where Father Tobias was working when he died. They went into the library. Peter told her that his death had come as such a shock to the little community who ran the library. Rev Tobias had been such a frequent visitor and such a good friend of them all, they were all so upset by his death.

Lisa walked into the main room of the library with bookshelves from floor to ceiling and with bookcases set at right angles into the floor. There were many small alcoves with desks and chairs where readers could work and consult the books. Lisa was shown an alcove at the far end of the room, so tucked away and hidden that it seemed to be in a different room.

"Here is where Rev Tobias liked to work, a little out of the way but he liked the peace and quiet."

The table had a simple wooden chair and on the table a lamp and a pile of books. "Are these the books Rev Tobias was consulting?"

"Yes, not his usual selection of Victorian poets or church history but a rather rum selection."

"Can I look at the books he was consulting?"

"Of course you can. I'll leave you to yourself, just let us know if you want anything."

Lisa sat and looked at the books almost in a trance, not even reading the titles. The last few hours had been such a shock. Tobias had seemed troubled after yesterday morning's communion, the last time she had seen him alive. He had said something odd, she now recalled. "I'm just an old fool Lisa but I've got to check this out or something could be very wrong and a great injustice done." Why hadn't she asked him what he meant? He had said he was going to St Deny's and booked himself in for a night and would Lisa take care of the parish while he was away? Nothing unusual in that, she thought. He was always coming here, it was like a second home for him.

Lisa's eyes focused on the books and she picked them up, examining each one and reading the titles. The warden was right, it was a rather rum selection and not the usual things which interested Tobias, she thought, as she read the titles:

An Illustrated Book on Tattoos
Famous Railway Journeys of the World
An Unknown Person in an Unknown Land (about Paraguay)
The Oxford Dictionary of English Surnames
The Register for Stoneyhust Public School 1975
Sports Clubs of South America
A Biography of Butch Cassidy & The Sundance Kid

She sat staring at the library shelves wondering how she could make sense of the seeming jumble of books with little or no connection. South America? Tobias had never been there, or at least had never spoken about it. He was interested in railways, like most clergymen, but tattoos?

Sarah walked past. "How are getting on Lisa? Any luck?"

Lisa sighed. "Not really. It's a pretty hopeless task if you ask me. I shouldn't have bothered. After all, I don't even know the order he looked at the books."

Sarah smiled. "Oh that's easy to work out. We keep a record of each book people ask for and the counterfoils will be in order. I'll go and get them."

Lisa stared after her, mouth open, marvelling at the wonders of the library service, seemingly so quaint yet so efficient!

When Sarah returned she was carrying a bundle of counterfoils and soon arranged the books on the desk in a very different order.

She stood back admiring her handiwork "There now. I'm pretty certain that's the order Father Tobias consulted the books."

Lisa again looked at the books, this time with a new determination and purpose.

The top of the pile was the book on English Surnames. There was a marker in place and she opened the book at the page. It was the letter 'V'. What on earth could Tobias be looking at? She scanned down the page, looking for a clue in the names. Venus... Verner... Vickers... then she saw it. There was only one family she knew of in the church with a surname beginning with V and that was Verdugo, or rather Mr Verdugo, who had recently died and his son Paul had returned from South America to tidy up the estate.

VERDUGO: Spanish occupational name for an
officer of justice or public executioner.

Quite appropriate for old man Verdugo, she thought, a former
churchwarden who had been a local magistrate, and a pretty severe
one at that if all the stories were to be believed.

Verdugo had died about two months ago and his son, who hadn't
been seen in Greenford for almost 20 years, had returned from Brazil
to inherit the estate, and, if local rumours were correct, sell up and
return to Brazil as soon as possible. Local gossip also said that there
had been a rift in the family and old man Verdugo had not been on
speaking terms with his son for many years. Still, he had left him
the estate, which would be a tidy sum at today's prices. She had met
Paul last week in the village. He seemed a personable young man;
he was certainly turning the heads of the young ladies of the parish.
Maybe it wasn't just his good looks though, but also the thought of
the inheritance would make him extremely attractive to some.

Right, the next book: 'The Illustrated book of Tattoos'. What was
Lisa to make of this? Some of the pictures were quite horrific as to
what people would do to their own bodies for the sake of art! She
flicked through the pictures trying to think of why Tobias would want
to consult such a book. She tried desperately to remember when the
last time was that she had seen someone with a tattoo. Then it came
to her. Paul Verdugo, of course, had one, a very strange one on his
arm, a horse with two sticks and 'PV' underneath, presumably his
initials.

Lisa went through the illustrations trying to find one that was
similar. Yes, here it was, a Polo player on a horse with two crossed
sticks, that must be it. She closed the book and picked up the next:
one. 'Sports Clubs in South America'. This was easy. She went straight
to polo and then hit a brick wall as there were over 200 in Argentina
and 40 in Brazil.

Lisa picked up 'Stoneyhurst College Registers 1960-1975'. She
flipped through the pages and then realised there must be a Verdugo
link. She looked closely at each year's register of leavers, and there it was,
in 1973, Paul Verdugo along with 30 other students. A photograph of the
year was there on the opposite page. Not much help there, she thought.

The next book was 'Famous Railway Journeys of the World'. Africa, Europe, The Flying Scotsman, but which one? There was one in South America, 'The Old Patagonian Express', but after reading the account she was none the wiser.

'Butch Cassidy and the Sundance Kid'. What was she to make of this? She couldn't remember Tobias reading westerns, so she put the book down feeling that her search was going to be fruitless. She couldn't understand why Tobias would be interested in these books, even with the link to South America and Paul Verdugo.

What were his last words to her that morning in the vestry? 'I'm just an old fool Lisa, but I have to check this out or there could be a great injustice done? Why was he so interested in Paul Verdugo and why was he checking him out?

Then it all fell into place with the next two books. 'An Unknown Person In An Unknown Land' was about life in Paraguay. She didn't need to open the book, the title was enough. A thought flashed through her mind like an arrow. Yes, of course that's it, she thought. It was confirmed when she turned back to look at the Stoneyhurst Register for 1975. There was a photo of a boy on a horse winning a prize. It wasn't Paul Verdugo and the jigsaw was almost complete.

She got up to leave, thanking Sarah for all her help, and walked to the car park, her mind racing. There was something else, though. She thought back to the Monday morning when Tobias had been so agitated and left so abruptly for the library, leaving her in charge of the parish. What was he doing when she arrived in church that morning? She had gone into the vestry and found him putting away the marriage registers, not unusual except there hadn't been a wedding. What then had he been looking at?

When she got back to the vicarage there were 15 messages on the answerphone, most from parishioners sending condolences after the vicar's death; some from fellow clergy, but one was from Kate.

"Lisa, I think you should go to the police. That substance you gave me to look at isn't ink but a deadly poison, but not just any old poison. This one is quite unusual, it soaks in through the skin and is lethal. A small trace on the tongue or fingers and you could be dead. Where on earth did you find it?"

But Lisa didn't ring the police. Instead she went to Rev Tobias's rectory, wondering what she would find. She had a key and let herself in. There was a stillness and silence that would not be broken now. She went into his study, not sure if she was doing the right thing, and looked on his desk. There were the usual collection of letters and Orders of Services, a half-finished address for the Mother's Union and, underneath them, a desk diary for the week, which Tobias usually filled in so that he could plan his movements. Monday was the meeting with herself at church, but afterwards, at 11am, another meeting, at Lingards', the solicitors. So that's where he went in such a hurry and that's where she was going now.

Mr Lingard was just about ready to leave promptly at 5pm when Lisa was shown into his office. He didn't like calls at this time and wondered why his secretary had allowed such an intrusion when most business could wait until the morning. Lisa thought she had better come straight to the point.

"I believe Rev Maybury came to see you on Monday morning?"

"Yes, that is correct," Lingard replied cautiously. "Could you tell me what this is about as I was just about to leave?"

"Could you tell me why Rev Maybury consulted you?"

Mr Lingard's patience was now exhausted and he reached for his hat and coat. "I'm sorry but the relationship between a client and his solicitor is, how shall we put it, like the confessional." He gave Lisa a cheesy smile.

"Even when the client is dead?"

Mr Lingard froze; his hand reached for his hat but never got there. He turned and looked at Lisa. "I'm so sorry, and here he was sitting in my office, just yesterday."

Lisa launched her attack. "I'm afraid he died rather suddenly and I'm not satisfied. I think it may have something to do with what he came to see you about yesterday."

Mr Lingard now sat down, producing from his top pocket a rather large red handkerchief, with which he began to mop his brow.

"Have you been to the police? Oh! This has come as such a shock! Tobias was such a gentle man."

"No, I haven't yet because there are still some loose ends I need to tie up before I present my suspicions."

Mr Lingard now regained some of his composure. "But this doesn't alter anything. I still can't tell you what we discussed."

Lisa raised herself to her full height of barely five feet and tried to tower over Mr Lingard, who was still sitting at the desk.

"Look, Mr Lingard, it would reflect well on you if you are seen to be co-operating. After all, you don't want the police crawling over your office and all your files do you?"

"No, no, I suppose I don't." Lingard continued mopping his brow.

Lingard looked beyond Lisa out of the window. "It was an odd request and I don't know why he asked for it, but I gave it to him as he was such a dear friend. I didn't ask any questions. Perhaps I should have."

"What, what was it you gave Tobias?"

"A photocopy of the signature of Paul Verdugo when he came in to sign for his fathers papers."

"Can you give me the same copy of his signature?"

Lingard was looking a little pale now, wondering what he might be involved in. "Yes, I suppose so but what's all this about?"

Lisa didn't answer but waited until he returned bearing a photocopy of a signature. She snatched it from his hand and rushed out of the office, leaving in her wake a rather worried and forlorn-looking solicitor.

This was it, she thought. Just one more piece of evidence and she would be able to go to the police But first the church and the marriage registers. It was now quite dark as she let herself into the vestry and unlocked the safe. She took out the register for 1979. There it was, the marriage of Paul Verdugo, a marriage which only lasted two years, and they were divorced without children. But that was not what was important, it was the signature to the marriage. The signature she held on the paper was similar, but anyone could see it was a poor copy of the original. She closed the book in triumph and as she did so she looked up into the pale blue eyes of Paul Verdugo standing above her.

"How did you get in?" Lisa asked rather nervously.

"Through the door, as most people do, the door you left open. But I locked it after me. What's that you've got in your hand?"

Lisa instinctively screwed up the piece of paper and anxiously moved away from the desk that was separating them.

Paul smiled and snatched the piece of paper from her hand. "Now then, vicar, what would you be doing with a copy of my signature? What were you comparing it with?"

Lisa's mouth went dry. "I don't know what you're talking about. I'm here on church business."

"Is that why you went to see Lingard and ask for a copy of my signature? It's alright, he told me. I just happened to call round there after you'd left. The poor boy was quite shaken, not sure he'd done the right thing... professional standards and all that."

Lisa felt sick. What was she to do? Attack being the best form of defence, she went for it.

"You killed Tobias, didn't you?"

Paul smiled, "That's a bit harsh. Let's just say I helped him along on his way. A little something I picked up from the indians in Paraguay, especially good for people with weak hearts. He liked books, so what better way to go than sitting in the library reading?"

"How did you poison him?"

"The old fool was sleeping when I went into the library. Just a few dabs of the poison on his thumbs and the end of his pencil. At his age and with his weak heart, if he put it in his mouth he would be dead. I watched from the other side of the bookshelves. When he woke up he put the pencil to his lips and he went back to sleep, never to wake up." He smiled and looked menacingly at Lisa.

"He was on to you, wasn't he Paul? Or should I say Peter Vincent?"

"Very clever, a real life Miss Marple and an old fool of a meddling clergyman. I thought I had the perfect plan and he had to come along with his questions about trains."

"The Patagonian Express?"

"That damn train! How was I to know that it was narrow gauge? Tobias went bumbling on about the train, asking how he'd always wanted to travel on that line and asking me questions about it. I'd never travelled on it, but Paul had made the journey many times to the gold mines. And then questions about Butch Cassidy! I thought the old fool was going senile."

Lisa retorted quickly. "They disappeared in Patagonia, Butch Cassidy and the Sundance Kid, that's where they were tracked down and killed. So what made Tobias suspicious of you?"

"When he met me he remembered that Paul didn't like horses. He had fallen off one when he was a boy here in the village and almost died. Tobias remembered that and, seeing my tattoo, asked what it was for. I told him about playing polo. I think that started his suspicions. With Paul and I having the same initials I thought the tattoo didn't matter. He then started asking questions about trains and Patagonia."

"His lifelong passion outside the church; he knew all about them."

"Stupid mistakes. And it was all going so well, even the solicitor was fooled."

"Who exactly are you?" Lisa edged around the desk.

"I'm Paul's best friend, his flatmate in Rio and for the last ten years his lover."

"But what happened to Paul?"

"He died last month in Rio, of Aids. I nursed him to the end. It was, believe it or not, Paul who thought all this up."

"I don't believe you."

"Look, it was, but what does it matter now?"

Lisa realised she was on the wrong tack. "Tell me then, convince me."

"I was at school with Paul, Stoneyhurst. Like brothers we were, inseparable. Then when he left he came here to Greenford. He studied engineering and mining at university, then he went to South America. It suited him. He fell out with his father when he told him he was gay. His father, a churchwarden and local magistrate, didn't like that. He threatened to cut off his inheritance. They never spoke to each other for the last 15 years, not even to exchange Christmas cards. The hurt was so deep.

I met Paul when I went to South America on business. We just met by chance in a bar in Rio – it was a gay bar though! We've been together ever since, inseparable just like at school, except this time a more fulfilling relationship. Six months ago Paul and I split up. He contracted Aids after a one night stand and was only given a few months to live. I came back and nursed him. It was then, just before he died, that he received the letter from Lingard informing him that his father had died and, in spite of what he had said before, left him everything. Paul knew he was too ill to travel to England to sort out the estate and he couldn't make a will leaving me everything, other relatives would challenge it. So he said, why didn't I go to England and sort out the estate? Not many people would remember him back in Greenford and no relatives lived anywhere near the place. We looked similar, same build and features; sometimes people did confuse us, and he wanted me to have his father's estate. Paul died two weeks ago and so I came back to England to take his place, sell up the estate and return to Rio. Well, that was the plan until that buffoon of a vicar smelt a rat."

"He wasn't so much of a fool that he couldn't see through you, was he?"

"That stupid train journey. Why did I commit myself? Paul had done it loads of times, trips on mining business, how was I to know the trains?"

"So you murdered a good man just so you could get your hands on money that was not even yours, or ever likely to be?"

"He also noticed the tattoo, I thought it wasn't a problem as 'PV' are Paul's initials. I'd forgotten about Paul's aversion to horses."

"Tobias wasn't such a fool after all, was he?"

"You can do a lot of things with two million pounds, even get rid of two members of the clergy I suppose."

Lisa froze. Her next action was instinctive. She ran as fast as she could out of the vestry to the front door. Peter followed, his long strides catching up with her as she neared the church door. She found it locked. Turning to face her pursuer, she only had one advantage, her knowledge of the church building. Desperately she went forward and Peter went after her, only to be fooled by the dummy she had thrown him as, with a neat side-step, she went the other way with all the skill of a rugby three-quarter.

She now had a few yards' lead as she rushed for the bell tower, managing to get in and slam the door behind her, drawing the bolt across. At last she breathed more easily, but not for long. With her back against the door, she suddenly felt it shake as a heavy object pounded into the wood on the outside trying to break it down.

"You can't hide from me, vicar! I'll get you in the end!"

Then another great blow came down on the door. She knew it wouldn't last long under that kind of sustained pressure. She had to do something, but what?

Then she realised, the bells! She tumbled up the steps, two and three at a time in her rush to get to the top. Breathless, she paused to hear the splinter of the oak door as it began to crack and split under its heavy pounding.

She pulled for all she was worth on the bells, oblivious to the ear-splitting noise so close to her head as she swung the two bells, the sound almost deafening her.

At 10pm at night the bells of St Gemma's were not usually to be heard, so their ringing caused quite a stir in Greenford. The drinkers in the Axe and Cleaver spilled onto the street wondering what was going on and residents from nearby houses came out to see what was happening. The sexton ran out of his house to the church, fearing vandals had got in, but when he opened the door he found a sight which puzzled him. Paul Verdugo was breaking down the door to the bell tower. Others now arrived, taking the axe from him and rushing up the bell tower to find Lisa like, a latter-day Quasimodo, ringing the bells for all she was worth.

It took Lisa a long time to recover her full hearing, not to mention the experience of almost being murdered in her own church. She thought the experience might have put her off church bells for life! Paul, or rather Peter Vincent, was imprisoned for the murder of Rev Maybury and Lisa was acclaimed the heroine of the hour, gaining a new, if not very flattering, nickname of Miss Marple.

A VERY NECESSARY MURDER?

<hr/>

They should be well aware that the shepherd will have to bear the blame for any deficiency that God, as Father of the whole human family, finds in his sheep.

Gifts needed by an Abbot: St Benedict's Rule

<hr/>

THE ABBOT PUT down the phone thoughtfully. An odd request, but one he had to think about and ponder before deciding what action to take. But now more pressing matters were at hand. The great bell had rung summoning the community to Terce at 9am, not the first service of the day but the third.

The Abbot took up his place in the choir stall and bowed his head in prayer, offering his thoughts to God. Dilemmas and responsibilities were weighing especially heavily upon him today with his sadness at the death of one of the Brothers the previous night. Father Thomas had been a member of the community in the monastery almost as long as the Abbot, over 25 years, and his death had hit the him hard. He wrestled with these thoughts as he prayed. Had he favoured Thomas more than other monks? Had he followed the rule of Benedict, who said 'The Abbot should not select for special treatment any individual in the monastery'? Even our Lord had disciples closer to him than the others. He continued to wrestle with his thoughts as the short office of Terce ended.

He walked back through the cloisters aiming for his office, but instead turned out into the small yard which led through the garden and into the wood. He wanted more time to reflect and pray. His walk led him up a gentle hill to a plot of ground, which had a low limestone wall surrounding it. He opened a small wooden gate to where modest plain wooden crosses marked the graves of the community. On each cross was the name and date of each monk; nothing ornate, just plain and simple. He walked down the lines of the graves recalling each monk in his mind, sometimes smiling, sometimes stopping to reflect on some aspect of their lives. He committed each one to God, giving thanks for the privilege of serving them as Abbot. He retraced his steps through the monastery vegetable garden; his steps a little lighter as he felt easier and less burdened and now his prayer was that he would treat all members of the community the same and show no favouritism. He knew that this was what he was trying to do, sometimes failing, but it was his avowed aim.

His thoughts returned to Thomas, an outstanding monk by any standards, but again he was judging and perhaps he shouldn't. Thomas had come into the monastery at the age of 55 at the end of the Second World War after serving in the armed forces. It was quite difficult for any person to adapt to monastic life, even more so for someone older.

Thomas had adapted though and took everything in his stride; the discipline, the rule, the obedience; it all became second nature to him. Monks coming into the monastery later in life can be given a hard time. Some people think it is an escape, a retreat from the world, but monastic life is never easy and takes all the reserves of courage and mental ability a person can muster. Thomas had those reserves seemingly in abundance and no matter how hard he was tested would come through, even looking for more difficult challenges. After only a year in monastic life he had asked if he could go and be alone for two weeks in the small hermitage at the far end of the monastery grounds. This could be hard as the monk was completely alone with only books of prayer and the Bible. Food was left daily some way off so that there could be no human contact, only complete isolation and silence. Thomas did this every year, coming out at the end, not haggard and desperate for company, but refreshed and renewed as though he had been on holiday. He even began to call it his holiday villa. It quickly became clear in the monastery that Thomas's gifts were many; he was experienced in mechanical engineering and could fix almost anything with a minimum of tools, but his real gifts were with people. After a few years a steady stream of people would come and stay at the monastery, always seeking out Thomas for counsel and direction. Over the last 20 years the monastery had become renowned for the quality and depths of its retreats for both religious and lay people.

Thomas had one vice though, if chocolate could be seen as a vice! The Abbot had observed on more than one occasion that bars of chocolate were being given to Thomas by grateful recipients of his counselling. The chocolate did not always find its way onto the common refectory table, to be shared by the community on feast days. The Abbot had told Thomas off about it more than once. He felt he couldn't let it go unnoticed when he observed a bar of chocolate, the size of which he never knew existed, passed to the monk who secreted it under his robes. Now Thomas was no more. But that wasn't quite right. The community were mourning but really should rejoice for a Brother who had passed through death and was now at peace with his Lord.

His death had been quiet and peaceful. He had fallen ill some weeks ago complaining of pains in his stomach. The tests in the local hospital diagnosed cancer and it was found to be very advanced. He came back to the monastery for the last three weeks and those days were good. He wrote letters, rang people and many people came to see him. In the last two days, when he was confined to bed in the infirmary, each of the community came in turn to pray with him and take their leave. Finally, the Abbot came to anoint and pray for him. Thomas had asked the pardon of the community 'for whatsoever trouble, annoyance or ill example he may have given them'. The Abbot had given him absolution and he received the sacrament for the last time. It was during the office of Compline that he died. The community was in chapel and when the service ended the great bell tolled, not just for the normal 12 times but went on tolling, 77 times one for each year of his life. The monks stayed in their stalls, each one with his head bowed praying for their fellow Brother and giving thanks. How fitting that Thomas had died during this service, the office at the end of the day, committing one not just to sleep 'But to rest in peace, as if his bed were his grave'.

Later on that day the Abbot summoned the monks together for the weekly chapter meeting. The main business was the arrangements for the funeral of Father Thomas, and the Abbot would have to say more than he would like to. He knew it would set certain tongues wagging in the community.

"As you are all aware, the arrangements for our Brother Thomas's funeral are to be made. The service will take place at noon on Friday. There will be guests of course, and little family as Thomas seemed not to have any immediate family." He paused, surveying the faces of the monks, each in their black cowl with their heads bent forward listening intently to what he had to tell them. "There will be some visitors, lay and religious, who Thomas gave spiritual direction to." There was the briefest hesitation as he chose the exact words to say. "Father Thomas, as most of you know, came into community late in life. He spent many years in the armed services and members of his regiment wish to be present and pay honour to his memory. I have given my permission for them to do so." There was no indication from the faces or demeanour of the chapter that this was a surprise, but the Abbot knew that there would be talk and questions as to what all this meant. "On Thursday night Thomas will be laid in the chapel and the Office of the Dead will be said after compline. Thank you Brothers" The Abbot stood, followed by the monks, and pronounced the benediction in Latin to end the chapter meeting.

The monastery fell back into its usual pattern very quickly. The basis of monastic life was routine and knowing what each part of the day consisted of. For some people who wanted excitement and adventure this would seem tedious and dull, but they would miss the sense that routine can free an individual and help them reach heights of spiritual and human fulfilment not known in the outside world.

Thursday Evening

The Abbot was sat in his office reading when a knock on the door announced his visitor.

A slim muscular man with tanned features was shown into the room.

"Ah! You must be Colonel Fitzroy." The Abbot stood up and moved towards his visitor, his hand outstretched.

"Very pleased to meet you Abbot, I take it as a privilege that you have allowed us to come and participate."

The Abbot looked quizzically at the Colonel. "But where are your men? You said there would be a party of six to carry the coffin."

The Colonel coughed and moved uneasily in his seat. "I hope you don't mind, Abbot, but I've put them up in the local pub. As soldiers, I didn't want them disturbing the peace here in your beautiful monastery."

The Abbot smiled. "We don't mind, we are quite looking forward to seeing them. They will be in full uniform tomorrow I hope."

"Of course." said the Colonel. Realising that perhaps he was being a little too cautious, he had come to the monastery in civilian dress, not sure of the protocol on such an occasion as this.

The Abbot asked if his visitor would like a drink. The Colonel said yes, wondering what beverage he would be offered. Tea, or even water, he mused to himself. He was both surprised and relieved when he saw a bottle of single malt whiskey produced from a cupboard along with two glasses. Generous measures were poured and the bottle put between them. How wrong can you be, thought the Colonel, as he took a gulp of the warm honey-coloured nectar.

"Now, Colonel, about tomorrow. There will be a lot of people here. Thomas was very popular and much loved. Your involvement will, how can I say, cause a few raised eyebrows and questions to be asked."

The Colonel moved forward slightly in the chair. "I realise that, Abbot, and we are very grateful for being allowed to take part. As a regiment we wanted to honour one of our own, one of our most distinguished and decorated officers."

The Abbot smiled, looking intently at the Colonel. "I know Thomas's history. I was his confidante and close friend when he entered the monastery, a long time ago now, over 25 years. I thought at first he would never last. We had many enquiries from people coming back from the war. Some wanted to escape from the horrors they had witnessed, others, well, they liked the discipline in the monastery and they were looking for some meaning in their lives. A soldier and monk have a lot in common you know, Colonel. We both have to learn a disciplined and regimented life of obedience. Replace the gun with a prayer missal and you could have a good monk."

The Colonel smiled. "I've never thought of it like that before, but I don't think you'd want some of my men in your monastery."

The Abbot went on: "Thomas when he came was troubled, very troubled. I thought he wouldn't last and that his demons would win. But I was wrong. He came through, showing great reserves of courage and strength. He proved himself to live a life of prayer and service which was truly exemplary. Now, tell me Colonel, why do you honour him and want to be here for the funeral?"

The Colonel helped himself to another drink. "We knew him by a different name of course, Joe, in the Special Air Service as it became known after it was formed in 1941. I didn't meet him until the end of the war but I knew of him. He was damn good, some say the best, the marker by which others are judged. I don't know, all I do know is that stories about him were legion and if it wasn't for the secrecy in the unit, the work he did behind enemy lines would have made him famous.

The Abbot poured himself another drink. "Fame is not to be looked for and sometimes it is like an albatross around the neck, cumbersome, unwanted and immovable. But I digress, please carry on with your story."

"The SAS was formed from volunteers, each member hand-picked, then trained in sabotage. They were dropped behind enemy lines, often working in pairs or sometimes alone seeking information, hindering enemy communications and identifying targets. Joe was the best; everyone wanted him as their team leader. On a mission, he was fearless, but never foolhardy, always taking care of the men in his unit. He showed courage and ingenuity in the face of overwhelming odds; he was a legend."

"And the killing?"

The Colonel again moved uneasily in his chair. "Yes, there was that, but it was war and no-one did it lightly or with a sense of satisfaction."

The Abbot looked into the eyes of the colonel. "I was Brother Thomas's close friend for many years, he told me everything."

"He told you then about the shepherd boy?"

"Yes, and I think that was what led him here to our monastery all those years ago."

The Abbot poured them both another drink. "Tell me the story from your side. I would like to hear it again and then I want to give you something."

The Colonel drew a deep breath. "It was a special mission to Yugoslavia. They were going in with a small team of four men. Their role was to capture and bring back alive an agent who was suspected of being a double agent. He had a codebook with names and addresses of other suspected double agents. We had to have that book and no-one had to know we had captured him. The mission had to be one of complete secrecy. The agent had to disappear one day without any clues as to what had happened. The agent thought he was safe, living in a small village in the hills in a remote region of Montenegro. There he thought he could indulge his game of playing one power off against another as no-one could reach him. Joe and three others were landed in Yugoslavia and made their way to the village. They were camped in the forests above the village waiting their opportunity when a young shepherd boy stumbled upon them. They had their orders, no prisoners. They would talk eventually, and everyone who threatened the operation must be killed. Even Joe hesitated. The boy was captured and tied up, but Joe knew that the whole operation rested on secrecy. If word got out that the agent had been captured, other double agents across Europe would have been warned off. Joe knew he had to do the execution, something he couldn't delegate. He did it away from the others, taking full responsibility. The operation was successful, the agent was captured and brought back alive. No one realised he had been captured until much later, and lives were saved and probably the war shortened by their efforts, as the popular myth goes"

The Abbot looked thoughtful. "What happened to Thomas, I mean Joe, then?"

"That was the last mission Joe went on. He asked if he could stand down. He was used to train others in the SAS, including me when I joined the brigade. When the war ended he left the SAS as soon as could and came here. You know the rest."

The Abbot sat back in his chair.

"Colonel, I would like to ask you a question? Can a murder ever be justified, or thought necessary?"

He thought for a few moments. "I think you would be more qualified to answer that question. I know that soldiers have to do things in times of war which could not be justified at any other time. Joe wrestled with that one. He couldn't forgive himself. I wonder if he ever came to terms with it. He always saw the acts which he committed as necessary to uphold the freedoms and ideals of his country, but it seemed as if he was carrying the weight of the sins of his fellow soldiers."

The Colonel paused, staring into the glass.

"War is a horrible business and there are no clean heroes, no-one comes out of it with much self-respect or sense of peace with what they've had to do. There were awful things done, bombings of cities with civilians in them, you try to fight a war with honour and with a code of conduct; it isn't easy."

"No, you're right, Colonel. Thomas certainly didn't have peace of mind when he came to the Monastery, but I believe he found it in his way. For him to become a good monk took a supreme effort. He was the best of monks; he had a lot to overcome, mainly inside himself. Perhaps this was the only place he could live and find any sort of fulfilment after all his experiences of war, murder and violence."

The Colonel thought for a few moments. "You know, Abbot, I wasn't looking forward to coming here today. When I rang earlier in the week, after we heard of Thomas's death, I thought you would refuse my request. You see our worlds are so far apart."

"Yes, they are, Colonel, but Thomas bridged them and tomorrow we must honour the whole of his life, not just the part spent in the monastery. But there is something else you've come for Colonel."

"You mean the medals?"

The Abbot got up and went across to a very large old safe sitting in the corner of the office. He opened it up and from the back drew out a small cardboard box and placed it on the table.

"You know, when a monk enters a monastery he makes a will and gives over all his worldly goods. Thomas asked if these could be kept by the monastery until he died, then disposed of. He was afraid of the publicity they would bring if he did anything with them in his lifetime."

He opened the lid and placed on the table an array of medals, each one with ribbons and some with bars. They glittered in the first light they had seen for 25 years. There was one medal which was different. It looked heavier, at first less distinguished than the rest, but the simple bronze cross out-ranked all the other decorations. It was a Victoria Cross.

The Colonel gave an audible gasp as he surveyed the medals and decorations.

"I didn't realise he had so many. We kept that sort of thing secret in the Brigade, but these, they are amazing. I knew he had the VC for a raid in Germany when he brought back his entire team against formidable odds."

The Colonel picked up the medals and began examining them. His hand went instinctively to the Victoria Cross, with its crimson ribbon and simple bronze cross made from metal which had reputedly been cast from cannon captured at the siege of Sevastopol in 1855.

The Abbot looked on bemused, not sure at the significance of these pieces of metal and ribbon.

"You know, Abbot, this is the closest I've ever been to a VC. "It's given for a single act of valour or devotion." He continued to hold the medal and turned it between his fingers.

"Did you know that King George V gave instructions that no matter the crime committed by anyone on whom the Victoria Cross has been conferred, the decoration should not be forfeited? Even if a

VC recipient was sentenced to hang for murder, he would be allowed to wear the Victoria Cross on the scaffold."

The Abbot looked thoughtful and smiled. "A bit like ordination Colonel! Thomas left instructions that your regimental museum should have them, and if you could give us a donation for them it would help."

The Colonel was still examining the treasure trove. "Of course, we will offer you the full market price. We have benefactors who buy items for us."

The Abbot again leant back in his chair. "The cheque can be made out to the monastery, but we are only administering the proceeds."

The Colonel looked up. "Can I ask where the money will be going?"

"Yes, certainly. It's going to a little village in Yugoslavia to help support an orphanage and school there."

The Colonel put the medals down and looked puzzled for a moment. "But that's where …"

"Yes," the Abbot interjected. "When Thomas came here he gave away his life savings to fund work in the village. His army pension was paid directly to the school and has helped to keep it going these 25 years. Now, with the sale of the medals, there should be enough to endow the school and orphanage for many years."

The Colonel looked up. "Was that his penance?"

The Abbot paused, thinking about the question. "No-one told him to do it, it was his idea and he didn't want any thanks. The school is in the name of the shepherd boy who was killed and Thomas's involvement is not known. I would want you keep it that way Colonel."

"Of course. We will respect his wishes."

"He talked to me about the project a lot. At first he thought he was doing it out of guilt, then he focused on the idea of the boy's life having some purpose and meaning and all this being done in the name of the shepherd boy whose life he had so cruelly cut short."

"Did Thomas find any peace after what he had done?"

"Yes, I believe he did, but not for a long time. He talked to me about it. He called it a murder out of necessity, if there can be such a thing. I am not a pacifist, Colonel. I too believe that war at times is sadly necessary in our fallen world. We cannot abandon our morals on the battlefield however. I couldn't have done what he did, but I realise that there are times and situations where even good men find themselves committing evil deeds."

The Colonel looked thoughtful.

"War is a peculiar time when normal law is suspended and one where it can be hard to find any moral purpose. Perhaps we need some of your monks as chaplains."

The Abbot smiled and swept the medals into the cardboard box. He handed them to the Colonel as the great bell began to strike for compline, followed by The Office for the Dead.

"Come on Colonel, please be my guest and sit with me for the service to honour our friend."

The Abbot and the Colonel walked purposefully towards the chapel, each with their thoughts about the person they were remembering. A soldier and a monk, two worlds seemingly so far apart yet embodied in Brother Thomas.

Compline lasted barely twenty minutes, the plainsong of the monks echoing around the Abbey, now in almost darkness as the shadows of night crept in. There was silence after the office for a good ten minutes, a silence that the Colonel wasn't used to but welcomed.

Then, seemingly from far away, a slow sound of plainsong could be heard gradually getting louder. From the far end of the Abbey four monks processed into the nave carrying a simple wooden coffin. The monks in the choir took up the refrain of the psalm:

> *Dominus custodit te ab omni malo:*
> *custodiat a ni-mam tu-am Dominus. Euouae.*
> (The Lord will guard you from all evil:
> The Lord will guard your soul.)

The monks had now reached the choir stalls and laid their Brother down in front of the altar.

The Office for the Dead continued, more like a dirge but one which the Colonel found very moving, with the softness of the chanting and the words echoing in the darkness of the Abbey, lost in its great vastness yet resonating into the soul.

The Colonel sat captivated through the service, not moving, just aware for one of the few times in his life of a spirituality he had rarely experienced before.

The following morning the Colonel was dressed very differently: his uniform, crisp and smartly pressed, the medal ribbons across his chest, his cap pulled over his eyes and his cane held between his gloved hands. The party of six soldiers arrived in the small car park; their uniforms seemed strangely incongruous in such a setting. The sergeant barked out the orders as they leapt out of the truck and hurried towards the door of the Abbey to take up their positions.

The Abbey was full well before 11.30 as it seemed that people from far and wide had come to pay their last respects to their beloved monk. As they passed the two lines of soldiers at the door of the Abbey, there were some curious glances and questioning stares as to why they were there.

At last the great bell began to toll and the service was ready to begin: a solemn Mass followed by a burial in the monks' wood. The Abbot led the procession of monks, swelled by members from other abbeys, and also clergy. The coffin stood at the front of the nave, looking small and insignificant, a single red rose on the lid.

The service proceeded with hymns and then a Mass for Brother Thomas. At the end of the Mass, the Abbot climbed the steps of the pulpit to address the congregation.

"It is with both sadness and joy that I stand here today. Sadness for the loss of a dear Brother who has died and who will be missed by so many, not least the members of this community that he served so faithfully for over 25 years. But also joy, for our Brother Thomas the trials and tribulations of this world are over and death is past, his soul rests in peace and in eternity with our Lord.

"Thomas was known and loved by us all. For some of you he was a wise counsellor, giving spiritual direction and a friendly listening ear. To the Brothers here a much loved and respected member of our community.

"Many found him to be wise. He didn't judge and understood the frailties of human nature better than most of us. People would seek him out, and travel many miles just to get his guidance and wisdom. We will all miss his wisdom.

"Thomas was human, though; he had his faults. I am sure the chocolate-makers will shed tears today at the loss of such a good customer (laughter echoed around the Abbey). But it was his human nature that God worked through. Thomas was a man of the world. I am glad that today members of his regiment are here in the Abbey, as it is part of his life we wish to honour. He gave brave service to his country, 'mentioned in despatches' is I think the term which is used, and he was decorated with medals, but you never saw him wearing them. (The Colonel tried in vain to place the service sheet across his chest to obscure his row of medals.) He saw and took part in the horrors of war, something that left a deep mark upon him. Perhaps that's why he could understand human nature so well; he always saw himself as the least and most unworthy recipient of God's Grace.

"Thomas did things in the war he was not proud of; here in the monastery he faced his demons and came to terms with the life of a soldier when he had to do things contrary to the life of the Christian disciple.

"There were two very distinct parts to the life of Brother Thomas. It is right that we honour both of them as they are embodied in the man and recognised by God. Let us give thanks for his life, for how his life touched and influenced ours, and let us commend his soul to almighty God for his infinite mercy. Amen."

The voices of the monks softly and solemnly chanted from *De Profundis* for the soul of the dead Brother. "From the morning watch even unto night, let Israel hope in the Lord," they sang. "And He shall redeem Israel from all his iniquities."

As the service ended, the soldiers came forward to take the coffin out of church followed by the procession of monks and mourners led by the Abbot. The long procession wound its way around the back of the Abbey, first through the gardens and then up the slight hill to the monk's wood. The monks continued the plainsong chants as they walked singing the Psalms of Jerusalem:

> *I will lift up my eyes to the mountains,*
> *From whence help shall come to me.*

Also from the Psalms of David:

> *'If you, O Lord, should mark our guilt,*
> *Lord, who would survive?*
> *But with you is found forgiveness.*

After a few minutes the procession reached the edge of the small wood and the clearing where the simple graveyard was set against the hillside.

The Abbot said the final prayers as the coffin was laid in the freshly-dug grave.

"Grant, we beseech thee almighty God, that by command the soul of thy servant Thomas our Brother may be counted in the company of the righteous in everlasting bliss. Amen"

He took some of the earth from the grave and sprinkled it upon the coffin; other monks and then some of the mourners came forward and followed his example.

As the Abbot closed his breviary the soldiers took up position at either side of the grave. They raised their rifles, pointing to the skies. Six shots rang out, shattering the quiet of the woods and making the birds take flight.

The Abbot surveyed the scene, silence had descended again upon the cemetery. Soldiers and monks were standing together and for the first time he noticed that the rows of graves of the monks were laid out like a military platoon.

As they returned back down the path from the small graveyard the Colonel and the Abbot walked together. They didn't speak; they didn't have to. Each had his own thoughts of Brother Thomas, the soldier and the monk united in death in a way that had never been in life.

THE COLLECTOR

They like to think their obsession is under control, that they can stop at any time; after all, they say to themselves, 'I have almost given up'. Yet in their heart of hearts collectors know it's not so simple. They cannot stop collecting.

Anon.

THE REV SARAH Mowbray liked the good things of life. That she had expensive tastes, no-one was in any doubt; that she did it on a clergy salary, few thought was possible. Relatives who left her with a comfortable income was the story Rev Mowbray allowed people to believe. The truth, however, was much more interesting, if not decidedly more sinister.

You see, Rev Mowbray was a collector. Some people collect stamps or postcards, others porcelain figures; she, however, collected something far more interesting and valuable. For Rev Sarah Mowbray collected inheritances.

It had begun like most collections, in a small way. An aunt had left her a few hundred pounds unexpectedly. She had used the money to go on a holiday where the bug really struck and the collecting started. You see, while on holiday she met up and made friends with a couple of elderly ladies. They had teamed up and enjoyed a great time together. When she had returned home she thought nothing more of it. They kept in touch and Sarah visited when she was in the area, but then, six months later, she received a letter from a solicitor saying that one of the ladies had died and left her £5,000 in her will. Sarah was amazed, and it was then that the thought entered her head... just a thought mind you, nothing too sinister, but a bit naughty, especially for a member of the clergy! She had not gone looking for this inheritance, but if she did were there more to be had?

Rev Sarah Mowbray had been a curate for over eight years now. Single and in her late forties, she knew she would never marry, but she also thought she may never be given any preferment and be a vicar with a living of her own. Her work was diligent and she tried hard, but there was no charisma, no sparkle. Her sermons, well thought out and delivered in a relaxed manner, failed to move people, and her ministry could never be described as distinguished, rather as ordinary and routine. Parishioners had no complaints, but then there was a sense that her ministry was hardly noticed and very much taken for granted. Her ministry matched her features: plain and ordinary, not really noticeable.

But then there was this other life, the holidays that Rev Mowbray threw herself into. Not excessive, just the normal entitlement of six weeks a year, but they were always exotic. Cruises were the preferred option but there were also train journeys across Europe. In this other life she was quite a different person, exciting, glamorous, popular and even a little hedonistic. She always went by herself but was never alone for very long.

The first few days of any holiday were always the busiest. Let's take a cruise as an example. She always got hold of the passenger list, usually on the pretence of being hopeless at names. That was quite wrong. She had an excellent memory for names and one she put to good use. Couples on the list had the red pen scored through them straightaway, so did single men as she didn't want any entanglements. No, it was single ladies she was looking for, and elderly rich single ladies with a bit of a health problem were like the rare signed copy of a first edition to a book collector.

She always aimed to have the passenger list sorted, as she put it, within the first three days of any cruise. That meant likely people identified, passengers discarded and a list of "possibles" drawn up, which she would then track down, befriend and, like any good collector, add to her collection.

Let us look at what she desired for her collection. The person had to be single, no children, and rich of course, although that could mean just a good house. There was also the problem of nephews and nieces and other well-meaning relatives. A few questions lightly asked about visits etc. and frequency of contacts would usually elicit the right information. If the person had good contact with relatives then she was quickly dropped. Sarah was looking for better acquisitions, like collectors who will exchange a dishevelled item in their collection for one in more pristine condition.

Let us suppose that the latest addition to the collection has been identified. What happens next? On a cruise a friendship will be struck up, quite a close one as Rev Mowbray ingratiates herself with her new target. As a woman and a member of the clergy it gives people a sense of trust and confidence in their new friend. They would go to places together when the ship docked and sit on the same meal table, nothing will be too much trouble for Rev Mowbray to undertake in the cause of the new-found friendship. When the holiday comes to an end, addresses will be exchanged and promises made to keep in touch. Nothing wrong so far you say, most people will do the same thing, though more often than not they will never see the person again. That is where Rev Mowbray shows the skills and devotion of a true collector and one dedicated to her hobby.

Two months later, and not a day earlier mind you, there will be a knock at the door of the new friend. Rev Mowbray will be standing there, usually with flowers or some such gift. She will be welcomed into the house like a dear friend, for that is what she has become. She will say that she was in the area on business and thought she would look in. This visit will give Rev Mowbray a true picture of her potential subject and if she is worth adding to the collection. There have been many that have been discarded at this stage, not worth the trouble of going on with. Nosey neighbours can be a problem, and even too many visits by the local vicar can be a nuisance. The condition and state of the property is of prime importance. Once, she was taken in by a lady she met on a cruise, very well to do she thought, and very rich. When she arrived at the house and saw it was a council property, she dumped the flowers in the waste bin and never even bothered knocking at the door!

The visit could last a few hours and afterwards, sitting in the car, detailed notes would be made: people talked about, the state of health. Elderly people were so ready to give out information on themselves, the medicines they were taking and the planned hospital visits. Nothing so vulgar as money would be mentioned, but a good look around the house, the quality of the furniture and possible antiques would help with any calculation. A visit to an estate agent in the local vicinity to ascertain house prices would all go down in the notes.

But still, you say, nothing has been done that is wrong. Yet! A collector is nothing but patient, prepared to wait for that item which will enhance their collection. Rev Mowbray had the patience of a true collector. The next visit would be in another couple of months, something special would be brought as a present this time, something she knew her friend would really like and appreciate. It is on this visit that Rev Mowbray would talk of money, of how she was only able to go on the cruise where they met because of an aunt who left her some money; of how she wouldn't be able to afford a holiday this year, the problems in the parish and the lack of money for vital work. Usually the chequebook was out by this time and a cheque written for her work. "Whom shall I make it out to?" the pen poised over the chequebook. "Oh! Just make it out to me. I can cash it and use it in the different funds. It's better that way."

The friendship now cemented would develop quickly. Letters and phone calls would be exchanged. Christmas and birthdays were always be busy times because during a visit then she could find out who really cared and kept in touch with her new friend. The new friend would, of course, be flattered and pleased that someone so caring and thoughtful would be taking such an interest in her.

It was only when she really felt sure of her ground that the subject of wills was introduced. She usually introduced it by telling a story about one of her parishioners who had died recently without leaving a will. A cousin in America, who was very rich and who never visited, would now get all the money and the house because no will was made. "Wasn't it shocking!" Of course, her friend would be aghast and then talk about her own provision. Had a will been made? Was it kept up to date? The words which would send a tingle down the spine of Rev Mowbray were: "Well, I haven't got round to making a will yet." Those words were music in her ears. She could almost feel the new crisp £50 notes as she quickly made provision for helping her friend to make a will.

Witnesses tended to be a problem. She liked to pick neighbours who weren't too fussy and who were preferably old themselves. Usually, though, a will had already been made and somehow she was going to have to get herself written into it. This was not too difficult, that is if she had chosen the person well and done good research. Collectors are always those who have done their research. Twenty people can walk past something at an auction and not notice its value, but the real collector, the real connoisseur, they can spot the genuine article every time.

Getting written into a will usually resulted after a friendship where the friend would be concerned for Rev Mowbray and wanted to leave her something to remember her by. Concern about the curate's retirement, where she would live and who would look after her, questions which she encouraged, and usually the answers brought forth genuine concern from the friend. Once those words, "Well, I'm going to leave you something in my will" were spoken it was as if the collector had found the prized and coveted item they had sought for many years. Rev Mowbray, though, was never satisfied with the words. Keen interest was taken as to instructions to the solicitor, when it would be done and what would be said in the wording of the will.

"I wouldn't want money. It may be an embarrassment for a curate to receive a large inheritance, and I would have to give it away. I am only worried as to where I shall live," Rev Mowbray would say, modestly.

"Well, you shall have this house then. The Cat Protection League wouldn't know what to do with it."

Here was the collector now with her prized acquisition, so she could rest easy. But anyone knowing anything about collectors knows they are never satisfied with their collection; they always have to go on collecting.

In six years Rev Mowbray had been on seven cruises, staying first class, of course (you meet a better sort of person there), one trip on the Orient Express and three trips to Switzerland, a place she loved and decided she would like to retire to, if she could afford it! Of course, she had to be rather economical with the truth when she mentioned holidays in the parish. She usually said she was going to stay with her aunt in Cornwall, and that could explain the suntan when she returned, but not usually in February!

During her holidays she always added to her collection. There had not been a holiday without an acquisition, sometimes two. Within the six years two of her "friends" had died, leaving her a house and money to the value of well over £100,000. This, of course, helped to fuel the other holidays and the rather expensive tastes she was acquiring. People in the parish did wonder sometimes. The vicarage was well furnished, but they didn't notice that the prints on the wall were not reproductions but signed originals, and Rev Mowbray was careful not to dress too lavishly. After all, she didn't want to draw attention to herself.

Any good collector will lavish attention on their collection, spend time with it, admire the pieces, feel a sense of satisfaction on a new acquisition. Rev Mowbray was no different. She would write letters to her "friends", visit them, always remember their birthdays, become like a daughter to them and never want anything in return. Well that's not exactly true but that's what she liked to make them think. Casually dropping by when she was in the area was her trademark, usually unannounced and always welcomed.

Then the problem happened. It was with a Miss Gladys Benbow. Rev Mowbray had been cultivating her for over four years after meeting on a cruise and it looked very promising. No relatives, only a nephew in America who didn't seem very interested in her. It had been very easy to make herself the largest beneficiary of the will. Gladys had promised her the house, which was very attractive and a similar one had sold for £120,000 at the local estate agents. The problem was when Rev Mowbray had dropped in 'when passing through' she had found Gladys in tears. She had just been told by social services that she could no longer live by herself and would have to go into a nursing home. She would have to sell the house and go somewhere she didn't want to go. Rev Mowbray felt a genuine concern for her, tinged, it must be said, with a little self-interest. The thought of the house being sold and the money going to pay for the bills at the nursing home made her wince. Gladys insisted that she wanted to die in her own house and that she didn't want to go into a home with a lot of dribbling old folk who didn't know what day it was. What was she to do?

That was the problem Rev Mowbray took away with her when she left the house, determined to find a solution, but what? The true collector is nothing but determined and nothing will stand in the way of them and a prized acquisition. There had to be a solution.

It was while Rev Mowbray was in the bath that the solution came to her. Could she? Dare she? Who would notice? After all, it would be granting the friend's wishes. Yes, she would do it. But she would have to make sure that it was something that was really wanted and the only solution.

Over the next three weeks Rev Mowbray spent a lot of time with Gladys. She rang almost every day and made numerous visits, taking Gladys to see various nursing homes in the area, none of which she liked. She usually ended up in tears, saying that she wanted to stay in her own home. It was after one of these fruitless visits that Rev Mowbray and Gladys Benbow sat having a cup of tea back in Gladys's house.

"This is the only place I want to live. Here is where I want to die. I don't want to go into one of those awful nursing homes where all you do all day is stare at the television and you have to wear other people's clothes."

Rev Mowbray tried to console her and thought to herself, 'Why don't I grant her request? Surely, she would thank me for it.'

Any collector knows exactly the right time to acquire a new item for the collection. Timing is everything. If it is bidding at the auction room or buying from a dealer the correct moment to clinch the deal is of the utmost importance.

It was after nine o'clock at night that Rev Mowbray visited Gladys for the last time. She had rung her from the phone box on the corner of the street to make sure the call couldn't be traced. She parked the car some way off and came the back way through the garden so she couldn't be seen by anyone. She explained to Gladys that she wanted to see her garden and check one of the flowers. She was welcomed in, but Gladys was about to go to bed. She was just making herself a drink, some hot chocolate. "Oh let me do that for you, it won't be any trouble."

It wasn't any trouble to stir into the drink four times the amount of sleeping tablets she should have, plus some other tablets which were there.

Gladys drank the hot chocolate, remarking how nice it tasted and how content she was in her own house and that she would like it to stay that way. After Gladys had fallen into a deep sleep in the chair, Rev Mowbray was careful to wash her own cup up and place it back in the cupboard, making sure there was no trace of her visit. She left through the back door and retraced her steps to the car parked a few streets away. She wasn't sure what she felt. Sadness, guilt, but also contentment that she had made someone's wishes come true, and she thought that if Gladys knew, she wouldn't be angry but very pleased that someone thought about her so much as to grant her last wishes.

It was a few days later that she received a phone call from the solicitor informing her of the death of Gladys Benbow and asking if she would take the funeral, something which she readily agreed to. It appeared that Miss Benbow had confused the number of tablets she was taking and had taken an overdose, accidentally. She had died in her sleep.

Over the next few years there would be another three 'friends' who would meet the same fate as Gladys Benbow.

There is always the suspicion with collectors that it is not the acquisition of a particular item for the collection which brings the most satisfaction, but the thrill of the chase. Few collectors would relish having 'everything' because there would be nothing to hunt down and look for. No, it isn't the collection that is of greatest importance but the collecting.

Rev Mowbray thought she needed a holiday. The travel agent found her a cruise at very short notice and she was off again. The thrill of the chase was back, checking the passengers, eliminating people on the list, and drawing up a shortlist. A book collector will have the same sensation going into a new town and discovering half a dozen second-hand bookshops they haven't visited before. The cruise was successful on a number of counts. She had needed a good relaxing holiday and she also returned with the names and addresses of two more "friends".

There was one aspect of collecting that Rev Mowbray didn't share with other collectors, that is the need to show off and talk about her collection to others. Hers, by choice, was a solitary obsession and one which could not be discussed, and her collection could not be seen by others, just appreciated and cherished by her. That's exactly how she liked it.

One particular cruise she did think she spotted a fellow collector, someone who was doing the very same thing she was, but it was only a suspicion and collectors usually don't wish to share their secrets or let others steal their potential acquisitions.

The reader must be worried about the profession of Rev Mowbray. Surely, as a member of the clergy, she could not do such a wicked thing. It would be against all the morals she professed. I agree with you, but you see, have you missed something? Have I misled you in anyway, telling you this story? To any normal person her behaviour is quite scandalous, and to any other member of her profession quite outside the acceptable bounds of behaviour. But Rev Mowbray is a collector, a person whose first duty is to satisfy that desire of collecting. Most collectors are innocent creatures with their rooms full of stamps, cigarette cards, even oddities like flat irons or milk bottles. It is not what they collect that is the important thing. People just look at the collection and either stand back in awe and admiration, or scratch their heads and say, "How can someone devote a life of collecting different samples of barbed wire?!" No, it is not the collection which has any importance, it's the collecting where the power and attraction lies. You see, Rev Mowbray would be thought of as an innocent little creature if her collection had been about tea pots or thimbles, but because it was with inheritances she first became hooked, then she is thought of as somehow sinister.

Rev Mowbray was not a murderer, at least not in her own eyes! She had granted a few old people their wish to die in the home they loved. That she herself had made monetary gain from the deaths didn't seem to bother her unduly. The true collector will always believe that the means justify the end. If you study the art of collecting, you see, it is littered with collectors who will do anything to get their prize. Nothing will stand in their way.

How then is this story to end? I have heard of collectors who sell their entire collection before they die, consign it to the auction room and never again collect. They are few in number. Most will say they are going to do that but leave it too late. You see, the drug is not the collection but the collecting.

Rev Mowbray was almost at retirement age. She had never been a vicar, just a perpetual curate and someone's dogsbody, always at the beck and call of others. Her ministry had been satisfying, but only as a fairly stodgy plain meal can be said to be enjoyable. No, her real satisfaction had been in her other life, one where she lived in a different way. She could afford expensive and lavish things, go to exotic places and meet exciting people. She could also indulge her favourite passion of collecting inheritances.

It was one Tuesday morning, just a dull grey day, when the postman knocked at her door with a letter which had to be signed for. She came back into the kitchen looking at the postmark. Letters from solicitors were not uncommon, and they usually heralded good news – another inheritance for the collection. This letter was a little different however. She read and re-read the letter, at first excited, then puzzled, and finally worried and anxious.

COBDEN & CURZON SOLICITORS

Dear Rev Mowbray,

We beg to inform you that we have executed the will of the late Gwendolyn Penbury.

She has named you as sole beneficiary of her will and all her estate, including house, contents, stocks and shares, are to be sold and you will receive a cheque from ourselves when we have finalised the estate.

I would appreciate it if you would ring and arrange an appointment about the estate. At a conservative estimate I would think the estate would realise in excess of one million pounds.

I should warn you that it will not be possible to keep this out of the press and there may be some publicity once the terms of the will become public.

Yours faithfully, James Cobden.

She read and re-read the letter, not quite taking it all in. You would think that she was overjoyed with such a large inheritance, but no, there was disquiet and unease in her manner. There were at least three things troubling her.

One, she didn't know who Gwendolyn Penbury was; she had never heard of her and she certainly wasn't one of her 'collection'.

Secondly, one million pounds was too much. What would she do with that kind of money?

Thirdly, and linked with the last point, publicity. That was the last thing she wanted and one million pounds would certainly be picked up by the press and she definitely didn't want any publicity.

She rang the solicitors and spoke to Mr Cobden. It was, however, too late. The press had already heard about the will and wanted to know who the beneficiary was. As to who Gwendolyn Penbury was, she was a lady from the first parish Rev Mowbray had been in. She had been kind to her many years ago. She could hardly recall the incident but she had taken the funeral of her sister and it made a deep impression on the lady.

About a week later the story was printed, first in the local papers and then the nationals picked it up and ran the story. 'CURATE LEFT A MILLION' was splashed across the inside pages. Why was Rev Mowbray so fearful? Was it that most collectors are solitary creatures, fearful of the bright light of publicity? Or that they would rather work where people don't see them? Yes, it was this, but also something else, a fear lurking inside, and her worst nightmares were about to become reality.

Many people read the newspaper stories. People in the parish tended to be good-spirited about it and wished her well, hoping that she would see her way to using some of the money for the church. The begging letters started arriving. She could deal with them though, that was not the trouble. No, the trouble was the papers that were opened on breakfast tables across the country. All her friends would either read or hear about it. "Oh, she is well provided for now. I don't have to remember her in my will." Her collection and collecting destroyed in an instant. But there were also others who would read the report of the curate and a million pounds. "Rev Mowbray. Now where have I heard that name before? Wasn't that the women who inherited aunt Jane's house? I wonder if she makes a living out of this? Perhaps I should make a few inquiries."

It took just two enquiries to do it, both made to the Bishop and from different parts of the country. They were from disgruntled relations, nephews and nieces, who thought that as the only relations it would be they who would inherit their aunt's house when she died, only to find that she had given it to a curate who she had only known for a few years. They contacted the Bishop wanting to know why a curate was going around the country inheriting vast sums of money and houses from people she was not even related to. The Bishop, after interviewing Rev Mowbray, felt he had no other alternative but hand her over to the police.

Sarah Mowbray has now been deprived of her title. She is serving 20 years in prison for murder and deception. She has reached a stage of contentment though and found a new hobby. She collects stamps. Vast bags full of unsorted stamps arrive at the prison where she willingly spends her days sorting and classifying them, the more unusual ones going into her own private album, of course!

What, dear reader, is the moral of this tale? I will let you draw that out for yourself; it is not for me to tell you. Suffice it to say, this whole sorry episode could have been averted by one simple thing. If only Rev Mowbray's aunt had been a little wiser all those years ago and instead of giving her an inheritance to spend on a holiday she had bought her a stamp album instead!

THE DEAN

*If there be any man, who is not or has not been a Dean himself,
who can distinctly define the duties of a Dean of the Church of
England, he must be one who has studied ecclesiastical subjects
very deeply. There is something charming to the English ear
in the name of the Dean and Chapter. None of us quite know
what it means, and yet we love it.*

**Anthony Trollope,
Clergymen of the Church of England**

THE RATHER SUAVE, tall, attractive woman slowly uncrossed and crossed her long legs with the unmistakably smooth swish of silk from her black-stockinged thighs.

The Bishop moved uneasily in the chair opposite, a little redder in the face and with slight beads of sweat breaking out on his brow. Talks with his clergy were not usually like this, he silently reflected, but then Adelaide was a remarkable vicar as well as an extremely attractive woman.

The Bishop continued to muse. Adelaide must be approaching 50, he thought, but dressed elegantly with a sophisticated air, very different to the usual clergy he had seated before him: scruffily dressed, unkempt, unpolished shoes and with the remains of yesterday's breakfast showing on the front of their clerical shirts.

Adelaide was very different, one of the most promising clergy in the diocese. The Bishop wanted to believe that it was in spite of her attractiveness, but perhaps even he had been overwhelmed by her charms. Then there was her record. She had been in the church for 20 years and ordained for 15, a model curate, and then a vicar for the last six years. An excellent pastor, commendable preacher and the Bishop only received good reports about her. That was why she had been summoned to the Palace.

Adelaide coughed and the Bishop came back to the matter in hand. He had invited her here to recognise her achievements.

"How would you like a challenge Adelaide?"

Adelaide smiled. "I always respond well to a challenge, Bishop."

"I would like you to become a canon of the cathedral?"

Adelaide flushed slightly, the first sign that she was a little taken aback and surprised. "I would be honoured, your grace, if you think I have the qualities?"

"No doubt at all. You have been in the diocese long enough and know your way around. I want to appoint you as a canon to bring a bit of fresh air to the cathedral. I think it's got a bit stuffy of late, so we need to shake up the other canons, even keep the Dean on his toes." The Bishop gave an impish smile and winked.

Adelaide also smiled, thinking of how the news of her appointment would be received by the other canons, and especially the Dean. It was no secret in the diocese that the Bishop and the Dean did not see eye to eye and disagreed about almost everything.

"How do the other canons and the Dean feel about the appointment?" she asked, trying to be diplomatic.

"The Bishop stirred in his chair. "Oh, I haven't told them yet. They will welcome it though. We all have to move forward and accept change."

"And the Dean, what will he say?"

The Bishop looked a little anxious for the first time. "I'm seeing him later today and I am sure he will welcome you with open arms."

Adelaide thought that a more ill-fitting image she could not bring to mind. The Dean, who opposed almost every change in the diocese, including women priests! He ruled the cathedral on fear and subjection to his ideas. She would like to be in the room when he was told by the Bishop who was to be the next canon.

The Bishop added: "Of course, in recognition of your extra duties, I am going to give you a curate so that you can carry on with your excellent work in the parish."

Adelaide was pleased. At last her talents seemed to have been recognised and people had begun to notice that she was good at her job, and a woman as well!

Adelaide slipped into her powder blue MG sports car (it was second-hand) and sped away from the Bishop's Palace, the gravel crunching under the wheels. Her thoughts were on her new position. She had been surprised to be offered it because she knew there were other clergy in the diocese who had been there longer who could well object to her preferment. And what about the Dean? It would be an unusual relationship and one in which she would have to have all her wits about her in order not to be cowed down and subservient to such a bombastic character.

The ten mile journey went quickly as she thought of the new opportunities ahead. Opening the front door of the vicarage, she was greeted by Biggles, a grey haired Persian cat who mewed his greeting. Picking up the pile of post, she deposited it on the desk in the study. She paused to switch on the answering machine as she continued opening the post. The messages were the usual… a member of the Parish taken into hospital, would she visit… a request to speak at a neighbouring parish's Mother's Union meeting… the choirmaster ringing for the hymns… an enquiry about a baptism… and a researcher wanting to consult the parish records looking for a long-lost relative. Adelaide decided to change into something a little more casual as she climbed the stairs.

If you looked around the vicarage you would be impressed by the tasteful decoration and the style of furnishing, a sumptuous white leather settee with a few antique items of furniture scattered around the room. The pictures on the wall were just modern prints at first glance, but when you looked a little closer you realised they were signed limited editions. A Lowry, a couple of Ashley Jackson's and a John Straytton. Quite a nice little collection.

The Bishop's second appointment of the morning was ushered into the study. The Dean strode in purposefully, well over six feet in height, his long strides seeming to give him a sense of urgency and purpose. His features were like the cathedral tower, tall, angular and lean, with the same colour to his face as the sandy-brown colour of the weathered stones.

"Ah Dean, so pleased you could come." The Bishop stood up. Somewhat smaller and a lot rounder than the Dean, he always felt uncomfortable in his presence, a strange sensation for one who was supposed to be his superior!

"Always time for you, Bishop." A forced smile came from the pursed lips.

The Bishop leaned back in his chair, tapping his fingers together rather nervously. "I'll come straight to the point, Dean. It's about the appointment of a new canon for the cathedral."

The Dean smiled. Yes, he'd known it would be about this and he was well prepared as usual. "Well, Bishop, I've been giving it some thought too and have drawn up a list of three candidates in order, I think, of preference, but I could be persuaded to alter their ranking." The Dean, looking very pleased with himself as he took a piece of paper out of his inside pocket and slid it across the desk.

The Bishop glanced at the list and put his hands on the desk. Looking directly at the Dean, he said, "I'm afraid, Dean, you do not seem to have picked the new canon. I hope your judgement on horses is a little more sound!"

The Dean was caught unawares. Not used to his ideas being treated with mockery, he returned to the attack. "Well, obviously our thinking differs, Bishop. Who had you in mind that I had not considered?"

The Bishop picked at one of his nails and, without looking at the Dean, said, "The vicar of Little Budlake"

The conversation did not last much longer and the Dean could be observed striding across the cathedral close, his head bowed and face flushed with anger.

Adelaide came down the stairs, buttoning up her blouse and slipping a white collar on her neck. A quick bite to eat and then she would be off on her visits around the parish. After setting the alarm and closing the front door, Adelaide decided to walk this afternoon. It was a pleasant day and the exercise would do her good. Pastoral visiting could be tedious at times, listening to the same old stories again and again, the pills and the hospital appointments. She felt sometimes she could be a dispensing chemist from all the tips and remedies she had picked up. Now, who was she going to see today?

First, Mrs Berry, who had been widowed for over a year. It was around the time of the anniversary of her husband's death and she would appreciate a visit.

Then on to Mr Briggs, three doors down the street. He had been widowed for more than seven years and, although over 70, always had a glint in his eye for the ladies. She smiled to herself as she remembered the incident about the kitchen cupboard. When she was newly-arrived in the parish, she had visited him and he was struggling to get something down from the top of a kitchen cupboard. Adelaide volunteered to get it for him. It had meant climbing on a stepladder, which Mr Briggs held dutifully. It was only when she reached the top of the ladder that she remembered that she was wearing a shorter dress than usual and the ladder began to shake slightly as she reached for the box. No wonder Mr Briggs was always pleased to see her!

A young woman was next, asking for the baptism of her child. Adelaide smiled and chatted with her as the children ran amok around the room, thinking of the offspring she had never had.

Then on to Mrs Clarke. She could always be relied upon for a good cuppa and a slice of home-made cake. She was a dear, always a useful source of information about the village. After all, nobody ever told the vicar anything directly! It all had to come second-hand.

A few hours later, Adelaide walked home across the village green, content in the knowledge of a good day's work. Just time to have a couple of hours relaxation before the evening choir practice, then off for a drink in the village pub with the choir to round off the day.

When Little Budlake had heard five years earlier that they were to get a woman vicar there was some disquiet, especially when they heard she was divorced. It said something for Adelaide's skills that she won over the parish very quickly and within a few months no-one would hear anything said against her.

Life for her had not been what had been expected. A high-flier at school, she had gone to university and then a job in the City with a recruitment agency. She had always felt that people were her strong point, a good judge of character and helping others reach their potential. Why then had she got it so wrong in her marriage?

She had only been working in the City a few months when she met Max, handsome, humorous and charismatic, but a real bastard underneath. Why had she ignored all her principles in judging people to fall in love with Max? Reason had flown out of the window and blind love had driven her forward into a relationship which nearly destroyed her. It had taken almost everything: her self respect, certainly her money, but also, more importantly, her self-confidence and trust. She loathed herself that she could not see what was so plain to others about Max: traits and flaws in him which were not even disguised but apparent for all but her to see. He was someone who worked in the City, a high-flier who lived and worked on his nerves, acting on his hunches, which were usually right, and not giving a damn for anyone else, least of all his wife. She could understand the initial attraction to him, but why did she give herself so completely to someone who was such a shit? The relationship had ended after only three stormy years and Adelaide was left a wreck, emotionally and physically. Max had taken her for all he could get. He left her penniless, the house had gone, the timeshare in France, the car, everything. She had been so naive. What made her walk out though was something else, something that she had found very hard to come to terms with. One Friday night Max had returned late with two business clients, who were the worse for drink but who insisted she join them for a nightcap. A bawdy video was put on and Max sat next to her on the sofa. The language and innuendoes were getting steamier. Max sat close to her, his hands all over her and Adelaide trying to fend him off, with the two friends seemingly enjoying the antics. Suddenly she could stand it no longer and got up and went into the kitchen. Max followed, asking her what was wrong.

"I thought that was obvious. The spectacle you were making of yourself in there."

Max came closer, still clutching the drink in his hand.

"You were being rude to our guests. Those two out there could help us a lot, and do you know how much their business is worth?"

Adelaide was staring out of the window her back turned. "What do you want me to do? A striptease perhaps, or shall we make love while they watch?"

"Don't be silly." Max put his arm on her shoulder. "Just be nice to them and remember, sometimes we all have make sacrifices. If things go well tonight the business could really take off."

Adelaide picked up the half-empty glass on the table and threw the contents over Max. His face contorted with rage and she thought how much like a little boy he looked, caught in a storm, bedraggled and forlorn.

"You're a shit, Max! You have no respect for me, just yourself and your perverted ideals"

Adelaide didn't see the blow coming towards her, she only felt the crack as she reeled backwards falling on the floor. It was not the first time he had hit her, but it would be the last.

When she came to she was alone in the kitchen, lying in a crumpled heap by the sink. There was blood on the floor and her jaw ached. She grabbed her handbag and stumbled out of the flat. It was two in the morning, but luckily she managed to hail a cab. She went to her sister's house.

The following day was taken up with visits to the doctor and then the dentist. When she returned to the flat the locks had been changed. Over the next few weeks she began to realise how stupid and naive she had been. Despite repeated attempts, she could not contact Max. When the divorce came through she was left with nothing. Max had everything tied up in the business, house, cars, all of them went down the plughole as the business crashed.

Adelaide stayed with her sister for a while but realised she would have to move on sometime. Then an old school friend contacted her out of the blue, and when she heard what had happened, invited Adelaide to stay with her. It was a religious community, all women, some more religious than others, but it would be a bolthole, somewhere where she could find her self-esteem again and build her life anew. She certainly did that in a most remarkable way, finding in the community first of all a sense of peace in herself and then, slowly, she began the long road back to achieving self-worth and fulfilment. She was surprised as to how well she took to the daily acts of worship after never being religious herself, and even spent a few months helping to lead them. People came for private retreats to the community and gradually more and more began to seek out Adelaide for those chats, which she never thought of as counselling, just common sense. They found in her someone who they could relate to. Adelaide stayed with the Sisters of Mercy for three years, fully accepted and an important part of the community.

Max was left far behind and she thought she could at last face the world again. She went back for a job in personnel recruitment, but very quickly found it unsatisfying and empty. One day, when she went back to the community to share a birthday party for one of the sisters, Marian said something which stopped Adelaide in her tracks. "You know, Adelaide, you would make a tremendous priest." The idea once planted took root and began to grow and develop. The books she started to read nurtured it and the questions she started to ask fed the new idea. Finally, she plucked up courage and went to see the diocesan officer responsible for vocations. She was surprised that no-one laughed at her, or tried to put her off. Quite the opposite; they would encourage her. Doors began to open and at last she was accepted for Theological training. Those were the two years that Adelaide loved, the late-night discussions over coffee, even the essays she didn't mind. As an attractive woman student she even found time for a few flirtations, but nothing too serious, she was single-minded in her pursuit of her new goal in life.

When she left college she was ordained deacon and sent to a suburban parish as a curate with a good man, if a little dull, as her vicar. She smiled as she remembered their weekly staff meetings every Tuesday morning at the vicarage. The vicar's wife did not like the idea of a single woman as a curate and seemed to think her husband was in need of protection. The study door was always left open and the vicar's wife would always be popping in with some excuse. "Some more coffee?" "Can I take the empty cups?" "Have you remembered... vicar? In every two-hour staff meeting there would be at least six interruptions. Adelaide could have reassured her that she had no designs on the vicar, although she did have to fight off a few men in the parish, and they weren't all single!

Four years later, another curacy, this time in the inner city. She'd enjoyed the change and the challenge. People were much more up-front with their problems, no pretence, and she liked that. They also accepted her, single and divorced. It didn't seem to matter at all. The four years spent there raced by and then, out of the blue, she was called in by the Bishop and offered her first living, Little Budlake. It was good to have independence and be her own boss. At last she felt fulfilled and a whole person again. Oh, there were those in the village who tut-tutted at a "divorced vicar", and those who looked for scandal, with an attractive single women in the vicarage, but they could find none. Biggles was the only creature that shared her bed these days and Adelaide had no regrets.

Some of these thoughts about the past flashed through her mind as she luxuriated in a bath listening to Elgar and musing over what the future held in store for her at the cathedral.

Her first chapter meeting at the cathedral went as bad as she expected: cold, business-like and only a small acknowledgement of her appointment as the first female canon. There seemed to be a reluctant, grudging acceptance of her and she could see it would take considerable reserves of energy to find fulfilment and purpose in her new role. The Dean hardly looked at her. He was probably thinking that by not seeing her, somehow she would go away.

Adelaide mused as she drove back to Little Budlake on what her tactics were going to be. She could give in, tell the Bishop it was no use, the cathedral was not for her, and she would be better sticking to parish ministry. Adelaide thought better of herself than that though! She had met men like the Dean before. Hadn't she been married to one? If the Dean wanted to play little games then so could she; she was not going to be beaten.

If the Dean's first tactic was one of pretending she didn't exist, well then she would show him that she certainly did and she would make her mark on the cathedral. The Dean had ruled the cathedral for well over twelve years; he had moulded it and shaped it to fit around him like a well-worn suit. The other canons were his disciples, if not committed to following him enthusiastically then too frightened to oppose him or bring in any new ideas of their own.

It was at the third chapter meeting that the fireworks began. The canons were assembled as usual in the octagonal chapter house, chatting together over coffee. Adelaide was leading the laughing and joking. The Dean stormed in. His face flushed, hands trembling, he banged his papers down on the large oak desk. There was silence. He turned to the canons; all ten were there and they all looked uneasily towards the Dean.

"Who is responsible for that... that display in the cathedral foyer?"

Adelaide smiled. "Why, me, Dean. I do hope you like it."

The Dean turned on her and glared. "Like it! Like it! A display celebrating 15 years of women's ordination in my cathedral! You dare ask me if I like it?"

Adelaide looked up at him, thinking for the first time that some men, when they are angry, actually appear more handsome. "I thought, Dean, that the cathedral belonged to God and the people."

The Dean flushed even redder. "I want that obnoxious display removed by the end of today!"

Adelaide leant back in her chair. "No, it's staying."

The other members of the chapter looked on amazed at such a confrontation. No-one had ever dared take the Dean on like this in all the years they had been there. He was used to getting his own way in all things.

The Dean stood behind the desk. Unused to resistance, he was not sure how to handle the situation. "I will order it to be taken down forthwith."

Adelaide stared the Dean out. "Then I will order it to be put back up again!"

The Dean picked up his papers and swept out of the room, declaring as he went, " I will not have this insubordination, I am going to see the Bishop."

When he had gone Adelaide smiled to the other canons. "Do you think I may have upset him?"

Rev Stapleton, a kindly man who had been a canon for over 20 years, smiled at Adelaide. "I wouldn't have missed that for the world, the Dean opposed in his own cathedral! I'm afraid to say, though, that the Dean usually gets his own way."

Adelaide laughed. "Maybe he's met his match this time with me."

Nothing came of the skirmish about the display. It stayed up in the cathedral for over a month, which was what Adelaide had planned. The Dean never mentioned it again. Chapter meetings were short and business-like, any points of conflict skirted over or avoided. Adelaide began to make her mark on her duties at the cathedral. She was much liked, approachable and popular. The congregation took to her very quickly and the Dean became more and more a remote and distant figure.

The Dean was in his early 50s and married. His wife, like the canons, obeyed him and followed his dictates. His children did not. Rebellious and different, one was a member of a rock band in London; the other, a girl, was looking after an animal sanctuary in Australia, vowing never to return home until her father altered his attitudes. The Dean's chosen drug was power. Wielded with an iron fist in the home and the Cathedral, it was usually not resisted. He was attractive to look at, lean and strong, his features displaying a charisma which often comes with power. People liked his decisiveness and determination, no hesitating or bumbling with him. He upset people, but he was no fool. He knew where he was heading in the church and the next stop would be a bishopric. But for now he had another problem, which demanded new tactics.

After six months Adelaide felt that she had made her mark. She had shown her ideas were not to be dismissed as those 'of a mere women'. She was more than a match for the Dean and she felt he had, grudgingly, begun to respect her. How wrong could she have been?

Adelaide had felt that the Dean was warming to her at last. He had started smiling at her, listening intently when she spoke, even promoting some of her ideas. There were even times when they could talk together, and she began to think he was mellowing slightly. Members of the cathedral chapter began to notice and make comments. Was the Dean changing and tempering his behaviour?

Adelaide felt pleased and content that things were at last beginning to work out for her. It was at this time that she began to let her guard slip, with unforeseen consequences. The Dean started inviting Adelaide into his office more often. They would sit and exchange ideas over a gin and tonic or a dry Martini. She began to like the attention he was paying her and, perhaps subconsciously, began to flirt slightly with her new-found friend. It wasn't much, just an odd wink over a joke, a smile, but there was something she was being drawn into without fully realising the danger. His whole personality exuded power and charisma and that was a heady drug for someone off her guard.

It was one Friday night when it happened. The cathedral had no services and the Dean had invited Adelaide to his house in the cloister for a drink before she went home. He said he wanted to give her some papers to read about the forthcoming building project. It was now quite dark, but light from the antique gas lamps gave a warm orange glow over the cold October evening as they walked and chatted together across the cathedral cloisters. The Dean invited her into his study, which was well-furnished with a desk and an array of comfortable chairs. He motioned Adelaide to pick where she would like to sit. She chose the long settee underneath the window. The Dean poured them both a generous measure of gin and tonic and then sat opposite her. They chatted and talked for over an hour. Adelaide suddenly looked at her watch and realised the time. Although she had nothing else to do that evening, she was conscious she was encroaching on the Dean's free time, time he usually spent with his wife.

It was then that a slight shiver passed down her spine. She had heard no noises in the house. Where was his wife?

Adelaide got up to leave, saying that she didn't want to encroach any more on his time.

"No, don't worry on my account." The Dean tried to put her at ease. "The evening is mine to do what I want with. My wife is away at her mother's. I'm a lonely bachelor tonight!" Adelaide should have been more alarmed at that remark than she was. But she wasn't. She, too, had nothing to do that Friday evening, so why shouldn't she sit and enjoy another drink?

As Adelaide took a sip of her drink she began to notice the first signs of a strange feeling she had never experienced before. Her head was spinning and she was beginning to feel drowsy. Ridiculous, she thought, on two drinks, but the sensation persisted. Her eyes were having difficulty focusing on the opposite side of the room, and what the Dean was saying was not making sense. She told herself she would have to pull herself together and asked to be excused to go to the toilet. While there she was sick and then felt slightly better. She returned to the study with the intention of leaving and going straight home or, if she still felt unwell, staying with a girlfriend who lived near the cathedral.

The last thing she remembered was opening the study door and the Dean standing in front of her. The room was going round and round and she fainted, falling towards him. He caught her and laid her on the settee.

Three hours later she awoke. She was lying on the settee with a rug pulled over her. Her dress was lying over a nearby chair. There was no one else in the room. She tried to remember where she was and what she was doing here. The dizzy sensation in the head had gone and was replaced with a feeling of her whole body aching and, somehow, things not as they should be. She looked at her dress and wondered why she had taken it off, but she hadn't. At least she couldn't remember doing so. Where was she? Then she remembered falling into the Dean's arms, that was the last thing she remembered. Just then the study door opened and the Dean came in, carrying a tray with two cups on.

"Ah, you're awake, you've had quite a nasty turn, my dear."

Adelaide pulled the rug up for protection in front of her. "Where am I? What's happened? Why am I lying here? "

Again the Dean smiled reassuringly. "You passed out, you've been asleep for the last three hours. I was going to call the doctor, but you seemed so peaceful. I was going to wait until you woke up."

Adelaide looked in panic at him. "Who took my dress off?"

"Why, I did. You had been sick down the front of it, I couldn't let you sleep in that mess. I sponged it off and there it is drying in front of the fire."

Embarrassment and then anger welled up inside her. "What the hell were you doing undressing me? What else have you been doing to me?"

The Dean handed her a cup of what looked like tea. "Don't be silly Adelaide, I've only been looking after you."

Adelaide pushed the cup away and it slipped off the table onto the floor. "Get away! Get out! I don't want you near me!"

The Dean bent down to pick the cup up. "Now look what you've done. You're not well Adelaide. Have a little more rest. You can stay here as long as you like."

Adelaide was now in a panic and sobbing uncontrollably. "Get out! I don't want you near me!"

The Dean looked agitated. "Alright, I'll leave you to come to your senses." He left the room and closed the door.

As soon as he was out of the room Adelaide leapt up and grabbed her dress. There was a damp stain on the front, which was not quite dry, but she quickly put it on and fastened her shoes. She looked around the room and grabbed her bag and coat and burst out of the study. She ran out of the house, leaving behind her the Dean in the doorway imploring her to stay and saying she wasn't well.

Adelaide stumbled around the side of the cathedral using the wall as a support. She thought she must have appeared drunk to anyone who was watching her. No-one was though as it was three o'clock in the morning. The sharpness of the air cleared her brain sufficiently for her to find her car and get in, locking herself in. She sat slumped over the driving wheel, sobbing inconsolably. How long she was there for she didn't know, and how she drove the ten miles back to Little Budlake she would never know, but finally the MG swung into the vicarage drive and came to a stop before the front door.

Biggles greeted her with a stretch of the front legs and a meow, but there was no greeting for him. Adelaide ran up the stairs to the bathroom, where she was violently sick again, then she passed out.

It was Biggles she was aware of, walking on her and meowing. She opened her eyes and blinked, trying to adjust to the light and work out what was happening to her as she found herself lying on the bathroom floor.

She stumbled into the bedroom, and it was when she caught sight of herself in the mirror that slowly the full horror of what had happened began to sink in. She looked awful. Dishevelled, make-up all smudged and her eyes red; she was a mess. But that wasn't the real reason she felt uncomfortable. There was a slow realisation of what had happened. She didn't feel right, not just in her head but her whole body. Her clothes felt funny, not just because they were a mess, but it was like someone else had dressed her. It was then that the first moment of sheer panic and terror struck her. My God, she thought. I could have been raped!

She sank down onto the bed and cried and cried, but there was no consolation, only a feeling of complete hopelessness, horror and shame.

The Dean

When she woke later that morning the bright October sun was streaming in through the window. At first she smiled, then the full horror and realisation of the previous night was upon her, giving her no respite. Her mind raced trying to remember details, but there was just a blank, nothing, only the sensation of feeling ill and falling into a deep sleep. Later she remembered stumbling into the Dean's study and a vague realisation that something had happened which she had not consented to, or even been conscious of. Then another thought entered her head. What was she to do?

The police! Why hadn't she gone last night after she got out of the Dean's house? Did she want to go? What would she say if she went? Had she been drugged? What about any evidence? All these thoughts raced through her mind as she ran herself a shower. It was like washing off the grime and dirt as if she had been down a coal mine. She spent a long time in that shower wondering if she would ever be clean again. At last she got out, and then another thought hit her. If she had been raped, what was she doing having a shower, washing away all the evidence? What a stupid fool she was!

When she finally emerged from the bathroom, she put on a dressing gown and went downstairs with the intention of making herself a hot drink. As she passed the phone in the hall she noticed the light flashing to say that she had new messages. Tentatively, she switched on the machine. There was a message from her organist, one from a parishioner, and then one which made her stand frozen to the spot as she felt powerless to move. It was from the Dean.

"Adelaide, I hope you are alright. You seemed quite ill last night and I was worried when you left, you didn't seem like yourself at all. I hope you are feeling a bit better. I'm not going to mention last night to anyone, best forget it." There was a long pause and what sounded like the phone being put down and then some mumbled words which she couldn't make out.

Adelaide picked up the machine and in one movement wrenched the cable from the socket. She hurled it across the living room, smashing a picture and shattering the plastic phone into myriad tiny pieces.

Adelaide sat in the hallway weeping in extreme anguish, unable to understand what was happening to her.

It was three days before she felt she could face the world again. The only person she had talked to was one of the sisters from the community. She had come over to stay with her and been a great strength. They had talked a lot about what could have happened, of how she could have been drugged. There were drugs which were used in rape cases that made the person forget everything and were difficult to detect. The sense of shame and embarrassment Adelaide had felt had changed to anger and the need to pursue justice. She was not going to let the Dean get away with what he had done to her. She made an appointment to see the Bishop.

The Bishop looked at her very cautiously as he showed her into his office. This time there was a different kind of air about him, something which Adelaide had not seen before. Before she could say what she had come about, the Bishop launched into a speech. "I'm glad you've come Adelaide. If you hadn't then I was about to send for you. I've had some disturbing reports about your behaviour."

Adelaide looked non-plussed. "My behaviour! But I've come to see you about…"

She didn't finish the sentence before he went on. "You're an attractive women, Adelaide, but I must warn you to be careful where your relations with the opposite sex are concerned."

Adelaide was furious. She stood up and went closer to the Bishop. "My relationships... I've come here to tell you that I was raped last Friday by a member of your clergy."

The Bishop turned to look at her. She thought he would be surprised, but no, there was no look of shock, only one of disbelief. "That's what you may call it, but I have had a very different account."

Adelaide sank back into the chair, her mouth open. What was going on? What had been said? There was only one person who could have initiated all this.

"What has the Dean told you Bishop?"

He looked at her sternly. "That your behaviour towards him of late has been… how can I put it… too familiar… how you have made no disguise in your attentions to him. I've heard it from others at the cathedral and I thought it was mischievous tittle-tattle, but when the Dean himself came to…"

Adelaide's eyes blazed. "The Dean's been here! What's he said?"

"That he always found difficulty dealing with you. How he realised that his initial reaction of hostility was wrong and how he should show more of a generous and kindly spirit. Of how he showed friendship to you and thought things were going well, but he had heard that you were going round making accusations about him. He came to tell me the whole story and how it has all been misrepresented."

"Did he tell you he drugged me and then raped me?"

The Bishop looked angry. "He told me you would say that. He told me that you came to see him the other Friday night... of how you got drunk and made a clumsy pass at him... of how you fainted and slept on the settee until the effects of the alcohol had worn off... of how you left upset and what a fool he had been to allow you into his house when there was no-one else there and his wife had been called away unexpectedly."

Adelaide shook her head. "I don't believe I'm hearing this."

"You say you have been raped. Have you been to the police?"

Adelaide realised her folly. "No. No, I didn't, but I should have."

The Bishop looked at her in a pitying sort of way. "I have no other option but to suspend you, Adelaide. I will give you three months paid leave during which time I would like you to consider your position, and I will be recommending that you find another position in another diocese. I forbid you to talk about this or make contact with anyone, especially the Dean and chapter."

Adelaide stood to go. As she was leaving, she turned and looked at the Bishop, her eyes blazing. "Do you know, Bishop, I'm disappointed in you. I thought more highly of you than this. You've not only let me down, but also the church." With that she stormed out.

On her way home she stopped the car in a country park and went for a walk to think and clear her head. What was she to do? Who would believe her now? It was her word against the Dean's and it was obvious who people were believing, especially as he had been clever enough to get his story in first. Then a flash of inspiration lit up her mind. Was it possible? Was there actually still some evidence she could use?

When she arrived back at the vicarage her first stop was at the dustbin. She turned it upside down on the path, spilling the contents all over the gravel. She searched through the used teabags, torn envelopes, empty cans and other sundry detritus. Then she found what she was looking for. She held it up in triumph. It was the small cassette tape from her broken answering machine she had thrown across the room; that was in pieces, but the tape looked as if it was still intact. When she went back into the house she made a number of phone calls.

It was three days later that she drove over to the convent of the Sisters of Mercy. In her previous life, one of the sisters had worked at the BBC in sound recordings and helped produce a record of singing at the convent. Sister Marian met Adelaide as she was shown into the convent. They went into a small office and sitting at a desk was a young man with a number of tapes and recorders around him. Sister Marian introduced him as Mark, a friend from the BBC who worked as a sound technician. He held in his hand the small tape from the answering machine.

"I've managed to amplify the sound and produce a recording which you should be able to hear."

Adelaide sat down and her breathing became rapid, sensing how important the next few moments were likely to be.

Mark went on, pushing a few buttons on what looked like a very sophisticated recording machine. "The tape contains three messages, the first two are not important you say, but the third one is interesting. The message is clear, then a small click, a silence, then something which is hardly audible and muffled. It's as if someone said something to himself, under his breath as we call it, not realising that the machine at the other end of the line was still recording it."

Adelaide looked at him, still tense.

Mark continued. "Well, I've managed to amplify it and take out a lot of the background hiss. It's still not very good, but you can hear quite distinctly what is said."

He leant back in the chair and pressed the switch. Adelaide caught her breath and looked at Marian.

The tape hissed, and after the Dean's message were the words spoken in the same voice but a very different tone: "Oh my God!... What have I done?... What have I done?... What a fool I've been!" The phone was then put down.

Adelaide jumped up. "That's it, it's the Dean, he's said it, he's admitted to it without ever realising it. He thought the phone conversation had ended, but it was still recording." Adelaide had a look of righteous triumph.

Marian put her arm around Adelaide. "I hope this helps to clear your name and show what really happened."

Later that day, Adelaide swept into the Bishop's Palace, ignoring the secretary's pleas that the Bishop was busy and could not be disturbed. Adelaide opened the study door and walked in to find the Dean and Bishop deep in conversation. The Dean looked agitated at the unexpected guest, the Bishop looked furious.

The secretary came scurrying after Adelaide. "I'm sorry, Bishop. I told her you were not to be disturbed but she just walked right past me."

The Bishop thanked her and told her it wasn't her fault as she apologetically left the room.

Turning to Adelaide, he glared. "I will not have this behaviour from one of my clerics."

Adelaide ignored him and turned to the Dean. "At least you won't be able to de-frock me like this man did."

The Dean had now regained his composure and looked sympathetically to the Bishop.

"You see Bishop, the kind of behaviour and accusations I've had to cope with from this woman."

The Bishop turned on Adelaide. "I'm very disappointed in you, Adelaide, and your total lack of respect for me."

Adelaide had now produced the cassette tape Mark had given her. "Play this, Bishop, and you will hear what really happened that Friday night."

A worried look appeared on the brow of the Dean. For once he was unsure of his next move. He was puzzled at what could possibly be on the tape.

The Bishop motioned Adelaide to the cassette player by the window. He then sat down in his chair, exclaiming, "We will hear what you have to say, then I must ask you leave."

Adelaide placed the cassette in the machine and turned to her audience. "I will leave after you have heard this. It was taken from my answering machine and contains messages on the Saturday morning after the rape."

The Dean interjected: "Alleged rape."

Ignoring him, Adelaide continued: "There are three messages, two from parishioners and one from the Dean and then some words which I thought were inaudible but they have been amplified. Here are the messages."

The two parishioners' messages were played, then the tape hissed and the unmistakable voice of the Dean could be heard. "Adelaide, I hope you are alright, you seemed quite ill last night. I was worried when you left, you didn't seem like yourself at all. I hope you are feeling better. I'm not going to mention last night to anyone, best forget it."

The Dean stirred uneasily in his chair. "I was only concerned about her after what had happened. I didn't want anyone to know for fear of embarrassing her. I told you the same story Bishop. There is nothing on that tape which you don't know about."

The Bishop turned to Adelaide. "I agree with the Dean, there is nothing new you have told us. I would like you now to leave us."

Adelaide wasn't finished. "Sometimes when you record a message, you think you've put the phone down and cut off the recording machine, but occasionally you make a mistake and it carries on recording, like it did after the Dean's call."

An expression of panic crossed the Dean's face. The Bishop leant back in his chair looking intently at Adelaide.

"The message afterwards is muffled, as if it was said under the breath and not meant to be heard, but I've had it amplified and here it is."

The tape hissed and after the Dean's message came the words spoken unmistakably in the same voice: "Oh my God!... What have I done?... What have I done? ..What a fool I've been!" The phone was then put down.

Adelaide switched off the tape recorder and sat down, a look of triumph on her face.

The Bishop, his hands drumming slightly on his desk, looked over to the Dean. "Well Dean, what do you have say? This is a very different account to the one you told me."

The Dean sank deeper into his chair, his head in his hands and his face flushed. He turned angrily towards Adelaide. "You bitch! I thought I would deal with you by first ignoring you, then when that didn't work, opposing and undermining you. But you thought yourself too clever, didn't you? So I came up with another plan, I thought I would charm you and then destroy you. It almost worked. That Friday night was to be your final humiliation"

The Dean got up and walked towards the door. He turned to face Adelaide.

"My career destroyed and by a women! You bitch!!"

Adelaide, her eyes blazing, stood to face him. "Don't you think you've done that yourself? What about what you did to me?"

The Bishop stood up and called after him. "Dean, I want your resignation on my desk by tonight."

"You shall have it!" the Dean snapped as he reached the door.

The Bishop had one last word however. "I will be contacting the police. You will be hearing more about this."

With that the Dean slammed the door and walked away from the cathedral.

THE LASHING HOUSE

A slave is one who is in the power of the Master to whom he belongs. The Master may sell him; dispose of his person, his industry, and his labour. He can do nothing, possess nothing, or acquire nothing, but what must belong to his Master.

Louisiana Law up to 1865

THE BALMY SUGAR cane grew tall and swayed gently in the sultry breeze, sweetening the day. Under the sun, now climbing to its zenith in the clear blue sky, three young boys sat beside the mighty Mississippi idling the day away.

Jeff Calhoun, Austin Grant and Jonboy Carter had been friends all their lives. It seemed to them a long time, but in reality it was only 12 years. No school today, so they indulged in their favourite pastime, doing nothing and lying beside the river, watching the steamboats working hard, tirelessly carrying the cotton and sugar cane up and down the river. They didn't have a care in the world, but the boys were too young to appreciate happiness, they only wanted adventure and excitement. Their world, growing up in Zachary, Louisiana seemed as dull and uninteresting as the day that was slowly slipping by, like the great river before them.

"Let's do something," cried Jonboy, always the leader who could be relied upon for bright ideas. He was the son of a preacher whose wife had died when Jonboy was very young. For the first years of his life she had called him Jonboy, a name that had stuck and now had special meaning as it reminded him of her whenever anyone used it.

"There is nothing." Jeff raised himself onto his elbows and selected a piece of grass to chew.

"I want to be a riverboat captain when I grow up," exclaimed Austin, who was the dreamer. A little shorter than the other two, his greatest exploits were always played out in his mind.

The boys sank back into the long grass, seemingly exhausted from their futile desire to do something different, and lazed again in the sun.

A faint sound could be heard rising above the noise of the breeze through the grass and the occasional steamboat whistle. It was singing. It was coming from the nearby plantation owned by Jeff's father; it was the slaves singing as they cut the sugar cane. The song drifted over towards the boys as they listened and then dismissed it. What were slaves to them? Little better than animals and more trouble at times. They had witnessed slaves twice and three times their age cowering like dogs as slave owners and foremen went past, always the whip by their side, just in case the 'niggers needed to know their place'.

The boys had only known slavery. To them it was a fact of life not to be questioned. Each of their families kept slaves, even Jonboy's, the preacher's son. His father kept slaves and could see no wrong in it. Who were they to question or think differently? They were only boys.

Jonboy sat up. "I know, let's go to Captain Pickett's."

The other two boys looked apprehensive. "Told we can't go there," said Jeff.

Austin also looked worried. "My Dad says if we're caught there again I'm to get a lashing."

But Jonboy was determined and usually had his own way. "Come on, who could tell? Captain Pickett is always drunk and no slave would dare say anything."

Reluctantly, the two boys rose and followed Jonboy, some way behind, and although not wanting to go, they knew that the Lashing House had a fascination for them like no other place in Zachary.

The Lashing House was at the centre of five plantations where the boundaries met, deep in the everglades. It was unseen from the road, yet many paths snaked their way towards it. When a slave required a whipping the owner or overseer usually sent the miscreant to Mr Pickett's bearing a note: 'Mr Pickett, will you give negro...........20 lashes and charge it to my account.' It was deemed unseemly for owners to whip their own slaves too much, and anyway they could plead innocence to the charges of those who opposed slavery, saying with a clear conscience, 'No, they didn't use a whip on their slaves.' They might not have, but Captain Pickett certainly did, a brute of a man whose pleasure seemed to be human misery and suffering. He seemed to take a particular delight in his work. Each day a steady stream of victims would arrive at his door, wending their terrified way from one of the nearby plantations, trembling as they handed him a note, which they knew he had to sign before they could return. They were taken inside, stripped and whipped, no mercy or forbearance shown to the old, women or even children.

The boys had come for one reason only though, to see the young negro girls being whipped. They had found that although the door to the house was closed and bolted every time the captain did his hellish labour, if they went round the back there were holes in the old wooden timber which afforded a view, usually of a nubile young negress stripped naked and being lashed, her screams piercing the air as the whip stung and lacerated her young flesh.

They had come here many times and not been disappointed, but lately Captain Pickett had grown morose and angry. He had told their fathers what they had been up to and they had given him permission to use his whip on them if they came near again.

For very good reasons the boys approached the hut very gingerly and waited. They usually saw Pickett sitting on the small wooden veranda smoking his pipe and drinking from a great flagon of home-brewed whiskey, waiting for his next victim. The veranda was empty. The pipe was there and so too was the flagon of whiskey. They couldn't hear any sounds coming from the hut, no screams or sounds of the whip, just the lazy buzz of summer in the sugar cane.

Jonboy was first to speak. "Let's go and see what's up."

The other two were more cautious and would have turned and run if it had been up to them. They followed though, like they usually did. Slowly the boys crept around the back of the hut, making sure they didn't make a noise. They took up their positions by the spy holes, which they knew so well and had given them so many delights in the past. They put their eyes to the holes and looked in. They could see nothing, that is until their eyes had got accustomed to the dinginess and darkness of the interior of the hut, but still there was nothing. It was Jeff who saw it first. He stifled a scream as he saw two boots slowly swinging to and fro in front of him. The other boys looked and saw the boots swinging and couldn't understand what on earth was going on. Jonboy took courage and stood up, looking directly through the small window and gave a shriek, not prepared for the sight that met his eyes.

Suspended from the roof beam hung the lifeless body of Captain Pickett. The body was gently swinging to and fro. The whip, which he had used so many times to such good effect, was wrapped around the beam and his neck hung limply from the other end.

The boys were in sheer panic. "What are we going to do?" shrieked Austin.

"I knew we shouldn't have come," said Jeff, almost crying. "It's all your fault Jonboy."

Jonboy was thinking. "Shut up will you, we've got to think and find out what's happened."

"I'm not staying here any longer." Jeff stood up and started running away from the hut, but he stopped as he heard someone coming up the track towards the hut.

All three boys were now frightened, thinking that they would get the blame for this act just because they were there with no real excuse.

They all knelt down in the long grass and lowered their heads as a tall young negro came walking slowly up the path, his head bowed and a note in his hand.

As he reached the hut he knocked on the door. "Master Pickett, I've come for the lashes."

No answer.

This time the slave raised his voice and spoke as loudly as he dare. Frightened lest he provoke more lashes, he repeated his request.

Still no answer.

What was he do to? If he returned back to the plantation without the note signed he would be beaten twice or three times as bad. They would think he had tried to escape his punishment.

The slave tentatively tried the door, lifting the latch; it was locked on the inside.

Slowly, the slave crept around the side of the hut, calling timidly "Master ar' you there?" As he reached the window he looked in, his eyes widening in sheer terror of the sight that was before him. He dropped the note and ran.

The three boys took their opportunity and raced back to the riverbank, resolving not to speak about what they had seen and hoping their presence at the whipping house would have gone unnoticed. They wondered what could have happened. Had the bad whiskey and foul job Pickett did finally got to him? Had he killed himself? Certainly it looked like suicide, the door locked from the inside.

That afternoon the boys were very subdued as they walked along by the side of the river. Not even the frequent whistles from passing steamboats could rouse them. All they could think about was the terrible sight they had seen as they looked into the cabin and seen the swinging, lifeless body of Captain Pickett.

It was almost supper time when the boys plucked up enough courage to return to the town, fearful of what awaited them. As they turned into the dusty main street they saw and heard a commotion taking place at the jailhouse. People were running towards it, a large group of men outside were shouting, women watched from the sidewalk.

Jonboy saw someone he knew. "What's happening"?

"A hanging! There's going to be a hanging! They have a nigger and he's killed a white man."

"Who's he killed?" asked Jeff.

"Captain Pickett and in his own Lashing House with his own whip. This nigger is going to die real well." The informant seemed to take great delight in the news.

The boys followed the crowd and stood at the front of the jailhouse.

Two deputies stood with rifles held across their chests at the entrance from where they could see men inside shouting and gesticulating.

The crowd were now getting restive. "Bring him out." "We want to kill him." "Dirty nigger." "String him up." "We'll teach 'em."

The boys looked around them at the faces contorted with anger and hate, yet soon they found themselves joining in.

A shot was fired by one of the deputies and the crowd fell silent.

The sheriff came out, a red-faced man, overweight. He too carried a rifle and looked as if he was not afraid to use it. Standing by his side were three of the leading officials of the town, Jonboy's father, Preacher Carter, Amos Turpin, the town doctor, and Aaron Goodman, the lawyer. The preacher strode forward and held up his hand for the crowd to be silent.

"They'll be no lynching today friends. If you want justice, you'll see it done, by God, I promise you. No nigger kills a white man and gets away with it, I know that, but we want an example, a public spectacle, everyone to see it. Especially all the other niggers. He'll stay here in the jailhouse and tomorrow we'll know what to do with him." He was no great orator, Preacher Carter, but his speech held the crowd off from lynching the slave there and then and even got them to believe that a bigger spectacle would be in the end a better and a more fitting justice.

Along with the rest of the crowd the boys began to move away from the jailhouse. The crowd was breaking up into small groups of men and boys discussing the momentous happening of that day and what should be done.

The three boys at first felt a great sense of relief that their involvement was not known and unlikely now to be discovered. They gathered around the back of the church, making sure no one else was around.

Jeff spoke first. "We did it, no-one knows we were there."

Austin quickly followed. "We must promise never to speak about this to anyone, do you hear that Jonboy?"

But Jonboy was looking down at his feet kicking a few small stones. Austin repeated the request.

Jonboy only looked down at the dirt he kicked up and then, challengingly, looked up and broke his silence. "He didn't do it, he couldn't have, the door was locked from the inside. You saw the slave come up the track after we saw him dead."

Austin looked mad. "Shut up Jonboy, if you say that to anyone they'll know where we were, we'll get a beating."

Jeff began to look worried. "No-one would believe us anyway. Let that nigger die, that's what they're for, ain't it?"

After some more talk they resolved to say nothing to anybody about the events of that day and to meet again in the morning.

As Jonboy walked slowly towards his house he saw carriages and horses outside.

He walked up the path to the wooden veranda where Sam, one of their slaves, met him and bowed offering to take his hat.

"What's up Sam, who's in the house?"

Sam averted his eyes, his large frame bent low and cowed. "Bad day for us black folk master Jon, they come to see what's to be done to punish us all."

Jonboy frowned. "What do you mean Sam?"

"Captain Pickett, his death go 'n mean bad things, not just for that poor nigger that killed him."

Jonboy went into the house, feeling for the first time in many hours the coolness of the shade, but his neck burned with fear and agitation. He could hear voices coming from the parlour where around a dozen men were gathered around his father.

"A good speech by you, at the jailhouse preacher, but we want justice done."

Another voice broke in. "Them niggers will kill us all if we give 'em any mercy, they must be shown a lesson."

"Hanging's too good for 'um. Let's think of some other way to kill that murdering nigger."

There was assent from others as more and more lurid ways of killing the murderer, now languishing in the jailhouse, were first discussed and then dismissed as impractical.

Again, Jonboy heard his father's voice: a voice used to speaking in crowds and, more importantly, getting it's own way.

"The bridge, let's hang him from the bridge and let's take all the slaves up to see the hanging! Then let him hang there for days for others to see what happens when you kill a white man."

Cheers went around as everyone now believed they had found a solution.

There was only one bridge. It was the bridge over the mighty Mississippi, around two miles from the village and the main roadway out of Zachary. It was made of wood; it's great timbers spanning the mighty river, the only bridge for 20 miles. Hundreds of people crossed the bridge every day and with the river traffic, any hanging there would be a very large public spectacle.

"But he didn't do it." Jonboy was now standing in the parlour, the faces of the assembled men turning towards him.

His Father looked puzzled. "What are you talking about Jonboy?"

Jonboy stood his ground, raising his face and looking at the men as they peered and leaned towards him. "He couldn't have done it, the door was locked, and Captain Pickett was dead before the slave arrived at the cabin. He must have killed himself."

There were gasps around the room. Jonboy's father got up from where he was sitting and towered over the boy.

"Have you been to the Lashing House when I told you not to?"

Jonboy was now unafraid of the consequences of what he was saying. "Yes, we were there, Jeff, Austin and me. We saw Captain Pickett through the spy hole, he was hanging from the beam, and he was dead. Afterwards, we saw the negro come for his whipping, he couldn't have killed him."

Jonboy was not prepared for the blow, which cracked down on his skull from his father's upraised hand. "I've told you not to go there! Disobey me would you! I'll teach you a lesson my lad." Another blow reigned down upon him and he crashed onto the wooden floor. He lay there, his head ringing from the blows and his father towering above him.

"Fetch the other two – we'll have this out right now and see whose telling the truth."

It didn't take long for Austin and Jeff to be brought into the parlour, held by their fathers, both of them were whimpering and showing signs of having being beaten already.

Rev Carter lined all three of them up, their heads bowed. Sobs could still be heard from Austin as his father told him to shut up and stop snivelling.

"Now then boys, you know what I say about telling the truth. How if you lie you're damned and will go to hell. Let's hear it from each of you. Have you been to Captain Pickett's today?"

Austin and Jeff both said "No", but from the lips of Jonboy came another exclamation. "Yes!"

"So, dear friends, we have a liar. I wonder who it is?" Rev Carter seemed in his element, taking a perverse pleasure in extracting the truth from little boys.

"Bring the Bible, let's see whose going to hell." A large black Bible was brought in and placed between the boys. All three were now cowed and forlorn, fearful at what would come next.

"Hold the book Jonboy, swear on the Bible that you're telling the truth."

Jonboy held the book and, in a whisper almost inaudible, said something.

His father, seemingly caring little for the sensitivities of fatherhood, dealt him another blow which sent him reeling again. "Speak up boy! No favours here, a son of mine has to speak the truth, otherwise I will cast him out."

Jonboy got up, wiping blood from the side of his mouth. "It is the truth, I was at Captain Pickett's and the negro couldn't have killed him."

Loud murmuring and gasps came from the others gathered in the room. The preacher seemed to be losing control of the situation, betrayed by his own son. He snatched the Bible from him and thrust it at Jeff.

"What do you say Jeff? Were you at Captain Pickett's today?"

"No." The answer came clear and sharp and a hush fell in the room. All eyes were now fixed on Austin. He moved uneasily, his face contorted as if he was about to burst into tears. The preacher towered over him and gave him the Bible. "Now Austin, it looks like you have the casting vote. What do you say about all this?"

Austin clutched the Bible and, looking away from Jonboy, burst out. "We weren't there, but Jonboy was. He went, he wanted us to go, he's always going, he wanted us to go spy on the girls as they get whipped. We didn't go Preacher Carter, honest, Jonboy's making all this up."

Jonboy turned to Austin. "It's a lie! You know it's a lie Austin!"

Before he could get to him he was restrained and held back. His Father now came to him. "Jonboy, I'm ashamed of you. My own son a liar and in front of witnesses! All this nonsense about Captain Pickett killing himself. Are you saying a 12-year-old boy knows more than his elders?"

"No Sir."

"Then why, my boy, do you persist in your lies? Why can't you tell the truth?"

"But I have told the truth."

"That's enough, take him away. I've heard all the lies I can stand from you boy! Later tonight you'll have the beating of all beatings, I'll teach you to lie to me, your father and a preacher."

Jonboy was dragged away, but not before he looked into the faces of Austin and Jeff. Behind the looks of sheer terror he saw two cowards who would do anything to save their own skins.

Jonboy lay on his bed sobbing, fearful of what was to come, confused at telling the truth and not being believed, and feeling a growing anger about the great injustice that was about to be done.

It was another two hours before he heard the heavy footsteps on the old wooden staircase. His father came into the room looking stern and carrying a whip.

"I'm not going to enjoy doing this, son, it's going to break my heart, but it's the only way for you to learn to tell the truth."

Jonboy sat up, his whole body shaking in fear at what was to come.

"I have told the truth pa. I did see Captain Pickett and he was dead before the negro came to the hut."

"Shut up, boy, I will not hear this nonsense, you will never speak about it again."

Jonboy found courage he never knew he had, his eyes blazed and he turned to his father. "You told me to tell the truth and I'm telling it, maybe you don't like the truth because you just want to kill a nigger."

With those words the preacher became frenzied, raining down blow upon blow with his whip, a beating the like of which he had never given before and never would again.

For two days Jonboy would not move from his room. The servants came up with food but he wasn't interested. He let Sam dress the wounds on his back, but he would not talk. It seemed as if his spirit was broken.

The third day was the Saturday. The execution of the slave was going to take place today. It had been declared a holiday and all of Zachary was going to assemble at the bridge and watch the hanging.

Even the slaves from the plantations were to be given a half day off so they could be present and see what became of one of their number who transgressed the rules and committed murder.

The house was still when Jonboy got up out of bed; not even the slaves were there. Everyone had left and gone to the bridge. Painfully Jonboy got up and went out to the barn. It took him a long time to mount the horse, but finally he managed it. He pointed the horse in the direction of the bridge but didn't take the main road. Instead he took the old twisty back road to the top of the ridge overlooking the river. When he finally reached it, he was alone. He tied up his horse and tentatively walked towards the ridge and looked over. Less than 250 feet below, the bridge was full of people. On one side of the bank, horses and carriages were drawn up with the white people, the plantation owners and their families; on the other side, the slaves, hundreds of them. They had walked and were now assembled, all eyes on the middle of the bridge as the sheriff and the leading men of the town gathered. There was Pastor Carter, standing beside the semi-naked body of Solomon Brooks, his hands and feet chained, his head bowed. Nearby a long noose dangled from the bridge like an enormous gibbet. At the back of the crowd he could just see Jeff and Austin looking sheepish and apprehensive.

The sheriff stepped forward. "Well folks, the time has come for justice. We've found this 'ere nigger guilty of killing Captain Pickett. There can only be one penalty for such a crime, death!" A loud cheer went up from the white folks but the slaves stood with heads bowed as if in prayer. The sheriff went on. "I've asked the preacher to say a few words before we do the hanging."

Rev Carter stepped forward. He looked pleased, thought Jonboy, such a large audience, far bigger than any of his congregations. He certainly wouldn't miss the opportunity to preach to so many."

He stood in the middle of the bridge and held up his hand for quiet.

"Friends and fellow townspeople," and looking over to the slaves, "Our slaves. We have seen an awful act committed amongst us in Zachary this week, an act of such savagery and barbarity that we cannot believe it has happened. But it has. Evil, my dear friends, has come upon us and we must root it out, no matter what it takes." A murmur of assent went around the crowd. "But, dear friends, it is not just this savage act of murder we are talking about. It is also lies and deceptions." Jonboy winced, fearful of what was to come. "This very slave not only kills a man, but when confronted by his crime only cries his innocence, even a beating has not dislodged the devil from his heart." More murmurs and shouts and threats came from the crowd. "Even my own son, dear friends, has been stricken with the madness of lies." Pastor Carter now began to wring his hands and look pleadingly to the crowd for sympathy. "But, dear friends, I would not have it. I have dealt with the devil – even in my own son." Loud cheers began to echo around the bridge. "We will not have lies and untruth and the devil here in Zachary. He must be rooted out, examples made! People must be made to fear the wrath of God!" He was now in full stream, his hands and all his gestures orchestrated to bring out the right emotion from his audience. "This devil amongst us must die!" He turned to Solomon, who still had his head bowed. "We must live by the law and truth, and if we don't, whoever it is in our community who transgresses must fear the consequences."

Loud cheers erupted from the white section of the crowd, silence from the slaves. For the first time in his life Jonboy knew the truth by which he would live his life, and it wouldn't be found in Zachary.

The sheriff stepped forward, put the noose around Solomon's neck and pulled it tight. Two men held him there until the sheriff gave the signal, then they hoisted the slave onto the bridge parapet. They pushed him out over the bridge, his body falling momentarily until the rope tightened around his neck and left him dangling over the Mississippi. There were gasps from the crowd, stifled screams from the women and then cheers from the men. From where the slaves were standing only a dumb silence and fear in the eyes of those who watched the body of Solomon Brooks as it slowly swung to and fro.

Jonboy turned and with tears in his eyes returned to the house, resolved more than ever to live by the truth, whatever that cost.

Later that night, when the house was quiet and everyone was in bed, Jonboy crept quietly from his room, stopping only in the kitchen to put some food in a canvas bag. He saddled the horse in the barn and led it out, trying not to make a noise. He walked some way down the path until the house was out of sight, before mounting and riding off. He rode past farms which were in darkness and no-one was about. He took the road out of Zachery and through the half-light of the moon, he could begin to see the great shape of the bridge coming into view.

He dismounted and started walking the horse across the wooden timbers. He stopped halfway and looked at the painted wooden sign.

Solomon Brooks. A nigger who kills a white man gets what he deserves.
Anyone touching the body without permission is liable to 30 lashes.
Signed, Sheriff of Zachary.

Jonboy pulled the sign down and threw it in the river. He looked out over the bridge and a few feet below hung the body of Solomon Brooks. He took out his knife. Cutting the rope, he despatched the body to a watery grave. He mounted the horse and rode north, as far away from Zachary as he could.

Twenty Years Later - during The American Civil War 1862

After the fall of Memphis, New Orleans and Baton Rouge, the Confederate army was left in possession only of that part of the Mississippi river which lies between Vicksburg and Port Hudson.

General Sherman was given the task of taking the river for the Union army and set about blockading Vicksburg. He sent one company downstream to take a small town on the western banks of the Mississippi and gain an important bridge to cut one of General

Grant's supply routes. A captain from the 6th Union Cavalry Brigade led that company.

The fighting was heavy around the bridge, but the Confederate troops were taken by surprise and no match for the guns and superior fire of the Union cavalry. The bridge was taken in three days' fighting and after leaving a party of soldiers to guard it, the captain led a small party of men into Zachary.

Their arrival was expected and there was no resistance in the town. The war, with all its hardships and atrocities, had weakened the resolve of even the strongest southerner for any more fighting.

As the blue uniforms of the Yankee cavalry rode into the town, people came out to witness the sight. Some slaves, fearful and not knowing what would happen, looked on from behind closed shutters. The mayor and sheriff came out to meet their conquerors.

The captain accepted the surrender of the town and told all the townsfolk to disarm. They were told to assemble in the main square; everyone, men, women, children and slaves. People tumbled out of buildings and soon the town square was full of white and black standing shoulder to shoulder, wondering what was going to happen next. No one could have guessed the order that was given and quickly carried out. The white men of the town were herded together on one side, the black slaves on the other. The cavalry stood in the middle. The captain addressed the assembly.

"We're all going on a journey, up to the bridge to see a little justice done!" People looked bewildered and couldn't understand what this was about. "First, though, we'll have a little justice here and now." Turning to the slaves he said, "You, my friends, can ride in the carts and the carriages," and then looking at the white men, "you will walk."

It was a very strange procession that wound its way out of Zachary that day, carriages and carts full of slaves and behind them a party of white men, stumbling and falling, being driven forward, herded like cattle by the whips of the cavalry.

At last the bridge was reached. The white men were herded across to the other side and then halted. The cavalry officer rode onto the middle of the bridge.

"Now gentlemen, I hope you enjoyed your journey and my men were not too harsh with you."

An older man, his clothes torn and dirty from where he had fallen on the journey, was pushed forward as spokesman. From his black frock coat, covered in dust, it was obvious he was a preacher.

"You've no right to treat us like this. We may be enemies but we have rights."

The captain smiled. "Rights, you have rights! Now let me see, are these the same rights you give these other gentlemen (he gestured towards the slaves), or are they the rights you keep for yourselves?"

A silence descended upon them. The captain continued.

"I said we were going to have a bit of justice and so we are. Bring forward Austin Grant and Jeff Calhoun."

There was a shuffling and turning of heads as two figures were pushed forward reluctantly. Soldiers grabbed them and held them before the captain. Both had aged, but some of their features from the age of 12 had stuck with them. After one look at them the captain told his men.

"String 'em up boys!"

Gasps and wails came from the crowd of men. The preacher again came forward. "You can't do this. It's barbaric, what have they done?"

The captain turned to the preacher. "We're looking for the truth, old man. You'll understand that, being a preacher, and these two, why, they lie, just like a jackass."

The soldiers had by now tied the men's hands behind their backs and were tying two ropes to the bridge, fashioning nooses out of the loose ends.

Austin and Grant were now shaking with fear, their bodies convulsed with terror, and they began shouting their innocence.

The captain turned to them. "OK you two. I'll give you one last chance to tell the truth. If you lie, you go over the bridge." The nooses were attached to their necks and two soldiers stood by each man ready to throw him out over the bridge to a quick and certain death.

"Twenty years ago a man was hanged on this bridge for the crime of murder. Was he innocent or guilty?"

They looked at each other and hesitatingly and stumbling over the words spoke together. "He was innocent."

The captain smiled. "I think you're going to have to speak a little louder."

"Innocent," they repeated, but this time so that everyone could hear. The biggest reaction was from the slaves, who cheered and clasped each other. Something a lot of them had believed, all the years the story had been told about Solomon Brooks, was at last being proved to be true.

The captain turned to the preacher. This time he dismounted from his horse and took off his hat. The preacher looked at him with a quizzical expression. "It can't be... can it?... after all these years... my... son... It's my son... Jonboy... It is...." He moved towards the captain.

"Stop right there preacher! I don't want you near me. The last time you touched me it was with a whip for telling the truth. Now, tell these folks here, your assembled congregation and fellow townsmen, the truth! Did you murder an innocent man in Solomon Brooks?"

The preacher for the first time in his life was lost for words. He sank to his knees, his hands pleading with his son. "We didn't know. How could we believe a 12-year-old boy? Someone had to pay for the Captain's death. Jon... don't be too hard on us... we're... your kith and kin... your people."

The captain turned his back on the preacher and walked towards the slaves standing on the side of the road. A few saw his eyes fill with tears as he quickly put on his hat and pulled it down over his eyes.

He looked at the soldiers and barked an order. "Release the men." There was relief on the faces of the crowd on the far side of the bridge as Austin and Jeff walked back towards them. The preacher, still on his knees, raised his hands and thanked God for mercy.

The captain wasn't finished though. Turning to his soldiers, he gave the order. "Burn the bridge!"

Shrieks of horror came from the men, disbelief and panic set in as they realised the full impact of what was about to happen. Their whole livelihoods would be threatened. The transport link across the river was vital for the town, and also it began to occur to some of them, if the bridge was burnt down, they were at the wrong side. How were they to get back to their homes?

Captain Jon Carter sat alone on his horse on the ridge he had climbed 20 years before, watching as the bridge began to burn. Tears started to roll down his face as the flames began to rise up from the old wooden planks and cast a bright orange glow over the water. Men stood and watched as their livelihoods were being slowly destroyed and they could do nothing. The slaves stood still, not knowing what to feel. A new sense of freedom when all they had known was hard toil and servitude. Could it be that a new day was dawning for them?

It was a few hours later when Captain Jon Carter turned his horse away from Zachary. The smoke from the bridge was still rising and the noise could be heard of burning timbers crashing into the river. The truth had been told at last in Zachery, and for once everyone had listened.

ASHES TO ASHES

———◆———

*We disapprove of the present custom of burying the dead, and
desire to substitute some mode which shall rapidly resolve the body
into its component elements by a process which cannot offend
the living, and shall render the remains absolutely innocuous.
Until some better method is devised, we desire to adopt
that usually known as Cremation.*

Aims of The Cremation Society of England 1889

———◆———

THE CREMATORIUM RAN like a precision instrument, everything governed by the hands of the clock. Each half-hour was accounted for, with all the funerals taking place in the correct order and precise manner. That's what Peter and Bill liked, order and precision, that's what governed their lives and it was the way in which they ran their place of work.

Woodlawn crematorium prided itself on giving a good service to its customers. That they were unaware of its care and attention didn't seem to matter. Woodlawn cared for them and their relatives just the same. People noticed, the well-manicured lawns, the tidy borders of flowers, even the little details, the hand towels in the toilets and the fresh flowers. Nothing seemed too much trouble for the staff at Woodlawn, no request viewed as outlandish or strange, each was accommodated and taken care of. Funerals ran like a well-oiled machine. Services on the hour and half-hour and woe betide the funeral director that misjudged the journey and arrived late. Or for that matter the clergy who overran the half-hour with their over-long eulogies and sermons.

Peter and Bill were different but were both neat and tidy in their work. In other circumstances they would have made a good couple, for they certainly not only got on with each other well but also had that sixth sense of anticipation, each knowing what the other was doing or was about to do. They could accomplish most tasks together without planning or argument. Together they were a good team and everyone thought how lucky Woodlawn was to have such attentive and conscientious staff.

Bill was the older and had been there for over 20 years. Rather stocky and jovial of face, his complexion ruddy, he liked his pint and watching a game of football or cricket. His was the humour that kept the day moving along and sometimes took the weight of seeing constant lines of bereaved relatives.

Peter was younger; he had only been there seven years and was much leaner and taller. You would think when they had to carry a coffin on their shoulders it would be lop-sided, but not a bit of it; each compensated for the other. Peter was into sport in a big way, swimming, karate, and running, not to mention spending most of his spare time at the local gym. He also seemed to know most of the clergy, and if it was Peter who talked to the clergy then Bill saw it was his role to cultivate the funeral directors. Both professions could be described as a rum lot. Each had the uncanny knack of being serious and consoling when being with the mourners. Then when they were not there, cracking jokes and lightening up. Perhaps it was the strain of the job, of always putting on a sympathetic face with bereaved people!

Peter and Bill liked their job. To them, dealing with the mortal remains of people was like a personal service they took great pride in. It was the last private act they could offer a person and why not make it the best they could? They had long been used to the more difficult side of the crematorium, the side the public don't see, around the back where the furnaces were. But if members of the public had ventured there, they would have been reassured. It was kept as everything else at Woodlawn, spick and span, orderly and clinical in its cleanliness. There were two modern furnaces; each encased in shiny aluminium, which naturally were kept polished and shining. They could burn up to temperatures of 1200 degrees centigrade and after an hour and a quarter the body and coffin was reduced to just five or six pounds of grey ash. It always seemed a sobering thought to Peter and Bill when they raked out the ash, here is what we would all come to one day, all who came through the doors; rich, famous, beautiful or ugly, we would all be reduced to just a few pounds of grey ash, indistinguishable from the next person.

In the back room there was row upon row of crimson plastic urns, each with a name and number printed neatly on the side. Each had the date of cremation and just to make sure there would be no mistake, the name and number was also placed on another tag and placed inside the container. In over 20 years Woodlawn prided itself on never making a mistake, no ashes had ever been mixed up. Bill and Peter were meticulous in this, like all the other facets of their work.

That Friday was just like any other day. Bill was in 'the front of house', as they called it dealing with the service and mourners, and Peter round the back, taking care of the coffins after they had been despatched. While the service was on Peter came into the small office next to the chapel to have a word with the funeral director, one who always knew the gossip and usually had a good story to tell. The service was going on, the vicar's words coming through the loudspeaker as Peter walked in and smiled at John Knowles, the undertaker.

"How are you John? Any good stories today?"

John was a tall man and his black frock coat and top hat made him look even more impressive.

"Only about this joker, pointing through the small window to the vicar conducting the service."

"What's up with him then?" asked Peter.

"It's the new man at St. Giles. He only got the name wrong in church. It's a Miss Sparrow we're cremating, he kept calling her Miss Swift during the service!"

I told him when he got in the car and he just looked at me and said, "Oh no! Wrong bloody bird!" I think he'll be a bit of lad, not like his predecessor, Old Canon Lyttleton, who was as dry as old bones."

Peter and Bill both laughed and as the vicar intoned… "Ashes to ashes… dust to dust…" Peter leant over and looked through the small window to catch a glimpse of the new vicar of St Giles.

As he looked the colour visibly drained from his face and his mouth fell open. It was Bill who first noticed him and held on to his friend's arm. "What's up old chap, you look as if you've seen a ghost."

Peter recovered slightly and apologised, saying he didn't know what had come over him. He quickly made an excuse and left. Bill was worried, he'd never seen his friend act like this before and so when the funeral cortege had left he walked round to the back of the chapel. There he found Peter sitting in the chair in the little office with his head in his hands sobbing uncontrollably.

He tried to recover when he heard the door open and Bill walk in but it was too late. "What's matter Peter, what on earth is wrong?"

"I'm alright, just a touch of flu I think." He got up and turned away so Bill couldn't see his reddened eyes.

Bill returned to 'the front of house', puzzled but not sure what to make of his friend. If he was ill, why not say so? Why did he react so when they were together in the office with the undertaker and why did he almost collapse when he had caught sight of the vicar of St Giles?

Bill wasn't a suspicious soul. He accepted life as it was and didn't look deeply into things, but he did notice a change in his friend, a change Peter wasn't prepared to elucidate or give an explanation for. He noticed something else too, whenever the new vicar of St Giles was down to take a service Peter kept himself in the back, not coming out until long after the service had ended and the mourners and undertaker had left. Bill almost said something but decided not too. Whatever was wrong was Peter's concern and nothing to do with him. Then one day it happened!

It was about two months after the occasion when Peter had taken a funny turn. There had just been another funeral taken by the vicar from St Giles. Peter had busied himself in the back, not to be seen as usual. Then when everyone had gone he came round to see Bill in the chapel. He was tidying away hymn sheets when who should walk in through the door but the vicar who had taken the last funeral.

"I think I left my service book and notes, I thought I'd better come back for them."

Peter turned and looked straight into the face of the Vicar of St Giles. A look passed between them and then on the vicar's face a look of recognition and an exclamation

"No, it can't be after all this time, is it you Edward?"

Bill continued tidying up the hymnsheets as Peter looked a little flustered. At last he straightened up and spoke.

"You'd better come into the office where we can talk."

Peter led the vicar into the small office and closed the door. Bill smiled to himself. Well, at last the meeting had happened. Perhaps he would get to know what it was all about. And why did the vicar call him Edward?

After about ten minutes he heard a car leaving and Peter walking down the aisle towards his colleague.

Bill straightened up. "What was all that about then?"

Peter looked as if he wasn't going to answer, then passing Bill casually remarked. "Mistaken identity, the vicar thought I was someone else."

Bill thought to himself. 'I don't believe you, my friend, you're hiding something.' But he didn't say anything, just shrugged his shoulders. He did notice though that it was about this time the relationship between them changed. It didn't seem to be much fun working together anymore and it was as if something or someone had come between them.

Late that night, there was a knock at the door of the vicarage at St Giles. Standing there in the rain, looking rather forlorn and bedraggled, was Peter. He was ushered into the study and was given a steaming mug of coffee. The vicar looked at him over the rim of his glasses. "I'm glad you've come Peter, or should I say Edward. It was quite a shock bumping into you this afternoon. I had no idea you lived in these parts or had taken a job at the local crematorium."

Peter hesitated, then blurted out. "Look vicar, I know this is difficult but I have to be sure."

The vicar looked puzzled. "Difficult? Sure? What of? I'm afraid I don't understand."

Peter continued to look agitated. "That confession I made to you all those years ago, is it safe, have you told anyone?"

"Told anyone? But why should I? I'm a priest, not a newspaper reporter, why should I tell anyone?"

Peter gave a great sigh of relief. "Thank goodness for that. I was worried after seeing you out of the blue after all this time."

The vicar smiled. "I don't understand why you are so worried Edward, once you make a confession to a priest, that's the end of it, it doesn't go any further."

Peter was sitting in the chair ringing his hands. "You see Father, you're the only one that knows, I never told anyone else. I moved here and turned over a new leaf, started again, new job, even changed my name. (Peter tried to laugh but it came out rather nervously.) I wouldn't want people here knowing about those things back then."

Father Joe looked at him, not in judgement but more in pity. "I must say your confession was, how can I say, quite startling when I heard it. It troubled me for a long time. I didn't know if I could keep it to myself. I am used to hearing confessions but yours, the details, the scale of deception and the way you catalogued it all, wrote it all down, so meticulously."

Concern again returned to Peter's face. "You did destroy it, didn't you? That's what I asked you to do after you read it."

"Yes, I did. I didn't want to keep it but I burnt it on the fire and sat there watching the papers turn to grey ash, all the dozens of pages."

Peter again gave a sigh of relief. "Thanks Father, that's all I wanted to know, now I can sleep easily in my bed." Peter made a move as if he was going to get up and go.

Father Joe motioned for him to stay. "Don't go just yet, tell me what your life is about now, quite a change from a salesman to an attendant at a crematorium."

Peter sat down in the chair. "Yes, when I came here ten years ago this was the only job I could find. I like it though, steady hours, the customers don't complain much and if you can get used to bereaved people then it's not a bad job."

"I seem to do a lot of cremations in this parish, the people speak highly of Woodlawn, you must be doing a good job there."

Peter mumbled something and seemed not to want to talk about it. Shortly afterwards he left and it was still raining as he walked briskly down the drive.

Father Joe watched him go down the road. He returned to his study and sat in his chair, mulling over a series of events which had happened some ten years earlier but which were still fresh in his mind.

That confession, it was unusual. It had been a night like this, rain sleeting down, a foul night and he was just locking up the church. He thought no-one would venture out on a night like this. Then he saw a figure silhouetted against the door at the back of the church. It was a bedraggled figure, one that looked desperate. Father Joe had gone towards him asking if he could help.

"Confession, confession," the man gasped. "You must hear my confession."

Father Joe heard the confession. It was obvious the man wasn't used to making one, but very soon he was pouring out his tormented soul. Some people think that priests are shocked by what happens in the world. It's rather the opposite really for they hear all kinds of problems and sordid details about life. This man's story was no different, except in its intensity and catalogue of sin and deception. Edward was a salesman, going around to people's homes. He was married, but that didn't seem to matter as there was a series of affairs and it was a sorry story. But there was something else. He moved on to prostitutes and he was ashamed of it all, of how far he had gone. Joe sensed there was more and suggested to Edward that he should come and see him two days later and talk further. When he had arrived Edward was carrying a large manila envelope, which he handed to the priest. Before he could say anything he was gone into the night.

Joe had sat in the vicarage and read the confession, the like of which he had never seen before. It was a story of man's depravity and to what depths a human being could reach. It started with the

191

affairs, seemingly dozens of them, and then the prostitutes, with all the graphic and sordid details. But that was not all, there was something which made the priest's blood run cold, sending a shiver down his spine. Edward was involved in a paedophile ring and in the confession he talked about young girls being abused. The confession ended with Edward saying how desperate he was to change, of how he wanted to tell someone what he had done and how he wanted to put it all behind him. This all occurred in a neighbouring town. He didn't say which one, and now he was leaving to go and live on the other side of the country and start afresh. He wanted to make a clean start and this was his way of breaking with the past and starting anew.

Joe had been greatly troubled by that confession. He thought about going to the police as criminal acts had been committed, but with what proof? The confession of an anonymous man who walked into church one night! The confession had been cleverly written, not putting in any details which could identify the writer or even the locality. No dates, places, people – nothing.

Joe had tried to trace the person, but to no avail. He asked at local shops and cafes, given the man's description and name of Edward, but no one could give him any leads. He hoped the mystery penitent would come back to church, but he never did. Had he done what he promised, made a full confession and then moved on?

And now, by a strange coincidence, they had met again. What was Joe to do? Go to the police? Tell the authorities? He knew they would take it seriously, even if the confession had been destroyed. But could Joe give evidence from a confession? That would break every rule of priestly confidentiality.

After some thought Joe knew what he should do. He must counsel Edward, or Peter as he was called now. He must make sure that the offending was really behind him and for the sake of the victims he had got to get him to talk to the authorities, no matter what that would mean.

His plan of action decided, he slept more easily that night, at least he thought he had until he awoke in the morning soaked in sweat with his mind racing. What a fool he'd been! This was all a trick, a set-up. Of course Peter didn't want to be traced. Why had the confession been so vague about places and events, so that even if Joe had shown it to someone he'd have no proof of who it was referring to. Also, Joe knew enough about human nature to know that guilt was something that people needed to off-load. Peter must have known things were closing in on him. What better way to get rid of his guilt than onto a priest and walk away, probably feeling a lot better, and then move to the other end of the country to start a new life with a different name. But there was one question which nagged at the priest and wouldn't let him rest. Was Peter still involved with the paedophile ring? Joe had to know.

It was a cold and rainy Thursday morning that Joe drove to the crematorium. He had a funeral but he wanted to get there early, hopefully to see Peter and arrange another meeting. When he arrived it was Bill who was in the 'front office' making preparations for the morning's work.

"Oh hello vicar, you're early for the funeral, it's not for another half hour."

Joe tried to reassure him. "I had another visit up this way but they were out. I'll sit in the back and read the paper. Is Peter in?"

"No, he's not. Off on a day's leave, some swimming gala somewhere. He drives the mini-bus for the youth team."

Joe felt a shiver run down his spine. And then he remembered. In the confession, although it was vague about events and places it did mention that a sports team was involved and that was the way of contacting young people. It didn't say which sport, but swimming and Peter, the driver of the mini-bus. This was too much of a coincidence.

Joe tried to be as casual as possible so as not to arouse Bill's suspicions.

"Is it far away then?"

Bill shrugged his shoulders. "Don't know, he never tells me much, like a closed book is Peter, never tells you anything."

Joe saw his chance. "Do you know where he lives?"

Bill pointed out of the window. "In the row of cottages about half a mile away, the last one in the row, with a green door."

Bill looked quizzical. "Anything the matter? You fairly spooked Peter that first time he saw you. Looked as if he'd seen a ghost."

Joe felt he had to say something. "I knew him from a time before in a previous parish."

Before Bill could ask any more questions the funeral cortège drove slowly up the drive and they both had to go to their duties, which was a big relief for Joe. He didn't wait around after the funeral and drove off, turning not the usual right turn back to his parish but left and made his way to the cottages. The end cottage had a door painted green which was peeling and some faded curtains at the windows, a typical-looking house for a single man to live in. What redeemed it was the garden. Not a plant out of place nor a weed to be seen, it was a riot of colour and obviously had the attentions of someone who knew what they doing in the garden. He tried ringing the bell but knew there was no chance of it being answered.

Joe drove back to the vicarage wondering what his next action should be. Would it be right to inform the authorities, and who were they? The police? Social Services? The swimming club officials? What would he say when he contacted them?

I believe this man to be a paedophile, but how could he prove it? With a written confession given to a priest and then burnt? Could Joe divulge the contents of a confession, no matter how horrific, to another person? The whole point and meaning of any confessional is that it is confidential with no conditions. But this was testing Joe's beliefs to the very limit. He decided he would have to talk to someone, and so he rang a friend who also was a priest of long standing. The housekeeper informed him that he was away at a conference for a couple of days but would tell him when he returned. Joe put the phone down with a great sense of heaviness. His problem was not resolved, but yet he knew he must do something.

It was after 11 o'clock that night that the doorbell rang. Joe was still up and went to the door wondering who it could be at that time. He peered through the small spyhole and saw Peter standing in the porch. He opened the door. "Peter, this is late but do come in."

Joe noticed a furtiveness with Peter, his eyes moving around the hall as if he was trying to find out if anyone else was in the vicarage.

"Are you alone vicar?"

Joe's brow furrowed. "Yes, but why such a late call, what's the matter?" Peter's eyes narrowed. "I hear you've been at the house and Bill said you were asking questions."

Joe realised that attack was the best form of defence. "Yes, I did. I haven't been happy with your confession and the way you are living now."

Peter's eyes flared. "But that's all in the past, it's over and finished with. You can't bring that up, it's against your code as a priest."

Father Joe looked intently at Peter. "Ten years ago I heard your confession, but you never returned to receive absolution and part of the conditions for that absolution would be to receive treatment and confess your crimes to the authorities."

Peter was now very agitated and marched up and down the hall. "But you can't say that. I confessed and that's an end to it, you can't bring it all up again."

Joe now spoke calmly and very clearly. "I can. If you are still doing the same things now you were involved in ten years ago, and especially with children."

Peter glanced at him with a look, trying to decide just how much the priest knew. "I told you it was in all in the past. I have a new life here."

Joe measured his words carefully knowing the damage he would do. "Ten years ago your paedophile ring was involved in a sports club. What do I find you are doing here in your spare time but driving young people around in a mini-bus to swimming events? A bit of a coincidence isn't it?"

Peter turned angrily. "You can't prove anything, you haven't got my confession and I can deny ever meeting you."

Joe spoke calmly. "You can do all that Peter. But I can ask questions with the right people here that will turn the spotlight on you and, believe you me, if there is anything going on, it will be uncovered."

Joe didn't see the blow coming but only felt the crack on his head and lights flashing before his eyes as he crashed to the solid stone floor. Blood started seeping into a small pool from his forehead as Peter stood over the priest like some avenging angel holding the cricket bat that had been in the hall. The priest was dead.

Peter moved fast. He had a lot to do and he had to be careful. First he got some sheets from upstairs and wrapped the body in them. He then dragged it outside to his mini-bus and with a bit of difficulty deposited it in the back. Fortunately the vicarage was not overlooked and as the trees were in leaf no-one could see the mini-bus next to the house.

He then returned to the house and started cleaning up. He took great care, putting on rubber gloves and wiping away any trace of blood and also washing down all the surfaces he had touched. He returned the cleaning materials with care to their exact places. He then went into the study and switched on the vicar's computer. He typed one letter and very carefully went around the house switching everything off, taking with him only three things, the letter, the cricket bat and the keys to the vicar's car.

He carefully drove the three miles back to his house, hoping that the mini-bus would not cause any suspicion so that no-one would have cause to remember it on the roads that night.

It was three days later that the police found the vicar's car. It had been sitting in a local beauty spot about five miles away, in a car park overlooking a deserted beach. Some locals had reported it. At first the police thought it was stolen. Then, when they tried to trace the owner, found that he too was missing. They then took a closer look at the car. In it they found a typewritten note.

I CAN'T GO ON. IT'S TOO MUCH. THEY ARE CLOSING IN ON ME AND I KNOW I COULDN'T BEAR THE SHAME. I AM SO SORRY I HAVE LET YOU ALL DOWN. PLEASE FORGIVE ME.

Joe's name was scribbled underneath in pen.

They also found some pornographic magazines, the like of which even some of the police officers had never seen before. It was child porn, but of a very extreme nature.

It didn't take long for the rumours to start. 'CHILD PORN VICAR WALKS OUT TO SEA' was the headline in the local paper, and although the Police had no other evidence of any link with child-pornography in the vicarage or on the computer, people came to the simple conclusion that the vicar had things he was ashamed of and had walked out to sea to commit suicide. That his body was never found didn't seem to matter.

Father Joe's shock disappearance was the cause for much gossip and speculation, not least with the local undertaking fraternity and at Woodlawn Crematorium.

Bill and Peter sat in the small rest room at the back of the crematorium, the boilers making their familiar hum, the dead being despatched with the usual efficiency.

Bill lowered his paper. "I still think that Father Joe's disappearance is a bit strange."

Peter still kept his paper in front of his face. "He got what he deserved, I'd string 'em up for what they do to children, and him a priest, he should have known better."

Bill was not convinced. "But he was such a nice guy, everyone liked him and no matter how far the police trawled back into his career, they could find nothing. A bit odd to me. Eh! Didn't you know him in his previous parish. He said he recognised you, didn't he?"

Peter moved uneasily on his chair. "No, he was mistaken. I looked like someone else." With that Peter got up and went outside to have a cigarette.

Things hadn't been the same at the crematorium for a number of months. There seemed now to be distance between the two attendants. Peter was more aloof than usual; he seemed to have changed and so it was with no surprise that one day Peter announced he would be leaving.

"Just moving on, going to stay with a sister up north" was all Bill could get from him.

So one Friday night, after the boilers had been closed down, Peter left with a handshake, that's all. He even refused to go for a drink. A few of the funeral directors had a whip round and bought him a silver hip flask and a cigarette lighter.

Bill thought long and hard that Friday night on what had gone wrong. Had he been the cause of Peter leaving? What had come between them. He couldn't work it out, no matter how much he thought about it.

Time passed like clockwork at Woodlawn. Five years on and Bill was contemplating retirement. The day came closer to the time he would hand over the crematorium to his new assistant, Mark. A good lad who learnt quickly and was good with the relatives. He had no fears the place would be in good hands. He planned his retirement well and wanted to make sure everything was correct, so he decided he would tidy the place up. He wanted to sort out the room where they kept the urns of ashes for relatives to collect and then dispose of. Some, of course, were never collected, and after five years had elapsed if no-one had claimed them, the crematorium scattered them in the grounds. It was these Bill was going to deal with. He surveyed the shelves. Line upon line of crimson plastic urns about ten inches high, each with a number on them, and it was now his task to sort out the ones which had been there longer than five years. There was great order and precision in the way they did their work at Woodlawn. The misconception by the general public is that you could get someone else's ashes, Bill knew that this was practically impossible.

Every time the boiler was fired and another coffin placed in the oven it would print out two identical numbers on slips of paper; each also had the date on. When the ashes were raked out, one number was stuck on the outside of the urn and the other placed inside. The numbers and names were entered in a large ledger.

Bill now sorted out about 20 urns which had never been collected and he started going through the ledger to tick off the numbers and write in that they had been scattered in the Woodlawn gardens, just in case a relative turned up to ask. One urn however puzzled him. It was No.555769. Yes, it had its number, both on the urn and inside, but in the ledger there was no entry. There was no name either on or inside the urn. What could have happened? How could a mistake like this be made?

It wasn't difficult to trace the day on which it happened and then Bill consulted another book, which told him which cremations took place on that day. There were 12. He checked off the numbers and the names in the book and they all matched. Then why was there a thirteenth?

He looked at the urn again. He examined it closely for any distinguishing marks and there were none. He looked again at the date and then his heart seemed to miss a beat. He reached for the telephone and rang the local library to check the date of a headline in a local paper. He put the phone down slowly and looked for the ledger which recorded who was duty on which particular day. He turned back the pages, not wanting them to reveal what they did, that Peter was on duty in the 'back office' on the day of the extra cremation.

When Bill arrived at the local police station the sargeant and constable looked a little mystified as Bill placed a large plastic urn on the counter and proudly announced.

"I think I've just found a dead body"

Footnote

They have not found Peter yet, although there is a national man-hunt out for him and his name and photograph have appeared on the television. The police think it is only a matter of time before he is caught. His mistake had been to follow the meticulous rules of the Woodlawn Crematorium too closely, especially for the thirteenth body he had cremated on that fateful day. Later that month Bill attended a thanksgiving service, held for the life of Father Joe, someone who, in death had been much maligned, but now his name was clear. His ashes were buried in the churchyard of St Giles.

STRANGE CUSTOMS

———⊰◆⊱———

The grave of the man believed to be the last "sin-eater" in England is located in the churchyard of St Margaret's Ratlinghope, Shropshire, and belongs to Richard Munslow, who died in 1906. Sin-eaters were paid a small amount of money to eat bread and drink ale across the body of a person who had died suddenly without confessing his or her sins. The sin-eater would take on the dead person's sins, so that the soul could arrive before God in a clean and pure state. Sin-eating was a practice peculiar to the English/Welsh Marches. Munslow appears to have taken on the job after losing three of his children in a whooping-cough outbreak.

Church Times, July 2010

———⊰◆⊱———

IT IS WITH SOME hesitation that I sit down to write this story as it will be difficult for any sane and rational person to believe it. My name is Henry Marlowe and I will be thought of as mad to have written it, as no such events that I describe could possibly take place in England in the year 1867.

I am a clergyman of the Church of the England and I swear on the Bible the truth of these words. I write them because I want people to hear the story of a good man, John Parsons, my closest friend, whose evil fate still sends shivers down my spine.

We were at college together in Oxford, studying divinity, both of us hoping to be ordained into the Church of England. We had rooms next to each other and were inseparable, sharing everything and enjoying each other's company like no other. John was a year ahead of me and left college before I did to take up a living in a remote parish in Yorkshire, at a place I never knew existed and would gladly have remained ignorant about for the rest of my life. When he heard the news of his appointment John was pleased, and although we would miss one another he was keen to start work and knew his first living would be a hard one and one he had buckle down to. How hard he cannot have imagined and what led to his fate I want to now recount in the form of the letters he sent me from that God forsaken place at Ugglethorpe.

****

1st December, 1867

Dear Henry,

I wanted to write to you and tell you my first thoughts about my new living. I don't think the Bishop could have sent me farther away, even if he had wanted to!

Thanks for seeing me off at the station in Oxford; it took four hours to reach Leeds. I then transferred to a local train for the trip to Grimton Bridge. The train was slow and almost empty, the only other occupant of the carriage being an old farmer whose dialect I could hardly understand. We made good, if slow, progress through the pretty countryside of the Yorkshire Dales. I began to notice the meadows replaced with rough pasture and the railway line started to climb through hills and valleys. The heather was dark and when you looked to the skyline, it seemed as if the leaden sky was touching the tops of the hills. Sheep were the only occupants of the moor sides and it was becoming more and more desolate and bleak. We passed small stations with funny names, Bogthorn, Pickles Hill, Hermit Hole, Marsh, Damside and Scartop. The names mirrored the places and I have never seen hamlets or villages like them before in their bleakness. Finally we arrived at Grimton Bridge and along with my luggage I got out onto the small station. It was an eerie feeling to stand on a platform alone, with only the steam from the train.

It was now getting dark and I could see no one else about. The train gave a piercing whistle and was off, leaving me alone, it seemed, in a strange and desolate land. I went into the waiting room and found a fire but no one to greet me. In the letter it spoke of being met at the station. I could do nothing else but wait. I must have been there over an hour, no trains or people. I was beginning to get worried when I heard the sound of a horse's hooves on the cobbles outside. Here was my transport, a buggy the like of which we have not seen in Oxford for twenty years, but still it seems the main form of transport here. The man motioned me to get in and gave a very gruff sort of greeting; no apology for being late, just a sullen air.

We quickly left the station behind and went out onto rough lanes. It was now quite dark and the mist was rolling down from the moors. The moors are bleak and weather-beaten, and the hills appeared as great black shapes against a skyline where the moon cast a yellow hue over the summits. It was almost an hour's drive from the station and we passed through no other village until I could see in the distance the shapes of some houses and chimneys set against a black forbidding hillside.

Henry, here's a funny thing, I distinctly heard a bell tolling, I could hear it across the moor and it was definitely not the wind. I thought it was the parish church and it quite cheered me up to think they were tolling it to welcome their new vicar. How wrong I was!

We passed through the narrow lanes of the town and on to the church, which stands on a slight hill at the edge of Ugglethorpe. It was all in darkness and looked in the murky evening light quite depressing, its great black steeple standing out and pointing, it seemed, like a defiant finger to heaven.

Next to the church was the graveyard and there, seemingly in the midst of the graves, my vicarage! I can tell you Henry, at that moment I longed for the comfort of my room in the college and the dreaming spires of Oxford.

Waiting to greet me was a small man with a huge black cloak. Getting close up to him I could see that his face seemed misshapen and his features quite out of proportion. This was Caleb, the churchwarden. He greeted me and helped me into the vicarage with my luggage.

First impressions are not always the best, but I could see that the house although large was austere and would be cold. It was furnished adequately but nothing pretty, just functional and plain. It certainly lacked any feminine touch and I would hesitate to bring any family into such a house as this.

Food had been left for me and a fire lit and Caleb said he would return in the morning after I had rested.

Henry, I sat in the parlour wondering where I had come to. It seemed to be so foreign to me. How could I make my mark on a place like this? What hope could I give the people who lived here and eked out their living on the harsh and bleak moors?

That night I went to bed, the room was as cold as I feared and the wind rasped at the windows. It took me a long time to get off and as I did I fancy I heard the bell tolling again. It seemed to be far away and muffled. I made a note to mention it to Caleb in the morning.

Will write again soon. John.

****

11th December, 1867

Dearest Henry,

Thanks for your letter and news of Oxford; it really cheered me up. It seems as if I'm a thousand miles from academia here amongst the hills and sheep.

Conditions here are a bit better since my last letter. The natives are friendly, if a little sullen and reserved. My first service saw the church packed; curiosity I think, as everyone wanted to see the new vicar. The last vicar only lasted two years then left without telling anyone, just disappeared. A very rum business! Anyway, they have been without a vicar since then, so they are very glad to see me, even with my Oxford ways!

It is an odd place Henry. Everything is fashioned by the harsh landscape. The people too take on the manner and characteristics of the moors around them, bleak and weather-beaten. It always seems to be raining, or just about to rain; not very hospitable, the Pennines!

I must tell you what happened at the first funeral. You will have to tell the other fellows at college, it will put their theology up the spout!

I went to the house as requested an hour before the service so that I could bless the coffin and accompany it the short distance to church. Imagine my surprise when I got there to be ushered into the front room and there was the coffin laid out by the hearth. But on top of it was a white cloth and plates and cups as well what looked like small cakes and a jug of ale. I asked what this was for, thinking it was when people came back after the funeral for refreshment.

But no! We were to eat and drink it now after saying the Lord's Prayer together. I didn't wish to offend anyone so went along with it. It was only afterwards that I found out that this was for 'sin-eating'! The idea being that the nearest and dearest just before a funeral eat and drink a funeral biscuit placed on top of the coffin. A good authority told me that it is supposed to represent the dead person's sins you are eating before they are buried! The fellows wouldn't find this in the theological books.

But more was to follow. When we had processed to the church, we were about to enter when I noticed Caleb at the back by the font with a small group of people and a baby. I asked what they had come for and they said a baptism!

Well, after the funeral I returned to the church and found them still there, so I did the baptism and then when they had left asked Caleb why they had come at such an inconvenient time; the baby wasn't ill or anything. He said that it was quite common for baptisms and funerals to occur together, as it was believed that the goodness of the person who has died will pass into the new-born baby if it baptised at the same time as the funeral. I later checked through the service register and found quite a number of baptisms and funerals happening at the same time! They are a superstitious and fearful lot here in Ugglethorpe in need of enlightenment, but am I the person to do it?

Write soon, John.

****

2nd January, 1868

Dear Henry

Happy New Year! How goes it with your appointment? You never know, they may send you to the wilds of Yorkshire like me?

Christmas was busy with large numbers of services, but so cold. I never knew I could feel the cold like I do here. It blows in from the moors and chills you to the bone. It certainly makes you keep the sermons short!

Had an invitation to the big mill-owners house for a meal over Christmas. A very good time and as they have two very pretty daughters, I may be making more than the odd pastoral visit! They live in the largest house round here and as it was built in the 16th Century there are many stories and legends attached to it. We sat one night by a great crackling log fire hearing some of them talk all about the witch trials, murders and ghosts. There was a great catholic persecution here and priests it was said used to hide at the hall in a priest's hole, which has never been found. There is also a room at the top of the house where on certain nights of the year a cross appears on the wall. I tried to be my rational self and laughed off this mumbo-jumbo, but the people here really do believe it and nothing you say will shake them from it. I despair sometimes and wonder what to make of it.

Oh, by the way, I found out about the bell. I asked Caleb, the great fount of local knowledge and superstition, who seems to be an authority on every subject, and certainly he has an old wives to tell about any unusual occurrence.

In the last century a bell was stolen from the church just before it was going to be re-hung. It had been lowered to the ground and left overnight. Some enterprising local villains broke into the church and loaded it on a wagon and made off with it. They obviously didn't realise the weight of the bell, for the first bridge they came to gave way, plunging them and the bell into the water. They were all drowned! It was said that the bell has been tried to be recovered many times, but every time was met with disaster. Finally, they left it there in the reservoir and it is said that those who are facing peril or death can hear a muffled ring.

When I told Caleb that I'd heard the bell on at least two occasions he just looked at me with those suspicious eyes of his and muttered, 'Tha's got to be careful vicar.'

Looking forward to seeing you next month. I can take you on some splendid walks over the moors and the Heatons have promised that we go grouse shooting if you are up it!

See you soon, John.

****

10th April, 1868

Dear Henry,

I did enjoy your visit. The time seemed to go so quickly, but we did manage to pack a lot in. You certainly made a big impression on the Heaton girls! They've never stopped talking about you and Caleb has designs on you to succeed me as the next vicar here, be warned!

I heard the bell again last night. It was a clear cloudless night and as I was lying in bed I distinctly heard the muffled tones. I strained my ears trying to work out which direction it was coming from. If I ask anyone else if they heard it they look at you strangely and move on quickly to another topic.

The Heatons are becoming good friends, but they are as superstitious as the rest of the people despite their education and culture. I go up to the Hall most weeks and have a meal. They have taken a liking to me, I think. Mr Heaton and I usually sit in front of the fire and talk after dinner. He tells me stories about the Hall and what happened in Ugglethorpe. For a small place there certainly have been some rum happenings. In the 1600s one of my predecessors, James Gatley, was a staunch evangelical who would have no truck with popery. It was during the time of the persecution of Catholics and so they were meeting, secretly sometimes in the Hall. One Sunday morning there were rumours of papists assembled at the Hall 'celebrating their idolatrous Mass'. Gatley led the mob, armed with clubs and swords, up to the Hall demanding that the priest be brought out. Nobody was found to be inside worshipping, although all the rooms were searched only the servants were there. Later it was rumoured there had been five people and two priests holding a service, but they hid in a secret room it and it has never been found.

With a log fire and two or three glasses of excellent wine it makes a good story, but I was intrigued. As you know, I worked with my father's architects' business before going into the church, so I know a little about buildings. I asked if I could see the plans of the Hall and try and find this secret room. Mr Heaton is arranging for this, so I will have a good look round the next time I have a day off, searching for secret rooms and the like!

Write soon, John.

****

4th June, 1868

Dear Henry,

Just a note to thank you for the books. A bit of civilisation and culture here on the moors! Spring is here and the moors have developed a new beauty. There is a freshness in the air and last week I went for a walk with the Heaton girls. They are such good fun! The heather is beginning to bloom and the curlews were circling overhead. It doesn't look as barren as winter and you could almost begin to like the place.

I went up to the Hall to look for the secret room. It was great fun, but fruitless. Amy and Jane helped me, but even with my plans and measuring sticks, I could find no place where it could possibly be. There is a strange room, which Mr Heaton would like me to exorcise. No one has ever stayed in it and it's this room where it is rumoured the Cross appears. I have volunteered to stay in it. My bravery certainly impresses the girls, but Caleb says 'Tha's a fool parson'. He continues to tell me old wives' tales about almost every superstition in the village. The trouble is everyone else seems to believe these foolish tales.

Last week I walked up to the Hall and decided to count the yew trees on the drive. There were 99. I counted them again on my return, just to make sure I hadn't made a mistake. When I asked Mr Heaton why such an odd number and why no one had planted the hundredth tree, he said they had but every time they planted one it died. They had tried over twenty times, but to no avail, and had now given up. Caleb says, 'Its folly to tamper with matters we don't understand, leave well alone.'

Henry, I am fed up with these locals and their superstitions. The power of them must be broken. I am looking for a way to do it and rid the place of idle custom and folklore. Everything you touch or do seems to be lucky or unlucky. I will not have it and I am determined to be rid of these things.

Write soon, John,

****

21st October, 1868

Dear Henry,

Your letter arrived today and I was pleased to get it. You warn me not to do anything that will put myself in danger. Don't worry, old man, I can take care of myself.

I preached against superstition and bad luck last Sunday. The sermon was met with a wall of silence and as people left the church they would not look me in the eye. I feel I am coming up against an evil spiritual force here, which needs casting out. Even Caleb it seems has fallen out with me and hardly speaks. He says, 'Let things bide. Don't disturb 'em.' I'm not sure what he means but I will not let these superstitions win.

You ask in your letter about the bell, if I have heard it again. I don't really want to talk about it as I think it is some trick. I hear it every night and sometimes if I wake it is there tolling, ringing in a muffled sort of way. Is it warning me? Or is it inviting me to something? I don't know. I think it is a trick and I will find a rational explanation soon.

Write soon, John.

****

1ˢᵗ November, 1868

Dear Henry,

I had to write to you. I don't know who else to talk to. I hear the bells all the time. It's there with its droning ring if I am awake or asleep. No one else seems to hear it, or if they do claim not to hear its muffled ring.

I've been to the bridge in the night but found nothing. Henry, I'm getting desperate, I don't know what to do.

Friday night is the time for the exorcism and blessing the room at the Hall. I am to go at 9pm and say prayers in the rooms. I have volunteered to stay there overnight to show people there is nothing to be afraid of.

But Henry, I am afraid. Please pray for me and let me be in your thoughts.

Write soon, John.

****

That was the last letter I received from John. As soon as I received the letter I went to the station to take the next train to Yorkshire. I arrived in Grimton Bridge at dusk and it was just as John described it, if not worse. As soon as you got out of the carriage the cold dank air met you, wrapping itself around you like a muffler. Luckily there was a carriage, which someone agreed to share with me. All the way to Ugglethorpe I fretted and worried if I would arrive too late. The mist was rolling down from the moors as we entered the village, with its mill chimneys belching out their filthy black smoke.

I went straight to the vicarage and hammered on the door. No-one was in, but Caleb appeared from the churchyard.

"Where is the vicar?" I implored.

"He's not been seen for last two days; sum says he went t'Hall and stayed in haunted room."

I grabbed him by the throat and came close to his ugly face.

"What do you know of that room?"

He cowered away as I relaxed my grip. "Only that no-one who has spent a night in it has lived to tell the tale."

"Drive me to the Hall and be quick about it."

Soon we were driving through the village as if the hounds of hell were after us. We arrived at the Hall and could see lights from the downstairs room.

I burst in and found Mr. Heaton looking anxious, talking to a police constable. They turned to look at me with questioning stares.

"Have you heard from John. Do you bring us news?"

I shook my head. "That's why I'm here, I'm worried for him."

Mr Heaton looked agitated. "He came here to spend a night in the room. He said that he wanted to rid of us of superstition and he wasn't frightened. I let him and he was alright when we all retired for the night. But in the morning he was gone. Nothing there, his clothes, nothing. I thought he may have got fed up and gone home, but he hasn't been seen since and he didn't turn up at church yesterday to take the services."

"Take me to the room," I said, trying not to show the panic and desperation I felt.

Mr Heaton led us up the steps to the second floor. We went through a couple of doors and entered what was obviously the older part of the house. We had to crouch low to enter a small room, which looked like a small bedroom, with just one tiny window at the far end.

Mr Heaton held the lamp so that we could examine the room. "As you can see gentlemen, there is nothing in this room and no-one here."

"What about the priest-hole, couldn't that be part of this room?" I said, my voice agitated as my eyes darted around the small room taking in every corner and crevice.

Mr Heaton frowned. "But it has never been found. People have looked and even John came here with the plans of the house and measured all the rooms. He could find nothing."

I lay down on the floor and started to examine every crack and minute detail hoping to find a clue, but there was nothing. We spent an hour going over that room but could find nothing.

We returned downstairs and sat exhausted in front of the large log fire, which crackled and sent sparks up the chimney. I must have dozed off as when I awoke, it was with a start as if woken from a dream. The fire had burnt down and there were only glowing embers in the grate.

Then I realised why no-one had found the priest hole before?

"The chimney! The chimney!" I exclaimed, jumping up out of my seat and startling my two companions.

Mr Heaton looked puzzled. "But what about it? There is nothing unusual, is there?"

I pointed to the roof. "It goes up through the floor and passes through the bedrooms. The room we were in is directly above us and yet there is no sign of the chimney!"

"My God, you're right."

We bounded up the steps two at a time and again reached the room. This time we headed for the wall where the chimney should be. I had picked up an axe by the fireplace and wielded it above my head, bringing it down on the plaster to reveal the sandy-coloured bricks underneath. There was nothing there, just solid bricks and no evidence of a chimney.

After 20 minutes of hacking at a solid wall I sat down, slumped against the other wall exhausted. "I'm sorry, I seem to have messed up your decorations."

Mr Heaton put his hand on my shoulder. "They don't matter, it's John that's important now."

Mr Heaton kindly said that I could stay at the Hall for the next few days until we discovered what had happened to John.

In better times I would have enjoyed staying in such a fine house, but now I could hardly sleep or eat, the only thing on my mind the fate of my beloved friend John. Even the company of the lovely Heaton girls brought no solace, just an air of complete and utter hopelessness about the situation.

The police said they had put out a county alert for the vicar. I telegraphed the Oxford colleges hoping that John may get in touch and for them to forward me any messages. But after three days there was nothing.

I spent a day poring over the plans of the Hall, but to no avail. I am no architect and couldn't understand where, if any, a hiding place could be located. I spent my time between Mr Heaton's library and pacing the grounds outside thinking and praying for some sort of answer.

In the library I spent my time looking through the old books relating the Hall and it's history. It had been in the hands of the Heaton family since the early 1800s, but the house itself was much older, parts of it dating back to the 15th Century. It was built by an old Catholic family, the Fitzwilliams, who it was rumoured hid catholics during the persecutions.

It was now a week since the disappearance of John. I reluctantly told the Heatons that I could prevail on their hospitality no longer and must return to Oxford. Mr Heaton drove me himself to Grimton Station and saw me onto the train. His features looked drawn and he seemed to be carrying the disappearance on his shoulders and blaming himself for his fate, whatever that may be.

On my return to Oxford there had been no news of John. I tried to return to my studies, but the words on the pages looked jumbled and had no meaning. In the lectures I found myself gazing out of the window, longing to hear one scrap of news from my friend. Even at night I found myself waking in the middle of the night, my mind going over the events at Ugglethorpe and finding no answer.

It was three weeks since John's disappearance. I went to bed and, as usual, tossed and turned into the early hours. It was about 4am when I awoke. The room was bright as there was a full moon that night and I had left the curtains open. I looked at the patterns made by the moonlight around the room, seeing shapes and shadows which only the subtleties of moonlight could reveal.

Then I sat bolt upright in bed, my eyes focused at the other end of the room, a sudden realisation and comprehension filling my mind now emptied of all thought of sleep. I'd got it, I had found the key to

John's disappearance, but would it be too late. I hurriedly washed and dressed and, grabbing an overnight bag, rushed out of the college. The streets of Oxford were deserted as I ran to the station. The first train north was 5.50am and I paced the platform impatient for its arrival. I telegraphed the Hall telling the Heatons of my return and asking if I could be met at the station. I didn't tell them the reason for my visit, the idea in the cold light of day seemed so fanciful and bizarre that I didn't have the confidence to share it with anyone.

The train journey seemed to take an age and the connections longer than usual. At last, in the middle of the afternoon, the train drew into the familiar drabness and bleak features which was Grimton Bridge railway station. As I leant out of the window a figure stood on the platform; it was Mr Heaton. He saw me and grabbed at the carriage door, almost falling over in his eagerness to see me.

"Have you any news?" he blurted out, his features more drawn and darker than the last time we had seen each other on this station.

I felt ashamed to tell him that I had none, but I had woken in the night with an idea. I told him I would disclose all when we got to the Hall. It was a drive at feverous pace and the horses fairly galloped towards Ugglethorpe as if the devil himself was behind us.

When we got to the hall Amy and Jane were waiting on the steps, anxiety written deep on their faces. They too looked expectantly for good news, which sadly I could not give.

After we had gone into the house I told them of my idea, preposterous as it may sound.

It all started when I looked through the books in the library. I was searching for something, but didn't know what it was. If I had come across it I probably wouldn't have known as I wasn't sure what I was looking for. This morning when I awoke in my room with the full moon shining through the window, I remembered something I had read in one of the books that a Cross appeared in the room at certain times and no-one could explain it. This was the room where the catholics had celebrated their Mass in secret during the years of persecution. When John had disappeared it had been the night of the full moon and tonight the moon would be full. I wanted to be in the room when the moon was full.

Mr Heaton listened intently during my story and only said it was worth a try. He then rose and went off to the library as the two girls fussed round me, insisting that I eat something as I realised I had not eaten anything all day.

After about an hour Mr Heaton returned carrying a number of books. He laid them down on the table. "You know, Henry, you may have something here. All the disappearances occurred round the time of the full moon and there have been numerous sightings of the Cross on that wall and no-one can explain it."

That night, as the moon began to rise in the sky, Mr Heaton and I took our places in the room. We extinguished the candles and waited for what, we were not sure. The room had been cleaned of all the rubble I had hacked off the wall thinking there was a concealed fireplace. The place had a peculiar odour, which you could not recognise. The room was in darkness, except for a small window high up on the wall behind us, its glass old and discoloured, scratched and dirty. Gradually your eyes got accustomed to the dim light in the room and after a time the moon's rays started to filter through the window. I thanked God that it seemed a clear night and prayed that clouds would not hamper our vigil. The moon's rays started at first to cast shadows and shapes at the base of the wall opposite us. Nothing unusual, just moonlight streaming through the window. Gradually the moonlight became stronger and more light filtered through. We were looking so intently at the wall that we thought we saw shapes and signs when there were none.

Then it happened. We had been in the room about three hours and the moonlight was now fully illuminating the wall opposite. Our eyes were focused, ready for any sign or symbol, and slowly, as if someone were drawing it, a large Cross appeared on the wall opposite. Its symmetry was perfect and drew gasps from both of us. But that was not all. In the centre of the cross, where the horizontal and vertical lines meet, another symbol appeared. We could not make it out; it looked like a hole, but no, it had a small shadow at the edge – it was some kind of marker. We both must have had the same realisation at the same time as we both leapt forward to touch it. My hand got there first and, sure enough, it felt different to the surrounding wall. I pressed hard and from the floor beneath a loud grating noise started and I was thrown off balance on to the top of Mr Heaton and we both ended up in one corner of the room in a heap, our legs and arms entwined. We struggled free, searching for the candles. As we lit them, we couldn't believe what was revealed. It seemed as if half the floor had gone and a black hole appeared in its place. As we edged nearer we saw that there were steps leading down into we didn't know what. The smell was overpowering, a mixture of stale air, dampness and something which smelt like death itself.

"Be careful Henry," implored Mr Heaton, "there must be some sort of timing device. Remember, if it opens it also closes and we don't know how long we've got."

The risk did not bother me as I scrambled down the steps and into another small room only a few feet high but the same size as the room above.

There at the bottom of the steps lay my friend John, his body crumpled up and seemingly lifeless. I cradled his head in my arms and wept, feeling his wrist for a pulse, which I thought I detected. I was just about to call out to Mr Heaton in the room above when the grinding and scraping noise started again, this time much louder, and I could see the flagstones above coming together. I let out a scream, but it was too late, the flagstones closed together.

I turned back to John, who emitted a stifled groan from his lips. His face was blackened and dirty; he looked a shadow of his former self and his clothes were like rags. I laid his head down as gently as I could and looked around the rest of the room. I brought the candle up and held it in front of me and saw what was like a vision from hell. Around me were bodies, or rather skeletons, some reduced to skulls and bones, their clothes long since disintegrated. There were six and the sight still sends a shiver down my spine when I think of it. I thought I was in hell itself and now I would suffer the same fate. It seemed I was in that tomb a long time, cradling my friend and shedding tears of both joy and panic. Then I heard the sound of the grinding and rasping of the stones as they moved once again. I saw the hand of Mr Heaton reaching down into the hole, imploring me.

"Come on, we have to be quick, we've only a few seconds."

I lifted John and pushed him back into the room above, quickly scrambling after him as once more the stones moved to lock together.

We moved John gently between us back into the main part of the house and laid him on the settee. When we got him into the light we saw the full horror of his predicament. He was hardly breathing, his body was emancipated and looking like just skin and bone. What clothes he had on hung off him and were torn and bedraggled. We gave him some water and a few drops passed between his lips. One of the servants went for the doctor and within an hour he was being tended and helped. It was another two days before he spoke. I was there sitting by his bed when he opened his eyes and smiled and he just held me by the hand and said, "Henry".

I write this in my rooms at Oxford. I can see John; he is sitting in his wheelchair underneath a large oak tree watching cricketers play on the common. The doctors are pleased with him and every day he grows stronger and there is hope he will make a recovery, but how much we do not know.

The events at Ugglethorpe, what are we to make of them? Well, John did find the priest hole, cleverly hidden by a master mason that built that part of the house. The mechanism for opening the room was hidden so that in daylight it could not be seen. Marks had been made on the window and at full moon, or when there was sufficient light, the mechanism was revealed.

And the other skeletons in the priest's hole? They were the unfortunates who had tried to spend a night in the room and discovered the room's secret, only for them to be trapped and be entombed. John only survived because water from the gutters leaked into the room and he could at least have water. He went for 35 days without food and it is still too soon to see if his body will recover.

Mr Heaton has written to say he is going to have that part of the house demolished and the bodies of those in the room (which included two former priests of the parish) buried in the grounds of the Hall. He is to plant a yew tree in their memory, so let's hope the hundredth yew tree flourishes and grows tall to give a lie to the superstition and folk-magic of Ugglethorpe.

POSTSCRIPT

Hopefully you will read this after enjoying reading the stories. I wanted to explain where they have come from and why I had written them. As a lover of crime fiction I have always thought that the clergy have a pretty poor time. They are usually inept or benign figures, either the murder victim or when presented with a murder not sure what to do and quickly removed from the plot, usually figures of fun and ridicule, Father Brown and Cadfael being worthy exceptions who bring all their skills and knowledge into play in order to solve murders.

I have found that clergy are well equipped to deal with the darker mysteries of life. Clergy are not protected species who faint at the first sight of blood. They are often in the front line themselves; family break-ups, listening to confessions, dealing with deaths on a weekly basis. They are also well placed to see good and evil in humankind at its most pronounced. I wanted to write stories where the clergy are the centre of the story, either as the victim, detective or the perpetrator. I wrote them initially for my own amusement and when I told the stories to friends they have encouraged me to see them published. I hope you enjoy them.

The usual disclaimer that none of the stories bear any resemblance to real people is nonsense! After 35 years in the Methodist Ministry there are little facets of people I have met in each of the characters. Snippets of conversations overheard, a chance remark, a good story, they are all in here. You never know, you may recognise yourself in one of the stories. Please let me know if you do!

THE GRAVEDIGGER

This was the first story I wrote and it just came to me out of the blue. I don't know why I thought about it but the story just unfolded in my mind and I had to write it down. The story begins at the end. I like this way of writing as, hopefully, the reader will be captivated enough to read the rest of the story after reading the ending. One of the problems you have with clergy and murder is that they have to be believable. Rev Charles Adams is not a mass murderer but a very weak character. I remember thinking while reading a detective story that there always seems to be a problem of where to hide the body? Where better to hide a piece of hay than in a haystack and a dead body amongst others in a graveyard? It seems so obvious. The scene about digging up the graveyard for a road widening scheme actually happened in my own village of Haworth where I grew up. I was about ten at the time and it made a deep impression upon me.

THE MINISTER'S BARBECUE

Readers always ask, where do you get your ideas from? As if there is some magic book full of them which writers can pull down off the shelf. A few years ago I helped organise a barbecue for the Church and bought the meat to cook. The evening went really well and it was only later, at two o'clock in the morning, that I woke up desperately ill with food poisoning. In the middle of the night I could only think that if I was ill (and I never usually suffer in this way), what have I done to the little old ladies at the church? I could have poisoned half the church! Your imagination does seem to race at that time of the morning. Early in the morning I started ringing round to see if anyone else was ill. Thankfully, it seemed as if I was the only one! It must have been a rogue sausage! I breathed a great sigh of relief. Then a thought came to my mind, what a wonderful way to commit a murder! Bring some uncooked food to someone else's barbecue and cook it for the person you want to eat it.

Whenever I have told this story I have had the reaction, does the dog have to die? You can kill any number of characters off in a story but woe betide you if you kill a cat or a dog! I wanted to write at least one story where the main character was the clergyman who solves the crime and what better name than Sherlock, after my favourite detective!

DOUBLE DELIGHT

I really enjoyed writing this. Not least because for research purposes I went along as a guest to my first horse racing meeting. It involved champagne and the winner's enclosure, but that's another story. I like comedy farces which are usually based on people impersonating others. I was a little nervous when I showed this story to an identical twin, but it passed the test and they enjoyed it. It poses an interesting question: "Is any crime committed in the story?" As for the ending, as

I wrote the story the ending just emerged. I don't know where it came from, but it made me laugh and think that perhaps justice had been done in rather an unconventional way.

A TWINKLE IN THE EYE

This story is based on a real life character, although he died many years ago. He was vicar where I grew up and a great family friend. He was a larger than life figure and one who loved life. In this day and age I am sure he would have been castigated by the church for his eccentricities, but he was a great clergyman. At the age of 16 he took me to Scotland touring for 10 days, sharing a room – something unthinkable today. When you write about good people it is very difficult. What, after all, is there to say? If, however, you put them in situations where their character has to come through and you see them at their best, then you can write about goodness. It also shows up the absurdity of church consistory courts and why they have had to be changed.

A (RATHER) MACABRE CRICKET MATCH

There had to be one story about cricket! I like the detective who hates cricket. He is a loveable rogue and contrasts with the bright female constable who loves the game. As to the ingenious method of murder, I think I may have come up with a new way to kill someone off, with a cricket ball. I did ask a few cricketers if it was possible and a brain surgeon if one blow with a cricket ball could kill someone. So watch out if you're standing on the dressing-room balcony!

THE BODY IN THE LIBRARY

This is the traditional whodunnit: body is found in the library. This probably took shape with my numerous visits to that wonderful residential library in North Wales, St Deniol's (now called Gladstone's Library). Sitting before a log fire, and with 400,000 books, it's a very special place. My thanks to the staff and, yes, you can tell the order of books which someone has read. They have a very unique way of filling out the borrowing slips. Also, after 'The Collector' I had to put a clergywoman in a good light!

A VERY NECESSARY MURDER

I have always thought some clergy who come late into the ministry have had different lives before they became priests or monks. This story explores a former member of the SAS becoming a monk and spiritual leader. There have been many people who have crossed over from the armed services to the monastery; after all, they are both believers in discipline and order. I wanted to pose the question, could someone cope with murdering someone in war and then become a monk? This story tells of such a man. After writing it I would have liked to have met the character I have created, a man who understood life and death and redemption in a very unique way. The monastery is based on Mt. St Bernard in Leicestershire, where I have spent many a happy and contented retreat.

THE COLLECTOR

How do you write about a clergyman or woman who commits murder? Not very easily as the character has to be believable. I decided to see the person in another light, as a collector. She collects inheritances and tries to justify to herself what she has done. That it is a female helps perhaps in the trust she gains from her elderly female victims. That I too am a collector (of cricket memorabilia) means that I know how the bug of collecting can infect a person.

THE DEAN

Well, in every collection there has to be one with sex in it! Not much though, but this story explores the dynamics of female/male relationships and about power and status in the church. The Dean is not a nice character and you wonder why he is in the church, but then he is a Dean! I don't think we have fully absorbed the implications of women in what has been for 2,000 years a very male-dominated institution and the Church still does things in very male ways.

THE LASHING HOUSE

I spent a holiday in the deep south of the USA a few years ago and stayed in some of the plantation homes around the Mississippi. Seeing some of the effects of slavery made a deep impression on me, not least part of the church's acquiescence to it. When I came home I read quite a lot of books on the subject, including a remarkable if distasteful one

Postscript

written by church leaders (at the time of slavery) of the south defending slavery from a biblical point of view. I always feel that this story is stronger than some of my sermons on the subject of truth.

ASHES TO ASHES

After conducting over 1,000 cremations in my ministerial career, you get familiar with crematoriums. Again, what a good place to get rid of a body! This story though is more about the confessional. The priest is a victim of someone who seeks both to use the confessional for his own ends and doesn't accept the consequences of his own actions. I would like to thank numerous crematorium staff, who do such a wonderful job in very trying circumstances.

A STRANGE CUSTOM

I have always been fascinated with locked room murders. They are probably the most difficult to solve. Growing up in Haworth I saw some pretty weird rural customs. None of the ones I include in this story happened there though. I hope I haven't been too hard on rural Yorkshire; it has its faults but it has given me all my inspiration and creative spirit. Not to mention the Bronte sisters!

I have enjoyed writing these stories, which have taken me around five years to complete. The book is ecumenical in that no denomination is spared. I hope I haven't been too unkind to my profession. I have always found clergy to come in all different types. Yes, there are ones like Derek Nimmo, characterised as "wet behind the ears", but there are also some remarkable men and women doing some very difficult and creative work in all manner of surroundings. I salute you. The bad apples I have found to be very few and are far outweighed by some very great human beings. But then writing about good people is not that easy.

The illustration on the front cover is done by Bob Bond, who for many years illustrated children's comics. I told him my idea about the book and he came up with the drawing. As soon as I saw it I loved it. If you have any comments about the book I would love to hear them.

E.Mail. Maxcricket@btinternet.com
Rev Malcolm Lorimer. November 2010